Evermore

Books by Jody Hedlund

Young Adult: The Lost Princesses Series
Always: Prequel Novella
Evermore
Foremost
Hereafter

Young Adult: Noble Knights Series
The Vow: Prequel Novella
An Uncertain Choice
A Daring Sacrifice
For Love & Honor
A Loyal Heart
A Worthy Rebel

The Bride Ships Series
A Reluctant Bride
The Runaway Bride

The Orphan Train Series
An Awakened Heart: A Novella
With You Always
Together Forever
Searching for You

The Beacons of Hope Series
Out of the Storm: A Novella
Love Unexpected
Hearts Made Whole
Undaunted Hope
Forever Safe
Never Forget

The Hearts of Faith Collection
The Preacher's Bride
The Doctor's Lady
Rebellious Heart

The Michigan Brides Collection
Unending Devotion
A Noble Groom
Captured by Love

Historical
Luther and Katharina
Newton & Polly

Evermore

Jody Hedlund

NORTHERN LIGHTS PRESS

Evermore
Northern Lights Press
© 2019 Copyright
Jody Hedlund Print Edition

ISBN 978-1-7337534-1-8

www.jodyhedlund.com

All rights reserved. No part of this book may be reproduced, stored in a retrieval system, or transmitted in any form, or by any means, electronic, mechanical, photocopying, recording or otherwise, without prior permission of the author.

Scripture quotations are taken from the King James Version of the Bible.

This is a work of historical reconstruction; the appearances of certain historical figures are accordingly inevitable. All other characters are products of the author's imagination. Any resemblance to actual events or locales or persons, living or dead, is entirely coincidental.

Cover Design by Emilie Hendryx of E. A. Hendryx Creative

GREAT ISLE

NORLAND

HIGHLANDS

HIGHLAND CONVENT

ST. CUTHBERT'S

IRON HILLS

STEFFORD MIDDLETON EVERLY

WEST MOORLAND

EASTERN PLAINS

MERCIA

EAST SEA

CANNOCK

CISTERN BOGS

LANGLEY

CENTRAL HEATHLANDS

CRESS RIVER

DELSWORTH

SMITHTIDE

WELLMONT RUINS

INGLEWOOD FOREST

WARWICK

Chapter 1

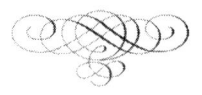

Adelaide

"I shall ride the final course." I grabbed the great helm. "You know I have the better chance at vanquishing Lord Mortimer."

"No, Adelaide." Mitchell reached to divest me of the helmet, but I sidestepped him and thrust it on before he could wrest it away.

"I shall pretend I am you, and Lord Mortimer will be none the wiser." My voice was hollow against the conical metal hood that covered my entire head except for the narrow eye slits and the small pricked breathing holes. I fumbled at the leather chinstrap, determined to tie it into place before Mitchell stopped me.

"Adelaide," he said in a puff of exasperation. But his voice wasn't as angry as it was frustrated. Whether he said so or not, I understood him. He was irritated more with himself than with me. Thus far during the jousting tournament, he'd tied with Lord Mortimer, which meant if we didn't win the fourth and final course, we'd go home without the coveted purse of gold.

If we returned to Langley without the gold, the physician wouldn't come to heal Aunt Susanna, and we would forfeit the expensive medicine she so desperately required.

"We need this victory more than any other." I stiffened my shoulders as Mitchell began to thread the belt from my cuirass to the cross-shaped hole at the base of the helm. Though I couldn't see Mitchell anymore, I sensed his troubled gaze upon me. With the customary Langley brown hair and eyes, he was small of stature for a man, more scholarly and interested in his studies than in tournaments. However, like any good nobleman's son, he'd been trained to use both his mind and body.

Much to the chagrin of my aunt and uncle, I'd trained right alongside Mitchell and my other cousins. Aunt Susanna oft lamented I was too much like my cousins and that she'd failed to raise me as a proper lady. I oft replied I would have it no other way.

The great helm lay heavy against my chain mail hood and padded coif. I was smaller than Mitchell, but we were close enough I'd jousted in his stead at tournaments. Always in the past, I'd enjoyed the challenge of taking part in competitions disguised as Mitchell. And always in the past, he'd humored my whims, relieved to escape his obligations.

However, the stakes of the tournament were higher this time. Not only did we need the purse of gold to pay the physician, but Lord Mortimer had also recently made known he had designs for me to become his next wife. He'd said as much to Mitchell during a recent hunting expedition.

As Lord Mortimer still mourned the loss of his first wife to childbirth, I hadn't given the gossip much credence. Mitchell, on the other hand, had been uneasy ever since, speculating what the lord might do if he became serious about the matter.

"That monster will not have you," Mitchell had declared viciously after the hunting party. "Though you would be harder to control than a wild coyote, I would sooner marry you myself."

I'd laughed at Mitchell's passionate declaration. Only months my elder, he wasn't my cousin by blood or birth. In fact, we weren't related in any way. But I saw him as none other than my true kin. We'd been inseparable growing up, and he was my steadfast friend.

Even now, I held out my gauntlet-gloved fingers and waited until I felt his hand in mine. "We shall prevail, Mitchell," I assured him. "And if Lord Mortimer ever discovers our duplicity, he will certainly put his thoughts far from me, for he will not be able to abide a wife who has knocked him from his horse."

I didn't wait for Mitchell's response. Instead, I shoved aside the tent flap and proceeded toward the lists. With spurs jangling and armor clanking, I joined the other knights with an air of confidence from years of training.

I rode Roland, Mitchell's bay roan, to the cheering of villagers who sat on the ground as well as the wooden benches that had been erected along the cordoned-off center field. The colorful pavilions with their more elaborate galleries provided seating for the nobility, a place to which I'd been relegated too many times in the past.

Disguised as a squire, Mitchell took his place next to me, straightening the caparison covering the horse. The flowing cloth was patterned with a red vertical stripe across white with a golden eagle at the center, the Langley family coat of arms.

"Remember everything I have spoken." He moved to the front of the charger and inspected the chanfron, making sure the iron shield sat securely in place over Roland's head. "Especially keep in mind that Lord Mortimer is weaker on the left side."

I nodded in reply and refrained from telling him I'd seen Lord Mortimer perform more times than he had and was familiar with every nuance of the lord's strategy and maneuvers.

Mitchell patted the charger one last time and whispered an endearment in his ear before going after my lance. I, too, leaned into Roland and rubbed the roan's shoulder with affection. He nickered his response as though he sensed how much was at stake.

"We shall do just fine," I said more to myself than to the horse. I'd ridden Roland as much as Mitchell—if not more. As a charger and medium-weight horse, he'd been bred for agility and stamina. He wouldn't be as muscular or heavy as Lord Mortimer's warhorse. But I'd learned size didn't necessarily equate strength, that strength could be found in many different forms.

Mitchell handed me a lance made of solid oak and decorated with red and white to match the Langley heraldry. I braced the long weapon under my arm and against my ribs, tilting it slightly forward to maintain my balance. I pressed my thighs into Roland's flank, needing to become one with the beast. This tournament was a partnership. I couldn't succeed without

Roland's cooperation—his measured speed, his balance against the pressure of our opponent, and the ability to sense my needs.

"God be with you." Mitchell gave my gloved hand a final squeeze. He spoke with confidence, but I could still distinguish a thin strand of anxiety in his tone. Not only was he worried about his mother the same as I was, but so many responsibilities had fallen on his shoulders, including the weight of the earldom, a weight that had been growing steadily heavier.

As the youngest of three brothers, Mitchell hadn't expected to carry such burdens. But Norbert had died in youth, and Christopher had run away five years ago. Older than Mitchell and me by two years, Christopher had a courage of both body and spirit I admired greatly. While I'd never been as close to Christopher as I had to Mitchell, I still held him in the highest regard.

A time had once existed when I'd fancied Christopher. Thankfully, my handsome cousin had been too preoccupied in those last days before his leaving to notice my increasing fascination. I'd surely have embarrassed myself if he'd stayed. Nevertheless, I'd allowed a secret hope to settle inside my young heart. A hope that someday he'd come back and fancy me in return.

Uncle Whelan had died unexpectedly, two years after Christopher's departure. We hadn't expected Christopher to return for the funeral since he was considered an enemy of King Ethelwulf. Thus, when he'd secretly visited, I'd been excited, wanting him to see me as the young woman I was becoming, not a little girl or his cousin. But he'd hardly noticed me and had remained only a day since his presence had posed a danger to us, especially because he'd pledged his services to the neighboring king of Norland.

With no one else to aid us, Mitchell and I had done what we could to survive. And now that he was twenty and I almost so—we'd learned to take care of ourselves and were doing what we needed to help Aunt Susanna.

Through my eye slits, I focused on my opponent on the other end of the list. Lord Mortimer was a formidable foe. Nigh on thirty, he was strong and experienced. But a greater weakness than his left side was his arrogance. He would expect Mitchell to come at him with his usual quick and powerful thrust. He would pride himself on knowing Mitchell so well.

But if God looked upon me graciously this day, I would deliver a thrust Lord Mortimer wasn't expecting.

I raised my lance high to signal my readiness, and Lord Mortimer did likewise. Then I couched my weapon in my armpit and settled myself more securely in the high-backed saddle. Although the April day was cloudy and the air heavy with moisture, sweat had already soaked the silk-lined doublet and padded collar I wore beneath my armor. The padded coif under my helm stuck to my head and my plaited hair.

Many times, I'd debated shearing my golden hair to a man's length so it would rest at my shoulders rather than waist. But Mitchell had cautioned me against doing so, convincing me I would draw unnecessary attention to myself and perhaps alert others to our duplicity.

The bugle call rent the air, clear and strong, quieting the crowd. Roland started forward, needing no urging on my part. His pace was perfect, providing adequate speed but smooth enough I could keep my balance.

With the thundering of horse hooves filling the silence, I focused on the part of Lord Mortimer's armor I intended to hit. I ground my teeth together, tightened my grip, thrust the lance, and then braced for impact.

My weapon glanced off the upper cannon protecting his arm and shoulder. But his made contact with my cuirass directly above my heart. The collision was hard and jolted me back against my saddle. I would have flown over Roland's hindquarters if I hadn't tightened my grip on the reins.

The crowd cheered at Lord Mortimer's contact. For a second, I wondered if I'd been too hasty in taking Mitchell's place in the contest. Perhaps I was the one with too much pride and needed a reminder to remain meek of spirit.

I rolled my shoulder and winced at the pain in my chest. "God, if you must teach me humility this day, I believe the bruise is a sufficient lesson." My whispered prayer was loud inside my helmet. "In fact, it will remind me for quite some days of the need to banish pride."

We returned to our respective corners of the list, raised our lances, and then began to ride toward each other once again. I bent closer to Roland, needing his strength, begging him for it. Then I put all thought out of my mind, save one—the target on Lord Mortimer's chest.

Roland's gait lengthened. His canter quickened. And the pounding of his iron-shod hooves echoed the thud of my heart. I sensed we were working together.

We were a team. And this time I had to hit my mark.

We drew nearer, but I waited, my gaze fixed and unwavering. Then at the last second, I drove my lance hard, feeling Roland thrust with me.

The crack of splintering wood was followed by Lord Mortimer's muffled cry of distress. The blow knocked into his chest at the same moment his lance hit me again. The power of the strike drove the wind from my lungs, and I felt myself sliding sideways. I clung to Roland desperately with my thighs. As though feeling my struggle, the charger compensated for my weakness, lowering himself just slightly so that I might jerk back up.

As I righted myself in my saddle, the crowd erupted into wild cheering. I ambled to the end of the list before turning Roland around. At the sight of Lord Mortimer sprawled on the ground and his warhorse at the opposite end of the field without him, a relieved thrill of victory coursed through me.

We'd won.

Tears stung my eyes, and I was glad for the great helm hiding them. I wasn't prone to fits of weeping or emotion. But this victory meant we could pay our debts to the physician. We'd already used his services countless times over recent weeks. Now he refused to come again until we paid him for his previous visits. With the diminished supply of the particularly rare and exotic powder that came from embalmed mummies, we needed the physician to bring Aunt Susanna more.

I glanced to where Mitchell stood and prayed I'd be able to convince my cousin of our need to ride out tonight after we were presented with our prize.

Mitchell was never one to forgo a feast when available. But with the direness of his mother's health, maybe he would listen to reason this time.

Lord Mortimer's squires had begun to assist him to his feet. From what I could assess, he'd been stunned but hadn't suffered any serious injury. Even if I didn't harbor fondness for the imposing lord, I still wished him no ill on account of our joust.

The herald blew the bugle again, quieting the crowd. Before he could pronounce me the winner, a harried and breathless man burst through the onlookers. "Sir Mitchell!" he shouted.

I swiveled toward Mitchell, and then realized the man was speaking to me. That he, like everyone else, believed I was Mitchell.

The newcomer towered above the other spectators by several handbreadths. I immediately recognized the thin stature and earnest expression. Tall John, our steward. From his red face and the perspiration ring at his hatband, I guessed he had travelled strenuously and without stopping.

"I have news!" he shouted. "Urgent news regarding your mother, the Countess of Langley."

My heart dropped into the base of my chest, leaving a painful empty void in its place. If Tall John had ridden several hours to find us, he surely didn't bear good tidings. I feared the worst.

"She is on her deathbed," Tall John called, heedless of the mass of people witnessing our exchange. "And she asks that you return home with all haste."

Chapter 2

Adelaide

I sprinted ahead of Mitchell, my boots slapping against the long passageway of Kentworth Castle. Upon reaching Aunt Susanna's chambers, I didn't bother knocking. I threw open the door and raced inside, praying we weren't too late.

I'd already sent Tall John straightaway to the physician's home, giving the steward a portion of the gold Lord Mortimer had bestowed upon Mitchell in a short ceremony. Though Lord Mortimer was proud and overbearing in many ways, at least he had the kindness of heart to allow us to be on our way as quickly as possible.

Mitchell and I had ridden well into the night before reaching home. We were exhausted and had pushed our horses much too hard. But I was determined to fetch the physician and purchase the costly medicine for Aunt Susanna.

"Aunt Susanna!" I crossed the room, which was lit by a lone candle on the bedside table. A maidservant rose from a pallet on the floor at the foot of the bed. At the sight of me, she curtsied.

"How is the countess?" I pushed aside the thick curtain surrounding the bed.

"She was restless all day," the servant replied, "but fell asleep a short while ago."

I peered down at the dear face of the only mother I'd ever known. The past months of illness had taken their toll. Her once full form was now skeletal and sunken, her lustrous hair thin and dry, and her body weak and lifeless. Whatever the malady, it had ravaged her until only a shell remained of the lively woman she'd always been.

Her eyes were closed, but her chest rose and fell with the breath of life. Weak with relief, I gripped the bedpost to keep from trembling. As soon as the physician arrived with more of his medicine, she would begin to revive.

"Thank the Almighty she is alive," Mitchell said next to me. We were still dressed in our armor, having removed only the most cumbersome of our attire and anything that might slow us down. Mitchell reeked of sweat and horseflesh and mud. If the room had been well lit, I had no doubt his appearance would match his stench. And I had no doubt I was his equal in my own filth.

All the long ride back to Langley, I'd been plagued with an impending premonition that the life I'd once known was about to end. No, we had not always had a peaceful or trouble-free existence. But Aunt Susanna's piety and devotion to God had brought a sense of well-being to the entire household. Her counsel had been my constant companion, and I could not live without her.

As if sensing our presence, her eyes flew open, landing first upon Mitchell's face and then shifting to mine. At seeing both of us by her bedside, she released a shaky breath, and her lips curved into a faint smile.

"You came," she whispered.

I divested myself of my glove and groped for her hand. "We are here," I replied. "Now you may rest easy."

Her flesh was cold and clammy, but I tightened my hold to reassure her of my presence. "Adelaide..." Her expression was taut with sudden earnestness. "I must tell you the truth before I go."

I shook my head. "You are not going anywhere. The physician is coming straightaway and will soon replenish your medicine."

Her lids fell, and for a long moment I almost believed she'd gone back to sleep. But when Mitchell shifted his feet and his armor creaked, she opened her eyes again. "You need to know—

"There will be plenty of time for you to speak on the morrow," I said.

"No." Her tone was firm, and her eyes grew brighter with determination. "I need to speak now."

I hesitated. Mitchell would acquiesce to whatever choice I made. It wasn't in his nature to object to my stronger will. However, at a time like this, I wished I didn't have to make the decision. For what if I made the wrong one?

Aunt Susanna glanced at the maidservant who was tucking in the coverlet more securely. I read the meaning of the glance and knew my aunt wished to be alone with Mitchell and me. I also realized she would not rest again until she'd unburdened herself with whatever news she was so desperate to share.

I sent the maid to retrieve food and drink. Once the door closed behind her, I leaned in and smoothed a hand across Aunt Susanna's cheek. "Are you sure this cannot wait?"

She shook her head, a new weariness already casting a pallor across her countenance. "Sit, Adelaide, and please listen to me."

I pulled up a stool next to the bed and gave her my full attention as Mitchell did the same.

"Your real name is Constance," she said without preamble.

I'd been called Adelaide for as long as I could remember. But my aunt's news didn't come as a surprise. Somewhere in the back of my mind, the name Constance resonated, and I guessed I'd answered to it before coming to live at Langley.

The kingdom had been in turmoil during my infancy. King Ethelwulf of Warwick had invaded and conquered Mercia, uniting Mercia and Warwick into one nation now known as Bryttania.

During those dangerous days when the new king had set out to purge the land of anyone who might oppose him, many people had gone into hiding or changed their names. It only made sense I'd been given a new identity for my protection.

I didn't know much regarding my real parents, only that my father had died in the Battle of Delsworth and my mother shortly after. At times during my childhood, I'd been curious about my origins, but my aunt and uncle had always told me they'd never met my birth parents and had seemed hesitant to talk about the past.

We'd always told visitors and neighbors I was Aunt Susanna's niece, the child of one of her many sisters, and everyone had believed us. I'd never questioned the falsehood and suspected the truth of my origins would have endangered me.

Apparently, now that I'd had ample time to put my curiosity regarding my past to rest and find contentment in my situation, Aunt Susanna was determined to enlighten me.

"Very well," I said softly. "Even if I was born with the name Constance, I shall continue to be called Adelaide since that is all I have ever known."

Aunt Susanna shook her head with a grimace of consternation. "No, my dear. You are not just any Constance. You are the Princess Constance."

Her statement was so absurd I couldn't contain my mirth, and a short laugh escaped before I could stop it. I expected her eyes to alight with humor too. But at the somberness of her expression, my humor faded to be replaced with a strange trepidation.

"You are Constance Dierdal Aurora, the crown princess and true heir of Mercia."

This time I couldn't find even the smallest sound to respond to her incredible declaration. Next to me, Mitchell sat just as speechless.

"The princesses were murdered by King Ethelwulf," I finally managed with a whisper. Even as I spoke the words, I reviewed what I'd learned about the Battle of Delsworth and swallowed hard. King Francis of Mercia had been mortally wounded. His wife, Queen Dierdal, had died giving birth to her newborn babes—twin daughters. The twins, along with their older sister, the heir to the throne, had disappeared.

No one knew what had happened to them. Rumors abounded that Ethelwulf had swiftly put the three princesses to death. In doing so, he'd assured his right to the throne. Whatever the case, they'd become known as the lost princesses.

"You were brought to us by a friend of mine," Aunt Susanna continued. "Sister Katherine. I knew her from the days when I was a postulant at St. Peter's."

Aunt Susanna had been sent to live in a convent as a young woman and had considered taking her vows but had married Uncle instead.

"Sister Katherine was a nun?" I asked.

"Yes, she went to live at St. Cuthbert's, an abbey hidden high in the eastern Iron Hills. After King Ethelwulf invaded Mercia, someone brought you to St. Cuthbert's for safekeeping."

My mind whirled as I attempted to grasp what Aunt Susanna was revealing. Though I wanted to protest, deep in my earliest memories, I had the vague recollection of standing in Kentworth Castle's great hall and clinging to the flowing gray habit of a woman with kind, blue-gray eyes. Had I been saying good-bye to Sister Katherine after she delivered me to Aunt Susanna and Uncle Whelan at Langley?

"What became of Sister Katherine?" Even as I asked, I wasn't sure I wanted to know.

Aunt Susanna's eyes filled with pain, from her illness or her memories I knew not. Her lashes dropped, and she seemed to gather inner strength before opening her eyes and meeting my gaze head-on. "Whelan learned that King Ethelwulf captured and tortured Sister Katherine. We feared for your life and prepared to move you. But Sister Katherine was strong to the end. She never revealed your whereabouts, though I have no doubt King Ethelwulf did everything in his power to tear it from her."

My chest expanded with an air of strange anxiety. I surmised without Aunt Susanna having to say so that she and Uncle Whelan had put themselves and their sons at great risk to harbor me. If Sister Katherine had given away my location, their entire household would have been punished. Most likely by a traitor's death of being hanged, drawn, and quartered.

What had they been thinking to take me in under such dangerous circumstances? Even now, my very presence at Kentworth Castle was putting them at serious risk.

I stood then, the stool tipping to the floor with a clatter.

"Adelaide," my aunt said reaching for me.

"No, I should not be here." I moved away from her and paced across the woven rushes to the window. "I will not allow harm to befall you on my account."

"No one knows," Aunt Susanna said, her voice pleading with me to come back to her. "Only your uncle and I. And once I am gone, just you and Mitchell."

"You are not going." I spun, my feet spread, my hand at the hilt of my sword. I was ready not only to fight any of King Ethelwulf's army that might come to hurt my family, but I was ready to battle death away from my aunt too.

Aunt Susanna didn't reply except to let her hand drop listlessly to the bed.

Through the scant candlelight, Mitchell watched me as though seeing me for the first time. His eyes were especially round in his angular face, filled with questions and doubts that mirrored my own.

"What if you are wrong about my identity?" I asked, hating to contradict this wise and loving woman who'd apparently sacrificed more for me than I'd realized.

"I saw Queen Dierdal once," Aunt Susanna said. "She was the most beautiful woman in all the land. And you resemble her so closely."

My cousins' friends, as well as neighboring lords, had always remarked what a pretty girl I was. But I'd been too busy attempting to be just like the boys to pay any attention to my appearance.

I shook my head. This was all too impossible to believe. "There could be any number of women who look like Queen Dierdal. Having a resemblance to the late queen is not proof enough I was her child."

"Of course not," Aunt Susanna said gently, beckoning me back to her side. Though the anxiety in my chest still raged, I crossed to her bed once more and took her hand.

She pressed something against my palm and squeezed my fingers closed over it. I took the item and inspected it in the candlelight. A ring. And not just an ordinary ring. It was a signet ring with the royal emblem that had belonged to the house of Mercia—two golden lions standing rampant as though holding up the ruby at the center.

"The ring belonged to your father, King Francis. Sister Katherine brought it with her when you came to us. And I have kept it hidden all these years."

Turning it over, I studied each detail. It looked authentic. Nevertheless, I couldn't shake my doubts.

"May I examine it?" Mitchell asked.

I handed the ring to my cousin, and he scrutinized it as carefully as I had. "It is indeed the royal ring," he said after a minute. "Long ago, when King Alfred divided his kingdom between his twin daughters, he gave them each a ring, one with a ruby and the other with an onyx. They are identical in every way except for the large gemstones at the center."

If anyone would know the authenticity, Mitchell would. He was a brilliant scholar with a mind that soaked in details like thirsty ground did a spring rain.

"We cannot be certain the ring was meant for me," I said.

"I have one other item. It will convince you that you truly are the Princess Constance." Aunt Susanna reached to her side, to the pocket she kept tied underneath her shift. She fumbled for a moment before pulling out a golden key.

At the sight of the object, Mitchell sucked in a sharp breath.

"What does it mean?" I asked as my aunt held it out to me.

"I see Mitchell already knows the value." Aunt Susanna studied her son's face.

"I have heard about the legend of King Solomon's treasure and the keys that unlock it." Mitchell's voice was low with awe. "But I did not know if the rumors regarding such keys were really true."

I fingered the length of the key, which was larger than my hand. It had an oval bow and a long, thick shank that ended in an elegant collar and pin. The bit on the end contained a pattern—what looked to be a pomegranate cut into two pieces with its seeds spilling out.

Though I was ignorant of the keys, I had learned about King Solomon's wealth during history lessons the same as Mitchell. The account came from the Holy Scriptures when God had appeared to King Solomon in a dream and told the young king he could ask for whatever he wanted. Instead of asking for wealth and a long life, King Solomon had asked God for wisdom and discernment as he governed his people so that he could distinguish right from wrong.

God had been so pleased with the king's answer He decided not only to give Solomon wisdom but promised to bestow on him wealth and a long life as well. The king had amassed so much that he'd ended up with thousands of chests of gold and jewels and other priceless treasures. Most of it had eventually been squandered by the kings who came after Solomon. But rumors had abounded of chests that had been dispersed and hidden for safekeeping.

I had no idea what a key to a rumored treasure might have to do with me. "Just because we have a key to a legendary treasure does not confirm I am the crown princess."

"Explain it to her, Mitchell," Aunt Susanna said, her voice faint, her gentle features lined with weariness.

Our conversation had taxed her as I'd feared. "Perchance later, Aunt dearest. For now, you must rest."

She shook her head, her eyes bright again. "There is not much left now. Prithee, Mitchell, carry on."

Mitchell hadn't taken his gaze from the key. "The kings of the Great Isle going back even further than King Alfred the Peacemaker have been charged with being keepers of the keys."

"Keys?" I interrupted. "So more than one exists?"

Mitchell nodded with excitement. "I have heard there are three. The ruling king was supposed to have the three keys in his possession at all times until his deathbed when he would pass them on to the next chosen keeper."

"If the rulers of the realm have been charged with being keepers of the keys, why have they not sought the treasure?"

"Perhaps they have," Mitchell continued. "I suspect the royal family's feuding over the decades has had more to do with finding the keys and treasure than uniting the land."

I'd been tutored alongside my cousins and had learned the lengthy history of Mercia, including the time when King Ethelwulf's grandmother, Queen Margery, had attempted to gain Mercia's throne away from her younger twin sister, Leandra.

Their father, King Alfred the Peacemaker, had no son to inherit the throne and hadn't wanted to choose one twin daughter over another to become the next ruler. Therefore, he'd divided his kingdom of Bryttania into two smaller realms, Mercia and Warwick. Upon his premature death, he'd given the succession of Mercia to Leandra and Warwick to Margery.

For a while, the twin sisters had each ruled their small kingdoms peacefully. But then, Leandra had died in childbirth, leaving a newborn daughter as heir. Margery had decided Mercia belonged more to her than to Leandra's husband and babe. After all, Margery was the firstborn, and the laws of primogeniture stated the succession should go to the eldest and their heirs.

Margery had fought but failed to reclaim the

kingdom. Since that time, her heirs had never ceased believing Mercia and Warwick should be united and that their family deserved to rule both realms. King Ethelwulf had been the one finally to succeed.

What if Mitchell was right? What if the fighting over the decades to reunite the kingdoms had contained ulterior motives? To locate the treasure? Did King Ethelwulf even now seek to find the keys? *What would he do if he learned I was in possession of what he sought?*

My key felt suddenly heavy and cold. "If I have one of the keys, then does King Ethelwulf have the other two?"

"It is possible," Mitchell replied, returning the signet ring to me and taking the key and examining it. "Although I have heard that when King Alfred the Peacemaker split the country between his two daughters, he gave one a larger portion of land and the other the keys in order to ensure that the keys were kept together as has always been done."

"If the keys have always remained together, then why would that change? Perhaps this is not an authentic key after all."

"It is authentic. How could it be otherwise?" Mitchell fingered the key reverently. "My guess is that someone decided to divide the keys to ensure their safety. Perhaps the two other lost princesses each have a key."

We were both silent for several heartbeats. The eerie quiet of the night settled around us, and the shock of the revelations threaded through the chilly darkness, making me shiver.

Aunt Susanna had finally closed her eyes. Her

breathing was slow but steady, and I didn't wish to disturb her again with any further discussion.

"I shall stay by her side," I whispered to Mitchell. "You must go meet the physician."

He turned the key over in his hand and opened his mouth as if to speak.

I halted him with a touch to his arm. "I realize there is much more to be said on this matter. But the rest can wait for another day, can it not?"

"Certainly." He handed the key back to me, but not without his fingers clinging to it just a moment too long.

Before he could move away from the bedstead, Aunt Susanna surprised me by grabbing our hands with a measure of strength I hadn't realized she'd retained. Her eyes were wide open again.

"Mitchell," she whispered hoarsely. "Promise you will protect Adelaide with your life."

"Of course, Mother," he started.

"Vow it," she gasped.

He lifted her hand and kissed it three times as was customary. "I vow it."

"And promise you'll forgive Christopher?"

Mitchell stiffened. "He is a traitor."

"But he is still your brother."

"Father disowned him. He is dead to me—dead to us all."

I wanted to remind Mitchell that Uncle Whelan had no choice but to disown Christopher. As a loyal advisor to the king, Uncle had done so to prove his allegiance to the king as well as to protect our family from punishment. But saying so wouldn't do any good. Christopher's betrayal had angered Mitchell perhaps more than anyone else. After all, Mitchell had been the one to ride after Christopher and had begged to go with him, only to have Christopher shout at him to go home.

Aunt Susanna shifted her attention to me. "God saved your life, Adelaide. Now it is time for you to give it back in service to Him as the ruler you were born to be. Promise you will do so."

Her words weighed upon my heart. I wasn't sure I could accept everything she'd told me about my origins, much less make a vow to her.

Her fingers gripped mine with an almost bruising quality. "You must vow it."

I hesitated. I didn't want to disappoint this dear woman. She obviously had the hope I would do something—perhaps rise up and become a ruler. She'd likely harbored such a hope all the years she'd taken care of me.

Even if I was one of the lost princesses, how would I rise up? I was only a young woman, alone except for Mitchell. What difference could the two of us possibly make?

Aunt Susanna lifted my hand to her lips and placed a kiss there. "Please," she whispered faintly, "Your Majesty."

Her address pierced my chest as surely as the blade of a dagger. The term *Majesty* was only used when speaking with a king or queen. No longer did she see me as her niece, or even a princess. She was acknowledging me as her ruler, her queen.

I wanted to shake my head, turn back time, and return to the way things had always been. But as I peered into her eyes, overflowing with love, I couldn't deny her. I loved and respected her too much. Maybe I couldn't promise to assert myself and be a ruler. Yet I could vow to serve God, couldn't I?

It was my turn to kiss her hand three times.

The moment I finished, her lashes fell. Her fingers in mine grew limp. And she released a long breath as though her job was finished.

I lowered her arm to the bed and waited for her to inhale, for the rise and fall of her chest. But with each passing second of stillness, panic crept into my veins.

I squeezed her hand, but it was lifeless. I shook her by the arm, but she refused to draw a breath.

"Mitchell!" I cried out. "We must do something to save her!" Even as the words echoed sharply in the silent room, my mind comprehended what my heart would not.

She was dead.

Chapter 3

CHRISTOPHER

I REINED IN MY STEED ON THE CREST THAT OVERLOOKED Kentworth Castle. My breath stuck in my chest at the sight of the majestic fortress made of local red sandstone. Its outer bailey wall was thick and crowned with numerous buttresses and towers at strategic locations. The great keep beyond the inner bailey rose tall and stately with enormous corner turrets.

Home.

The sight never failed to move me.

For early June, the land was vibrant against the cloudless blue sky overhead. I inhaled the sweet scent of the bright pink field roses that grew in abandon in the lush meadows. The cadence of locusts rubbing their wings and the hum of bees brought back memories of my childhood, of running the hills barefoot with my kin, swinging our blunt wooden swords, pretending to slay dragons and defending our land from evil.

How young and naïve we'd been. How little we'd known about the real world and the real evils. And how ignorant we'd been about regret and what a powerful force it could be.

I swallowed the bitterness at the back of my throat. After a fortnight of secretive travel across Norland, as well as through the Highlands and Iron Hills, I was ready for a hot meal and warm bath. Yet now that Kentworth was in sight, my reins slackened. I couldn't make myself urge my steed forward.

As the oldest living son, the castle and land should have belonged to me when Father died. I should have inherited all that belonged to him, including the title of earl. But by leaving Mercia to serve under King Draybane of Norland, I'd made myself an enemy of Ethelwulf.

Most of the time, I convinced myself the sacrifice had been worth it. But now, with the beauty of my boyhood home spread out before me with all its memories, I couldn't keep the regrets at bay... especially knowing Mother was dead and that I'd missed saying good-bye, just as I'd missing saying good-bye to Father.

The ache in my chest expanded and pulsed down my arms to my fingers.

I wasn't sure why I'd come. By the time Tall John's missive regarding Mother's death had reached my post in Norland, her funeral had passed. Nevertheless, I'd petitioned King Draybane for leave so I could return home.

Why? To check on the Langley holdings? To assure myself all was well with my brother and Adelaide?

If I was honest, I knew the real reason I'd come was to sever the bond with my past. It was time to officially sign over to Mitchell the earldom and relinquish the grasp of my old life. Perhaps in my deepest of hearts I'd harbored hope I could someday return and live at home again and assume my father's role in ruling his lands. But I needed to admit that would never happen. Not as long as Ethelwulf was on Mercia's throne.

A distant falcon in the sky drew my attention. It soared effortlessly, its long, smoky wings framing a bare chest. With its dark hood and cape, I recognized it as a peregrine and guessed either Mitchell or Adelaide was hunting. Or perhaps both.

I veered my steed in the direction of the falcon but then hesitated. How would they feel upon seeing me? Would they loathe me for my absence during Mother's suffering? Or would they open their arms in welcome?

As the peregrine swooped and began plunging downward at a steep angle, I urged my mount down the hill. Although the huntsman wasn't visible, I'd hunted with my siblings oft enough to know they were likely awaiting the falcon's return by Finham Brook.

The bird dove out of my vision but then flapped upward a short while later with a small hare in its talons.

"Adelaide," I said aloud, unable to contain my proud grin. Only my little cousin had worked hard to train her falcon to catch more than small fowl. Mitchell hadn't had the patience for the extra work.

My excitement mounted as I drew near the brook, but I pulled up short in surprise when I arrived and no one was there. I slid from my horse and bent to examine hoofprints in the mud along the marshy bank. Two horses. The tracks were fresh and told of a hasty departure away from the brook into the woodland.

On foot, I led my steed, following the easy trail. Had the hunters rushed off after a new prey? I trailed the two horses a hundred paces into the woodland before the prints disappeared. I frowned and studied the thick hardwoods and leafy shrubs for any sign of the hunters. But I could see nothing—no faint prints, snapped twigs, crushed leaves, or broken blades of grass.

How could two horses simply vanish?

I released my horse's reins and crouched. Pushing aside a thin layer of windfall, I once more caught a glimpse of the tracks. In that instant, I realized I'd lowered my guard. My mare whinnied a soft warning. But before I could rise, a blade bit into the tender unprotected skin at my throat.

I froze. And I calculated as much information as I could. The arm encircling my chain mail hood was slender of build. The leather falcon glove was not overly large. And the boot that was just in my vision was small too.

I could easily overcome this foe. But what of the other man? Where was he?

The cracking of branches to the rear of my captor gave me my answer. The weight of his footsteps told me the man was much larger but was still several paces away. I had to act now if I had any attempt at getting away.

I clasped the hand holding the blade against my throat and jerked hard, intending to flip the man over my shoulder to land in front of me. Before I could complete the move, he swiftly pressed a second dagger into my back thigh below my chain mail hauberk. The cutting edge pierced through my hose, forcing me to stand motionless once again.

I held my breath, my mind scrambling for a new plan. My opponent might be small but was apparently well trained. With the dagger firmly in place again at my throat and at my thigh, I couldn't move without drawing blood, and my captor knew it.

"Who are you and what is your business?" came a

commanding but distinctly feminine voice.

Chagrin burned in my chest. Had a woman bested me?

"Why are you on Langley land?"

The demanding tone sounded vaguely familiar. "Adelaide?" I asked. "Is that you?"

The knife faltered, and I realized at once it was my cousin. I took advantage of the brief lag in her attentiveness, jabbed the weapon from her hand at my throat, and swung around in a swift kick, knocking her feet from the ground so that she landed on her back. I rapidly stepped on her wrist and dislodged the other dagger.

My behavior was inappropriate toward a girl—that I knew. But this was Adelaide. I'd always treated her and Mitchell the same. And since she'd been the one to initiate the attack, surely a little wrestling in return would do no harm.

Before I could say anything or shove the dagger out of her reach, she kicked her legs around and slammed them into the back of my knees directly into the reflexive weak spot so that I buckled. My hold on her wrist fell away. In that small second, she retrieved her dagger and thrust it at my throat before my knees could hit the forest floor.

This time she yanked off my chain mail hood, grabbed the short plait of my hair at the back of my neck, and used it to twist my head, giving me no choice but to look at her. I found myself peering up into a face shadowed by a deep hood. Even so, I immediately recognized her eyes, which were the color of moorland sky at eventide. The blue was prettier than I remembered.

"How are you, cousin?" I gave her what I hoped was my most charming grin.

Her eyes narrowed, and the knife remained at my throat. She examined me, taking in the fortnights' worth of dark stubble covering my chin and jaw, the grit lining the grooves of my face, and the strands of my dark hair that had come loose since I'd last tied it back.

"It is I, Christopher," I clarified lest she try to harm me further. She would put up a good fight, as she had already, but I could disarm her and bring her into submission eventually.

Slowly, she released her hold at my neck and dropped the blade. I rubbed at the nick and came away with blood on my glove.

Behind Adelaide stood Tall John, my father's faithful steward. The falcon was perched on his arm, and a full sack lay slung across his back, likely the kill the bird had brought them. The old steward was still as thin as a sapling, with overlong arms and legs. From beneath his coif, strands of his hair had begun to turn brown-gray, the color of a winter woodland. But his eyes were unchanged, kind and alert. And at the sight of me, they filled with recognition.

"I see you are already planning a feast for my arrival," I said, turning back to Adelaide. "I hope you have at least one grouse in the lot. My mouth is watering in anticipation of a roasted leg."

Adelaide didn't respond to my mirth. Instead, she relieved Tall John of the sack. Then, with quick, nimble steps, she started away from me.

Tall John crossed to me, bowed, and extended a hand to help me to my feet. "It is good to see you, my lord."

"It is good to see you too." I squeezed his hand at his welcome. I probably deserved a rebuff from him too. But thankfully, he was extending grace. "My gratitude for sending me word regarding Mother's passing."

He bowed his head. "You have just arrived, my lord?"

"Yes, just." My gaze trailed Adelaide. "Is Mitchell hunting with you?"

"He's away to Delsworth for a fortnight."

"And he left Adelaide home alone?"

"She's old enough to fend for herself, as you can attest."

I tried to assess her more carefully, but her long cloak prevented me from seeing anything but her outline. When I'd left, she'd been but a wisp of a girl. She couldn't be grown up already, could she?

I jogged after her, easily catching up. "Adelaide."

She lengthened her stride. The horses were ahead, tied to a maple. If I didn't stop her now before she reached her horse, I would lose this opportunity to speak with her privately. I grabbed her arm and spun her around, giving her no choice but to face me. In the same motion, I threw back her hood so I could see her clearly.

Standing before me was not the girl I'd once known and played with. Instead, a stunningly beautiful woman met my gaze with her chin lifted and eyes blazing. I took a step back, though why I was surprised, I knew not. I should have expected maturity in her appearance.

She scowled at me, but nothing, not even a frown, could mar her loveliness. In fact, if anything, the liveliness of her anger lit her expression and exposed the high cheekbones that curved into a dainty chin. Her nose was narrower and more elegant than I'd remembered and her lips most definitely fuller.

"Do I meet your approval?" she asked, her tone cool and edged with steel.

I finished appraising her, noting the color of her hair remained unchanged. She'd pulled it back into a braid, but loose wisps framed her face—golden, like a fine, pale palomino, but thicker and luxurious in a way it had never been as a young girl.

"I hardly recognize you."

"That is what happens when you abandon your family for so long."

Her sharp words pierced me. So she was angry at me, not just for missing my mother's funeral but much more.

I wished I could apologize for leaving Langley. But I'd gone over that agonizing day a hundred times. Each time I'd concluded I'd had no choice but to follow my conscience. Father might have been able to make a deal with the devil and pledge his loyalty to Ethelwulf, but I never would. I'd rather die than sell my soul.

Even so, I regretted arguing with Father. I'd flung heated declarations at him that had been borne of my immaturity. I'd said many things I wish I could retract. But it was too late. He was gone, and the words would forever remain imbedded in my memory.

And apparently in Adelaide's.

"I am sorry about Mother," I offered, somehow needing to bridge this gap with her. "I came as soon as I received the news. I only wish I had known she was ill so I could have come sooner."

"Would you truly have come sooner, Christopher?" Again her tone cut me to the quick.

"Then you think so little of me to imagine I would not try to help Mother in her time of need."

She met my gaze frankly. The turmoil in the depths of her wide-open blue eyes reached inside and wrenched my heart in a tight grip. "Why are you here, my lord?"

I considered telling her I had come to offer my condolences. But I could see that not only had she grown into a beautiful woman but an intelligent one as well. I sensed she would see past any excuse I offered, that I might as well tell her the truth. "I am here to sever my rights to Kentworth once and for all."

Hurt flashed in her eyes. And perhaps disappointment. Was she disillusioned with me and with whom I'd become? At times I was disappointed in myself—that I had not been the kind of son, brother, or cousin my family had wanted. Even now, I was not the type of man Adelaide could respect and admire.

However, like everything else I'd given up, I would have to sacrifice her admiration in order to maintain integrity and honor. For without either, how could I live with myself? In the meantime, while I was home, I could do my best to repair the relationship with my cousin, could I not? Mayhap, by the time I left, we would at least be friends again. I could strive after that.

"Since you have come to see Mitchell," she said at last, striding again toward her horse, "you will be indisposed awaiting his arrival home. Whatever will you do having to tarry three days this time instead of one?"

Her sharp jab was well aimed. But my remorse at her verbal sparring waned. Instead, frustration slipped in to replace it. Adelaide had always been stubborn and willful. Clearly, she was more so now that she was full grown.

I stalked after her. If she'd been a child, I would have thrashed her for her disrespect. After all, I was her elder and superior. And I was still the Earl of Langley, at least until Mitchell returned home.

When she reached her mare, she stood with her back to me tying the sack of game to her saddle. Her motions were swift and sharp, her back as stiff as a pike.

I was tempted to whip her around and demand that she look at me, that she try to understand my perspective.

But the truth was I loved my cousin too much to command her affection. I wanted it of her own volition. I wanted her to look at me with the adoration and devotion that had always been present when we'd been younger. For as far back as I could remember, Adelaide had respected me and even attempted to be like me, much the same way Mitchell had. I had already lost Mitchell's affection, and I couldn't bear the thought of losing Adelaide's now as well.

Though we were no longer children at play and much had happened over the years to change us, I wished for the uncomplicated innocence of those days when she—and Mitchell—still regarded me as someone to admire rather than loathe.

I laid a hand on her shoulder. "Adelaide, please." My voice was soft and pleading. "I see I have hurt you. And it pains me greatly. I beg your forgiveness so I might regain your love."

Her fingers stilled against the strings of her bag. After a moment, she lowered her head and her shoulders slackened. I lifted my hand and combed back wayward strands of her hair the breeze had teased free. They were like the finest silk against my callused fingers, and I couldn't keep from brushing them again.

She leaned into my hand.

Slowly, gently, I turned her. She didn't resist. And when I pulled her into my embrace, she relaxed, letting herself fall against me. I wrapped my arms around her and drew her close. With the solidness and warmth of her against me, I pressed my face into her head and breathed her in. Everything about her reminded me of my boyhood, of home, of my parents, of the life I'd once had here.

"Oh, Adelaide," I murmured. "How I have missed home."

At my admission, she slid her arms around my torso and returned my embrace. My chest constricted with the regrets and sorrows I'd privately nursed these past years. I nuzzled my nose into her hair and let myself imagine for just a moment she was Mother, that Mother was hugging me and forgiving me too.

After a moment, I pressed a kiss against her brow and pulled back without fully releasing her to examine her expression and to ensure myself she was indeed willing to forgive me. This time, when she peered up at me, the haughtiness was gone. Vulnerability softened her features. Sadness filled her eyes, darkening them. I knew she, too, was thinking about Mother, that her grief was still deep.

"She was a good woman," I said.

Adelaide swallowed hard and then spoke in a low tone. "I loved her as if she were my own mother."

"And she, likewise, loved you as her own." Sometimes I forgot that Adelaide wasn't really my cousin, that Mother and Father had taken her in as a young child. "You were a gift and a joy to her."

"She was a courageous woman," Adelaide whispered. "I can only pray I have half the courage she had."

I didn't understand Adelaide's reference to my mother's courage. She'd lived in seclusion, rarely extending invitations to visitors, preferring a quiet and simple life. Nevertheless, now that I had this tentative truce with Adelaide, I wouldn't contradict her sacred memory of the woman we'd both loved.

"You are already courageous and strong," I said instead, my mind filling with images of Adelaide as a young girl insisting on learning to wield a sword and lance and bow. She'd been tough and quick and smart, so much so that at times I'd forgotten she was a girl. Even now, she stood attired in men's breeches beneath a hauberk and cloak. With her hood pulled up, she could easily pass for a man.

"I miss her terribly." Adelaide lifted her long lashes and met my gaze, her eyes filled with such sorrow I couldn't keep from bending in to comfort her. I embraced her once more and this time pressed a kiss upon her cheek. As my lips made contact, however, I was suddenly much too conscious of the softness of her skin.

I moved my lips away and pressed my cheek against hers intending to offer comfort, not intimacy. But with our cheeks touching, her mouth was near my ear, and I heard her quick intake of breath, reminding me of her beauty and the fact that she was no longer a mere girl.

Was I overstepping the bounds of propriety? I hesitated, suddenly uncertain how I should be treating Adelaide.

"I have missed you as well." Her statement was almost shy and echoed in the hollow part of my ear, sending strange warmth to my gut—a completely inappropriate reaction as her cousin. I pulled away and this time released her. Nevertheless, my sights lingered upon her face, exploring each curve, each perfect line, and each lovely detail.

When a faint, rosy hue spread into her high cheekbones, I realized my scrutiny was causing her discomfort. I smiled, hoping to put her at ease. "Since you have missed me, then you would not deny me a bath and hot meal, would you?" I nodded toward the sack that bulged with all the creatures her falcon had captured.

The softness and vulnerability fled from her features, replaced by hard determination. "You may ride on to

Kentworth and do as you please, my lord. Command the few remaining servants to tend to your needs. They shall do so willingly, I am sure."

She tightened the knot of the game bag upon her saddle and then slung her foot into the stirrup, glancing at me over her shoulder as she hoisted herself up. "However, they shall have to do so without the luxury of this game. This is intended for others."

With that, she settled into her saddle, gathered the reins, and urged her horse away.

Chapter 4

Adelaide

I knelt on the dirt floor next to the pallet and grasped the old peasant woman's hand, heedless of the open sores on her skin.

"You're a kind soul, my lady," Edith lisped through missing teeth and shriveled lips turned inward.

"I only wish I could do more." I squeezed her hand before rising.

"You 'ave done more than anyone, lady," said Mary, who cared tirelessly for her mother in spite of being busy with her own family. She hefted her lethargic infant son higher on her hip. With every visit I'd made during the winter and spring, I'd watched the child wasting away, his eyes becoming more sunken and his cheeks hollow.

The hungering time had taken its toll on everyone.

"The worst is over," I reassured Mary. "We shall have a plentiful year to come."

I prayed my prediction was true. Mary's husband and older children worked the Langley fields from sunup to sundown, plowing, tilling, planting, and weeding. As their payment for their labor, they always got to keep a small portion of the harvest.

Of late, however, the portion hadn't been enough. Not for anyone.

Though I'd resented Christopher for running away from Mercia, over the past year I'd begun to understand more clearly what had driven him, for I experienced the same discontent with King Ethelwulf and his rule whenever I rode the countryside and saw the sad, hungry faces of the peasants.

I felt the same smoldering anger when I visited the Langley-owned iron smelter in Everly and witnessed the poor working conditions. In fact, I'd even once convinced Mitchell to use our earnings from a jousting tournament to pay the income of the laborers rather than lay them off as many other smelters in the Iron Cities had been forced to do this past year.

With a final nod good-bye to Edith and Mary, I stooped under the dried herbs hanging in bunches from the low rafters. As I stepped carefully around the central hearth and the scant possessions the family owned, I was keenly aware of Christopher's scrutiny from the doorway.

Even though he was obviously worn and weary from his travels, he'd sent Tall John home with the falcon and insisted on accompanying me as I made my rounds to several of the small villages on Langley land. He'd gone with me from hut to hut as I divided the meat among each family.

After the drought last year, the scant deliveries were never enough. No one ever had enough anymore. We wouldn't until we harvested this year's crops. But

I'd instructed the children on how to look for early June fruits—gooseberries, wild strawberries, and even some cherries. More plentiful were turnips, spring onions, and beetroot. The wild produce along with the game my hawk caught would keep them alive, even if it didn't completely fill their bellies.

I did what I could to supplement with other supplies when I could purchase them. But the extras were rare since all of Mercia had suffered from the drought, and food everywhere was in short supply.

As I ducked out of the dark, unlit hut, I squinted into the sunshine.

"That is the last of the catch," Christopher said.

I nodded, well aware of that fact and also well aware of his presence. Ever since he'd embraced me, it was as if every nerve in my body had been strung tight and finely tuned to him. I could sense when he watched me. I could sense his nearness. I could even sense his shifting mood.

As we'd ridden between villages, he'd asked me numerous questions regarding the state of affairs in Langley and throughout Mercia. He'd gone from curious and surprised at how destitute the conditions had become, to angry and morbid. Even now he stood feet slightly apart, holding the reins of both our mounts, his expressive, honey-colored eyes churning with unrest.

"Where to next, my lady?" he said handing me my reins.

"Back to Kentworth," I replied. "We have done all we can for today."

He nodded solemnly. His chestnut hair was combed into a leather strip at the back of his neck. His cheeks and chin were covered in a dark layer of scruff. And he wore the dust of many days' travel. In spite of his ruggedness, he was still handsome with an aura of daring and dashing that had the same power as long ago to make my heart beat faster.

I couldn't deny that my immediate and strong attraction frustrated me. I'd wanted to remain angry at him for leaving us, to hold him at arm's length, or at the very least to stay indifferent. But all he had to do was speak a few endearments, hold me, and kiss my cheek, and I'd melted like wax against a flame.

Silently, I rebuked myself to be careful. He'd made no pretense regarding the nature of his visit. He didn't intend to stay, was leaving again, likely for good. And this time I wouldn't pine after him. I was, after all, more mature now. I could accept him for the wandering soul he was, could I not?

My anger toward him had been borne out of silly, girlish infatuation anyway. Surely, I was past that. While I might still appreciate Christopher's fine, dark looks and charm, he held no sway over my heart. And I would make sure things stayed that way.

The children and a mangy mutt followed us out of the village, skipping along behind our horses. Even with their tattered clothing and dirty bare feet, their laughter and cheerful good-byes were sweeter than any payment I could ever receive.

"How often do you bring them game?" Christopher asked, giving the children a final wave.

"At least once a week now that the game is plentiful. Sometimes two. Winter was particularly hard, and we had to do much more fishing than hunting. But Mitchell and I lifted the hunting and fishing boundary restrictions and allowed the bondsmen and laborers access to whatever food they could catch."

Christopher fell silent, the clopping of our hooves tapping out the storm I sensed brewing inside him. "Tall John's missive said Mother died from tumors and an excess of black bile," he finally said in a strained voice. "Was it from starvation instead?"

"No, ease your mind, my lord. We have fared better than our bondsmen, to be sure. Although I am afraid you will find the estate much reduced as we had to sell most of the valuables."

Christopher waved a hand to dismiss my comment. "I could not live in luxury if the people who depended upon me were dying."

I smiled at his passionate statement. For all my frustrations with Christopher, we did share the same heart on many matters.

Atop his steed, his profile was every bit as noble and manly as when he stood directly before me. His shoulders were straight and broad, his arms and legs thick with muscles that he'd developed during his time away. He'd always been bigger and stronger than Mitchell, but it wasn't his physique alone I admired. Yes, he possessed an irresistible charm with his easy smiles and teasing ways. But beyond that, he felt things deeply. He cared about people and principles more than he did personal gain. And for that, I respected him greatly.

My heartbeat spurted abnormally fast again, chopping against my chest. Before I could look away, his gaze slid to me, and his brow quirked as though to let me know he'd caught me staring. I didn't give him the satisfaction of a response and hoped my cheeks weren't flushing as they had earlier.

"You must be betrothed by now," he said lightly. "Or at least have many suitors vying for your hand."

"Aunt Susanna would not allow it." Not that I'd minded my aunt's decision. Even if other noblewomen were away at court seeking marriage partners among the elite, I'd been too busy, especially over the last year of drought, to think on such matters.

"Then you are secretly in love with someone?" His eyes twinkled.

I laughed again, this time with more mirth. "Aunt Susanna made no effort to introduce me to the eligible young men and discouraged Mitchell from extending invitations to his friends." In fact, now that I thought on the matter, it seemed my aunt had purposefully tried to isolate me. Had she worried that some nobleman might see me and recognize my similarity to the previous queen?

Though I'd pondered Aunt Susanna's deathbed confessions much over the past two months since her passing, I hadn't resigned myself yet to being one of the lost princesses, much less the crown princess. Regardless of who I was, my circumstances remained unchanged. It wasn't as if I could ride into Delsworth and demand King Ethelwulf hand the kingdom over to me.

In fact, as far as I could see, there wasn't much I could do. I was a young woman, alone, without means. Even if a portion of the nobility and ruling class would support me as the rightful heir, they would be risking everything to defy King Ethelwulf. Why would they take such a chance?

"I am surprised Mother did not think to secure your future," Christopher mused. "Now that job will fall to me—or more likely to Mitchell."

"Are you anxious to be rid of me, my lord?"

His grin inched higher. "You are quite troublesome and willful. I doubt many men would be able to tame you."

"Do I need taming?" I could admit I wasn't like most women who were interested in fashion and courtly love instead of hunting and fighting.

"I think we are all in need of taming," Christopher answered with more seriousness than I expected. "If we are blessed to find someone who is willing to kindly speak truth into our weaknesses, then we shall be better for it."

"Have you been blessed with someone who can do that?" I asked. "Surely you have taken a bride by now."

He ducked under a low branch and didn't respond right away, which left a strange hollowness in my chest.

"Though I shall not have land, titles, or wealth to my name, King Draybane has offered me the hand of his youngest daughter."

"Oh." My voice sounded weak, even let down. At the realization, I inwardly chastised myself. I ought to be happy for Christopher. Such an alliance was sure to prosper him in his new life. I forced cheer to my tone. "I am not surprised you have won the king's favor. He must think very highly of you to offer his daughter."

Christopher nodded, but his countenance contained no enthusiasm.

"Do you not harbor affection for the princess?"

"She is a good woman and will make a fine wife."

"Please tone down your excitement, my lord. It is too much to bear."

He grinned again. "A healthy marriage has more at its foundation than feelings."

"Then she is dreadfully dull?"

"I would not speak ill of her."

"No need. I can see that she is already too tame for you."

He seemed to ponder my statement as though he hadn't considered the possibility.

When he began to shake his head in protest, I spoke again before he could. "'Iron sharpens iron,'" I quoted the old proverb. "If she is made of fine silk and you of iron, she will smother you. Or perhaps you will shred her."

The cooling breeze of the evening was a refreshing change from the sultry heat that had been my companion all during my morning and afternoon of hunting. My stomach growled from hunger, but as with other times, I let it remind me of the plight of the people who depended upon me for their sustenance. For most of them, the gnawing never went away. Neither did their deplorable living conditions.

"You have grown into a wise woman," Christopher said.

His words of praise warmed my chest. "I had a very wise teacher."

"Mother was indeed one of the kindest, most astute women I have known."

My throat tightened with my fondness for my Aunt Susanna, along with all the grief lingering in my heart, made all the more acute in knowing how much she'd done to keep me safe.

Suddenly, I wanted to tell Christopher everything Aunt Susanna had revealed to me the night of her death. I'd borne the confusion in solitude. Mitchell had brought it up once. But when I'd informed him I had no wish to speak of it again, he respected my desire, and we'd both gone on with our lives as we had before.

What would Christopher think of Aunt Susanna's revelation about my identity? Would he find it laughable? Perhaps he'd be able to help me make sense of everything.

Before I could talk myself out of telling him, I plunged forward. "On her deathbed, Aunt Susanna confided something—"

He cut me off with a sharp shake of his head and then a finger to his lips. "Someone is coming."

A mound in the rolling hillside prevented us from seeing around the bend ahead of us, but I trusted Christopher's sharp instincts more than my own. A moment later, I caught the pounding of approaching hooves. I pointed to a thick hedgerow. "Hide over there."

"I cannot leave you alone," he whispered even as he began to veer his horse off the path.

"I am not the one with the bounty upon my head." I slapped the flank of his horse and then nudged my mount into a canter. I didn't wait to see if Christopher followed my instructions. Instead, I moved with measured purpose so that when the newcomers rounded the bend a moment later I pulled up short.

I was surprised to see Lord Mortimer upon his warhorse with several squires riding behind him.

"Lady Adelaide." The rise of his brow said he was surprised to see me too. He straightened to his full height. Attired in his chain mail and not his plate armor, he was less imposing than he'd been at the jousting tournament where I'd last seen him. Like most knights, his mail was black and matched his dark hair and his black beard that had been trimmed to a sharp point in an effort to imitate the king's style and thus show his support. With his angular features, long nose, and thick brows, he had an aura of aristocracy. And pride.

Had he finally discovered our treachery at the jousting tournament? Had he come to reclaim his purse of gold? After paying our debt to the physician, I'd planned to take the remainder to Everly when I next visited the smelter and make sure all the laborers had received their due pay. Perhaps now I'd have to discover another way to reimburse those in our employ.

"My lord." I bowed my head respectfully.

"Are you unaccompanied?" He glanced around with a frown and his squires did likewise.

"I sent my servant home ahead of me, my lord."

His sharp eyes assessed me almost angrily. "'Tis not safe to be out alone, my lady. Too many vagabonds and pillagers roam freely who would do a lady harm."

Lord Mortimer was correct. Of late, the conditions had worsened, with too many resorting to corruption in order to survive. Theft, assault, even murder went unpunished so long as it was done in the name of the king. Many lords resorted to bribery, intimidation, and even outright warring to gain what they wanted, regardless of the cost to those they hurt. As they were only following the example of the king, how could he fault their methods when his were often worse?

I pulled back my cloak to reveal my sword. "Have no fear, my lord. I am able to defend myself well enough."

Lord Mortimer sniffed at the sight of my weapon. "When you are my wife, you will not have need of a sword. Or men's breeches."

He spoke as if we were already betrothed, as though our marriage was a foregone conclusion.

"*When* I am your wife?" I asked carefully, knowing I would be wise not to offend him. He might be proud and foolish at times, but he was not cruel or lawless as some of the other lords had become.

"I am riding east to Delsworth to the royal court," he said. "Among my other business there, I will petition the king for your hand in marriage and purchase a royal seal. I am sure that is what your aunt and uncle would want now that you are nigh to twenty. It is far past time for you to be wedded."

The idea of Lord Mortimer bringing the matter before the king sent a rush of anxiety coursing along my veins. "No, I think not—"

"Your aunt will look down from heaven and rejoice to see your future secured." His smile and voice patronized me as if I was still a young child needing tutoring rather than an adult with a mind of her own.

"My brother, Lord Mitchell, will return soon enough from Delsworth. He will want some say in the matter."

"The king's authority is all we need." Lord Mortimer lifted his chin as he spoke. "Now, I and my men shall accompany you back to Kentworth Castle. In the future, see that you do not ride out without a chaperone."

"'Tis but a short distance, my lord." I prayed Christopher would remain hidden. Like most, Lord Mortimer wouldn't hesitate to go directly to the king with news of Christopher's return. Even if he wished Christopher no ill will, he wouldn't chance any hint of disloyalty by refraining from reporting an outlaw's presence.

"Besides," I continued, "I do not wish to inconvenience you or delay your travels."

Lord Mortimer was already motioning for his squires. "It is no inconvenience, my lady. It would be a great pleasure to have a few moments of your company and to gaze upon your beauty."

I closed my mouth over the caustic response begging for release. I couldn't rebuff or anger Lord Mortimer. But neither could I marry him. In our case, I was the iron shield and he the lance—we would shatter rather than sharpen each other.

I didn't know how I'd halt his plans to marry me. But I knew with certainty I must try. Without delay.

Chapter 5

CHRISTOPHER

With only a few kitchen staff and chambermaids left, the great hall was strangely quiet, as had been the inner bailey that had once boasted of stable grooms, a horse master, a falconer, yard servants, a butcher, and a blacksmith.

I sat at the trestle table, a pewter cup of ale in front of me. Gone were the silver goblets, plates, and utensils. The cushions from the benches were absent, leaving the hardness of the planks. The white walls were empty where embroidered tapestries had once hung. Only the most rudimentary of the furniture remained.

The direness of the situation in Langley had been a dagger in my side, as had Adelaide's conversation with Lord Mortimer from the previous evening. I'd respected the neighboring lord for accompanying Adelaide home. I'd have done no less had I come across her alone. However, he'd imposed quite strongly to insist she marry him.

Later, after Mortimer had gone on his way and I'd come out of hiding, Adelaide had explained she had no intention of marrying the widower, no matter what permission the king might give him.

Yet how could she refuse, especially if the king agreed to it? If she declined, she'd cause trouble to herself not only from Mortimer but perhaps even from the king. Especially from the king.

The king, though he claimed to be the defender of Mercia and Warwick, had ruled as a tyrant since the day he'd taken the throne from King Francis. Not only had he killed any magnate or nobleman who'd opposed him, but he'd declared the laws of Bryttania were within his own mouth, that the lives and property of his subjects were at his mercy and to be disposed of at his judgment. With his formidable army standing behind him and every enemy in the land subjected or vanquished, he ruled without judicial process, imposed illegal taxes, and had little concern for how justice was served on any local level of the realm.

I took several gulps of the ale noting its inferior quality compared to what I drank in Norland at King Draybane's court. Wiping a sleeve across my mouth, I shoved my mug away. Ethelwulf controlled the people with fear. Now as I considered Adelaide's fate, I felt the fear of the king once again, and my resentment came rolling back as strong as a summer storm.

I'd pondered the issue all day as I'd toured the estate with her and taken stock of what remained. And still, I had not formulated a viable solution to Adelaide's predicament. Perhaps the best plan was to find her a more suitable husband, a person of her choosing. If she divulged the name of another nobleman for whom she harbored some fondness, Mitchell could make arrangements with the family before I left. Then I'd be able to depart with a clean conscience, knowing she was secure and happy.

I drummed my fingers on the table now barren of its fine white linen covering. Somehow the idea of Adelaide marrying a different nobleman besides Mortimer didn't settle well either.

The door at the side entrance near the buttery opened. At the sight of Adelaide, I rose from my bench to greet her. As she moved into the light of the wall sconce, my salutation lodged in my throat. Her beauty stunned me to silence.

Her rich rose-colored gown was the same hue as the wild roses which grew on the hills. The vividness highlighted her eyes, making them bright and intense. The cut and style of the gown hugged her body, outlining a womanly form that had been hidden beneath the men's garments she'd worn since I'd arrived. Her hair, too, was fashionably styled into wavy curls that fell over her shoulders and down her back.

She held herself with a mature, almost regal bearing, one I'd noticed in her before but that now seemed to highlight how ladylike and elegant she'd become. As she glided across the rushes toward me, I couldn't make myself look away, and I couldn't find my voice. It was almost as if Adelaide's beauty had cast a spell upon me, turning me into a spineless, besotted fool.

No wonder Mortimer wanted Adelaide as his wife. He'd obviously witnessed her loveliness and had been captivated by her.

Even though I'd spent nearly every waking moment with her all day, and even though I'd been enamored with the changes both in her appearance and outlook on life, now seeing her this way suddenly awakened something inside me.

She stopped on the opposite side of the table from me

and lifted a hand self-consciously to her hair. "Is something amiss, my lord?"

"Yes." I swallowed hard. "Your beauty has rendered me speechless."

Her lips curved into a smile. "Speechless? I cannot imagine you without anything to say."

I mimicked the inability to speak, moving my lips without uttering a sound. At my jest, she laughed. The merriment lit her face, making her features even lovelier. The sound of her laughter seeped into my blood, spreading warmth through my chest with each pulse of my heart.

"Believe it or not," she said, smoothing a hand over her snug bodice, "I listened once in a while to Aunt Susanna's instructionn on how to behave and dress like a lady."

"She would be proud to see you so beautiful, as am I." I tried to keep my voice from betraying my reaction to her and silently chastised myself. Adelaide was like an adopted cousin. How could I think of her in any other way?

At the reminiscing of Mother, some of the sparkle diminished from Adelaide's eyes, replaced with sadness. Before I could contrive a witty remark to divert her attention from the melancholy thoughts, the doors at the far end of the hall swung open with a bang that echoed against the walls.

She produced her dagger faster than I unsheathed mine. Her speed and agility with weapons had matured as well, and I wasn't sure whether to feel proud or mortified that Adelaide was so accomplished in weaponry.

Her instincts and reactions were honed. Once again, before I could comprehend the situation, she tucked her dagger back into its resting place beneath her skirt and hastened to the newcomer even as he rushed toward her.

I moved into the shadow of a nearby passageway, knowing I needed to be wary about who I allowed to see me. Though I could trust the household staff not to betray my presence, I no longer knew who else might be friend or foe.

From my hiding spot, I barely had time to assess the visitor attired in chain mail before Adelaide threw her arms around him. "Mitchell!" she cried. "I had not thought to see you for another day or two."

Mitchell? My youngest brother? When last I'd seen him at Father's funeral, he'd been a thin, gangly youth who had refused to speak with me. This man, while not much taller than Adelaide, exuded strength and purpose. He reciprocated Adelaide's enthusiastic greeting by wrapping his arms around her in a welcoming embrace. Even from my distance across the room, I could see the delight on his features. And something more—something she couldn't see but that I clearly could.

Mitchell loved Adelaide. And not just as a cousin.

At the realization, my pulse rammed into my ribs with alarm. What did this affection mean? Did Adelaide love Mitchell too?

She pressed a kiss to his cheek. He laughed with pleasure, holding her, obviously unwilling to break his contact. "If this is to be my reception after a fortnight apart, I shall have to go away more often."

Adelaide smiled. "You would not dare to leave me behind again."

He pulled her back into his arms and held her tightly for another moment, his adoration for her evident once more.

"Then you purchased more food supplies and finished business early?" she asked.

"I hurried," he replied, "because I wanted to return in time to wish you happiness on your birthday."

I started with the news. I'd known Adelaide would soon turn twenty. But I hadn't remembered the actual day. Though Mother had always had a feast each anniversary of our births, I'd never memorized the dates the way she had. Even so, if I'd known today was Adelaide's birthday, I would have wished her felicitations and perhaps had the cook prepare a special supper.

"Now that you are here," Adelaide said, finally extricating herself from Mitchell's hold, "I must inform you that Christopher has come home." She searched for me among the shadows.

I stepped out into the open.

Mitchell's head jerked up, his sights locked upon me, and his expression hardened. The more severe expression reminded me of our father. In fact, Mitchell seemed to have much of Father in his noble countenance.

"Good eve, Mitchell," I said. "I am heartily pleased to see you."

Mitchell eyed me, all jubilance and excitement gone. "Why have you come?" The question was the same Adelaide had asked upon our meeting. Only Mitchell's was less curious and more hostile.

I decided to be as honest with him as I'd been with Adelaide. "I came to sever my rights to the earldom and Kentworth."

His eyes flickered with something akin to relief, but his face remained stalwart. "You needn't have bothered. When Father disowned you, you lost your inheritance."

Disowned me? The word raked at my insides. Even

though I should have expected the consequence, and even though it shouldn't have mattered, the realization stung anyway.

Mitchell watched my reaction and didn't seem to take any joy in my surprise. "What did you expect? With a son as a rebel, what other choice did Father have if he wanted to keep his family safe from the king's suspicion that we were all traitors?"

"I understand. He was wise to cut himself off from me." Ethelwulf had killed noblemen for much lesser infractions. Thankfully, Ethelwulf had respected Father's wisdom enough to overlook his wayward son.

"I have just come from petitioning the king to officially pass the title and lands to me," Mitchell continued.

"You did?" Adelaide's voice contained a surprise that mirrored mine.

Mitchell rapidly turned his attention back to her. "With Mother gone, and now that I am twenty, I believed it within my right to do so. Since Father had already disowned Christopher, the matter was easily settled."

"You could have told me of your intentions." Adelaide studied Mitchell's face.

"I was planning to eventually," he said. "But I thought it prudent to wait until I had word. I did not want to trouble your mind."

"Or were you afraid I would ask you to do the right thing by seeking Christopher's willingness first, rather than sneaking behind his back?"

Mitchell pulled himself to his full height, which was not much taller than Adelaide, and a surliness I'd seen many times in our childhood darkened his features. "I need neither Christopher's willingness nor his permission."

Adelaide, too, seemed to rise, her shoulders stiffening

in readiness for a verbal battle. I inwardly smiled, already knowing who would win. Adelaide was the stronger of the two. She always had been.

"Whether or not you need Christopher's willingness or permission," she was saying, "you must covet it nonetheless. It is the right thing. To take his inheritance without discussion would be the same as stealing it."

Mitchell glared at me. "Christopher gave up his inheritance when he left Langley. Thus, I cannot steal what no longer belongs to him."

"Lawlessness may be the rule of this land," she said, lowering her tone. "But it will not be the rule of Kentworth. We do things honorably or not at all."

The two held each other's gazes in a battle of wills. Finally, Mitchell looked away. "Since Christopher is here and has verbalized his intentions to give me his inheritance, let us cease our arguing."

Adelaide didn't respond.

"After all," Mitchell said. "I have something for you—something that will make you forget how peeved you are with me."

For an instant, I felt like an outsider watching their exchange. I didn't belong here or fit in. Nevertheless, I was too captivated by Adelaide and couldn't walk away and occupy myself elsewhere.

Mitchell retrieved a sack he'd dropped to the rushes. He loosened the drawstring and removed a small package tied in brown cloth. As the folds fell away to reveal a square piece of cake, Adelaide's smile returned.

"One of your favorites," Mitchell said smiling in response. "Gingerbread."

"Oh, Mitchell." She accepted the sweet treat, then lifted the cake to her lips and took a bite. As her lips closed around the delicacy, her lashes fell and she released a soft moan of pleasure.

My sights locked upon her ecstasy, and I watched each bite, wishing I'd been the one to bring her a sweet treat instead of Mitchell. If I'd but taken a moment to think about her, I would have remembered how fond she was of desserts. Over the past year of starvation, she likely hadn't had many opportunities for indulgences.

Mitchell watched her with as much fascination as I did. As before, his interest in Adelaide was as unsettling as my own. Perhaps Mitchell had already reconciled himself to the fact that Adelaide was no longer just a playmate and was indeed an eligible and heart-stopping young woman.

However, I was having a difficult time adjusting to her changes, scolding myself for viewing her as anything more than my cousin, and at the same time unable to keep my newfound enthrallment at bay.

Her eyes flew open, and she lifted the cake to Mitchell. "I am being selfish. You must have a bite as well."

He shook his head. "And give up the gratification of watching you devour it? No. I could not."

She smiled at his gallant answer. Then she turned to me and held out the cake. "I would share with you, too, my lord."

I began to cross the room, knowing I should deny her request as Mitchell had done, that I should allow her to eat the entire rare treat. But something drove me that I didn't understand.

When I stopped in front of her, I opened my mouth.

She broke off a corner and placed the piece past my lips, being careful not to touch them. Before she could remove her hand, I closed my mouth trapping her fingers inside.

It was the kind of trick I would have played on her if we'd been children. But as my lips closed around the cake and her fingers, a strange jolt rocked me at the same instant she sucked in a rapid breath.

I expected her to yank her fingers loose, to take a step back, to even shove me away for my antics. Instead, she froze, her gaze riveted to my mouth. I could only stand stupidly, letting the cake liquefy on my tongue, tasting the honey and molasses. More than the sweetness of the cake, the feeling of her fingers against my lips was a sensation that caused me to forget about food altogether.

Her eyes widened, her growing embarrassment reflecting mine, though I had no wish to let on my conflicted reaction. So I languidly released her, as if I made an everyday practice of allowing young women to feed me.

She withdrew her hand and stared down at the remaining gingerbread, refusing to meet my bold gaze. Only then did I become conscious of Mitchell's dark glare—one that said he was well aware of the changing dynamics with Adelaide, a change he liked for himself but didn't support for me.

Adelaide took another quick bite, clearly attempting to hide her discomfort. "It is delicious, Mitchell. I thank you for the gift."

"I would give you a whole cake if I could." The moment Adelaide ducked her head in acknowledgement of his compliment, he sliced me with another sharp glare.

"You are always so thoughtful." She squeezed his arm.

He placed his hand over hers.

I paused in my chewing to watch their exchange. Understanding finally penetrated the haze of my conscience. Mitchell not only loved Adelaide. He also wanted her for himself every bit as much as he wanted the inheritance.

Adelaide might not recognize Mitchell's feelings and intentions yet. But I did. Though something inside me resisted Mitchell's claim on her, I realized he was the solution to Adelaide's woes. She could marry Mitchell instead of Lord Mortimer and become the Countess of Langley. Once the arrangements were made, I'd be able to leave knowing she was safe and that Mitchell would do everything within his power to make her happy.

If only the prospect brought me more joy . . .

Chapter 6

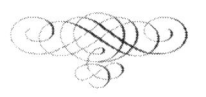

Adelaide

Sitting in the presence of both my cousins should have been a happy occasion. But I was riddled with memories of our family from when Aunt Susanna and Uncle Whelan had been alive and we'd all still been together. I missed those carefree days. More than that, I missed my aunt's calming presence.

With Mitchell next to me and Christopher on the opposite bench, the air between the two was tense. I wanted to punch them both and tell them to stop behaving like children. Instead, I tried to view the situation as Aunt Susanna would, attempting to be a peacemaker.

"We have but a remnant of our sheep left," I said in response to one of Christopher's questions. "The demand for wool has decreased. People cannot pay or trade for wool when they must use everything they have to secure food."

The windows in the great hall were still open, allowing the coolness of the summer night to bathe the stone walls and drive the staleness from the air. We'd already finished our simple supper of roasted hen, salad greens, and thick slices of bread. Now I indulged in another sweetmeat from the bowl at the center of the table. How Mitchell had managed to procure both gingerbread and sweetmeats I didn't know. And for this eve, I didn't care.

"So there is no income at Langley from any source whatsoever?" Christopher asked. "Not even from the Everly smelters?"

"We have taken care of the estate the best we could," Mitchell said testily. "Although I am sure you think you could have done better."

"Under the severe circumstances, I doubt it." Christopher reached for a sweetmeat, and I tried not to think about the moment when his mouth had closed over my fingers. Even so, the memory resurfaced along with a warmth deep in my belly.

"We shall do better this year," I cut in, trying to divert my attention away from the resurgence of girlish feelings for Christopher, mortified the infatuation had so easily surfaced and that he'd likely seen it. "The crops are abundant and healthy."

Before we could converse further, Tall John approached the table. He bowed before addressing me. "My lady, you have a visitor."

"Who is it?" I never had visitors and couldn't imagine who might seek me out, especially after darkness had descended.

Tall John would not meet my gaze even though I'd assured him many times that I counted him my friend more than a servant. "An old woman. Not from around here."

I rose, and Mitchell and Christopher did likewise. "She did not give her name or the purpose of her visit?"

"She said she could speak to no one but you, and that it must be alone."

"Send her away," Mitchell said. "We cannot be too careful whom we trust."

I met Mitchell's gaze and knew he was remembering everything Aunt Susanna had told us the night she'd died. If what my aunt said was true, then King Ethelwulf was in all likelihood still searching for me. Mitchell was right. We had to be careful about who we trusted.

Even so, if the woman was in need, if she was no more than a mere peasant asking for aid, how could I turn her away?

Christopher had raised his brow, his eyes radiating curiosity at our caution when yesterday I'd gone about the villages so freely.

The truth was if King Ethelwulf suspected me, he could have captured me yesterday when I was hunting or riding throughout the countryside. Besides, he wouldn't send an old woman. "You may bring her in here, John," I finally said. "Tell her I shall hold an audience with my cousins present or not at all."

"Adelaide," Mitchell protested. "Will you never heed me?"

"What harm can a lone woman do to the three of us? We are armed and able to defend ourselves."

Mitchell merely shook his head while Tall John bowed and retreated to do my bidding. We sat again, none of us talking.

"Are you in some danger I should know about?"

Christopher glanced first at me and then Mitchell.

Mitchell ignored his brother and focused on me. "You have not divulged anything of what Mother revealed?"

"Divulged what?"

"'Tis nothing of importance," I replied, not wishing to speak of something I longed to put behind me and ignore.

"If you are in danger, I would like to know." With the dust and grime of his travel washed away, his hair combed, and wearing clean garments, Christopher made a dashing portrait. I dared not look into his dark eyes lest he sense how attractive he was. He was already well aware of his charm and needed no further puffing up on my account.

"You have no need to know," Mitchell said. "You have not been here in the past to care, and you will not be here beyond the morrow. So leave off any pretenses that you care today."

"Believe it or not—" Christopher's voice turned hard. "—I do care. Very much."

Before the two could engage in a full battle, we were interrupted by Tall John returning with a stooped figure shuffling behind him. Again I rose, this time to greet my guest. With a dark cloak concealing her body and large hood obscuring her face, I could tell nothing except that she was hunchbacked and had a severely lopsided gait.

When she stopped in front of me, she lowered herself to her knees. Uncertain of the woman's intentions, my fingers found the rounded butt of my dagger. I could feel more than see both Christopher and Mitchell stiffen in readiness as well.

When the woman bowed to the ground before me and held herself in the low position reserved for royalty, surprise coursed through me. Tradition demanded that as her superior, I acknowledge her first before she could speak to me. For an instant, I sorely considered sending her away without a word, for I sensed I would not like what she had to say. But when her slight frame began to tremble, I relented.

"I am Lady Adelaide," I said. "Tall John said you wished to see me."

She lifted her head from the ground but did not look up. "Your Majesty," she said in a gravelly voice. "I am your faithful servant."

Even though she spoke quietly, her words seemed to reverberate off the walls as if she'd shouted them. They sent chills down my spine and over my skin. Only Aunt Susanna had called me that, upon her deathbed, in her last breath. Now this woman had not only bowed low before me but was using the royal title.

I could feel Christopher's attention shift to me, but I didn't want to confront his confusion when mine had surfaced once more.

"I have a message for Your Royal Majesty," the woman spoke again. "For Constance Dierdal Aurora, the queen and true heir of Mercia."

I wanted to object to her labels and calling me queen. But how could I? Not after everything Aunt Susanna had already told me. Not when I had the royal ring and the ancient key within my possession in the leather pouch beneath my kirtle. Not when deep in my soul I sensed the truth about who I was even though I'd tried to disregard it.

Again, I felt Christopher's scrutiny as well as his surprise. Thankfully, he refrained from questioning me.

"You may speak freely." I touched her shoulder gently.

Slowly the woman sat back on her heels and made as though to rise. Every move seemed momentous and painful for her. I was relieved when Christopher stepped forward and assisted the woman back to her feet. When she finally stood again in front of me, she lifted her head and removed her hood.

My heart stuttered to a stop at the sight that greeted me—a grotesque, deformed face. Patches of thin, wispy, snow-white hair grew in clumps about her scarred scalp, as if fistfuls of her locks had been pulled out at one time and had never grown back. Half her face was splotched and shriveled, as if she'd had burning oil poured upon her skin or been subjected to a fire. The socket of one eye was completely shut, and from the sunken appearance, I guessed she had no eye there anymore.

I swallowed my revulsion and prayed for this poor, tortured creature. Whatever had happened to her, she had indeed suffered greatly. As a result, she deserved my compassion and kindness.

"What may I do for you?" I asked. "Do you have need of food? I have not much, but I will give you anything I can."

She lifted her head higher. Her neck was threaded with scars that disappeared into a tattered gray habit.

A gray habit the color of stone. A nun. From St. Cuthbert's in the Iron Hills?

My gaze snapped to hers, to her one open eye, a

gray-blue that was as gentle as a mourning dove. More than the color, I remembered the kindness. It was still there, along with joy and pride.

"Sister Katherine?" I asked.

She nodded. From the wizened set of her mouth, I could tell she'd lost her teeth.

"Aunt Susanna said King Ethelwulf captured and imprisoned you. We believed you were dead."

"No. He did not dare destroy his only link to you."

Awe and gratefulness mingled together for this woman who had saved my life so long ago by bringing me here to Langley. I had an overwhelming urge to embrace her and started to reach for her.

"I am not worthy, Your Majesty." She tucked her hands into the wide sleeves of her cloak, but not before I glimpsed the numerous missing digits and stubs—all that remained of her hands. The sight confirmed that Sister Katherine had indeed been sorely abused, and the thought lit a flame of anger in my chest. Who would dare treat any woman, much less a woman of God, this way?

Before I could formulate a response, a gust of night breeze swept through the open windows and banged one of the shutters against the stone, shattering the silence. Sister Katherine jumped, and fear fell over her features, making her thin lips tremble and her chin quiver. She glanced to the door of the great hall as if expecting someone to barge in.

I could not say why, but an impending sense of doom fell over me as palpably as if the castle had suddenly been besieged.

She turned her attention back to me, a new urgency tightening her already taut skin. "Your Majesty," she said in a calm but ominous tone, "I have come to you today on your twentieth birthday to inform you the time has arrived for you to regain your throne."

Her one eye held me captive with its intensity—a strength that wouldn't let me push aside her wild statement, a strength that demanded a response.

"How will I regain the throne?" I asked the first question that came to mind, the one that had haunted me these past weeks. "I am one woman against a king with a powerful army."

"You are not alone. You must find your sisters. Together you will discover the treasure that will enable you to destroy the evil that has blighted this land."

I didn't know how finding two younger sisters would help me regain a throne I wasn't even sure I wanted. "Do you know where they are?"

"Emmeline is deep in Inglewood Forest, raised by a charcoal burner and his wife. And Maribel is at St. Anne's in the Highlands."

Emmeline and Maribel. The names were foreign to me. If I'd ever heard them, I'd long forgotten them. I tested them silently, marveling that I had sisters. Did they know anything about me or their true identities?

Again Sister Katherine glanced behind her to the door. "You must make all haste away. They will be here ere the night ends."

"Who will be here?" Christopher asked, his voice ringing with alarm.

"The king's men. They are following me here."

"Following you?" Mitchell asked, his eyes widening. "Then you have put Adelaide in danger."

"She's in grave danger," Christopher agreed. From

his intense expression, I could tell he was already plotting our next course of action.

"'Tis the only reason the king has kept me alive all these years," Sister Katherine remarked. "He knew if he set me loose close to your twentieth birthday, at the age of royal ascension, I would seek you out and give you the information you'd need to find your sisters."

"Then you have condemned her to death," Mitchell said, his face turning pale, "as surely as if you'd plunged the sword through her yourself."

"The battle must be fought before it can be won." When Sister Katherine met my gaze, I realized she'd purposefully set the course of my future into motion with her visit. Had she guessed I would be confused and complacent? That I would be reluctant to defy King Ethelwulf?

Even if I was the rightful heir of Mercia, I'd mostly been happy with my life in Langley. If I set out to find my sisters so we could rebel against King Ethelwulf, I'd have to leave everything behind. The life I'd known would cease to exist.

"How much time do we have before Ethelwulf's men arrive?" Christopher asked Sister Katherine.

"I was not so easy to follow as they expected." Sister Katherine gave the ghost of a smile. "I have given you several hours' head start. If you leave right away."

Her words were all the warning Christopher required. He darted forward, calling instructions for Tall John to saddle our horses.

"You do not need to trouble yourself," Mitchell called after Christopher. "You may as well be on your way back to Norland."

Christopher halted in the doorway and spun, his body rigid with the bearing of a man accustomed to not only a knight's life but of commanding others. "I shall see Adelaide to safety."

"You do not think me capable of protecting our cousin?" Even in this harried moment, Mitchell's tone condemned Christopher.

"We will be stronger together," Christopher replied.

"Adelaide and I have fared well enough without you so far. You cannot walk back in here and behave as though you care what becomes of us when you have given no care before. We do not need you now either."

Christopher stared at his brother a moment before shifting his focus to me. "Is this how you feel as well, Adelaide? I do not wish to leave until I know you are secure from Ethelwulf. But as I have been woefully absent during your previous hardships, I cannot claim any right to be here for you now."

I looked from Mitchell to Christopher. I was proud of the men they had become. In spite of the hurts and difficulties that had arisen since Christopher's leaving, I could not deny my affection for both. They were the only family I had known.

Truthfully, I didn't want to send Christopher away. He'd just returned, and I selfishly wanted more time with him. On the other hand, I didn't want Mitchell to feel slighted if I spoke against him and included Christopher in our plans.

Even now, his eyes demanded my loyalty to him above Christopher.

As my attention returned to Sister Katherine, to her deformed body, I realized exactly what she'd endured over the years. She'd languished in prison suffering the worst possible torture. For me. She'd sacrificed her life to keep me safe, just as my aunt and uncle had.

If she believed in me becoming queen, how could I not do the same? The possibility seemed so remote, even outlandish. But I couldn't dismiss it. Neither could I reduce our predicament to a sibling squabble.

I squared my shoulders, knowing I must make a decision quickly. "We are too outnumbered to refuse any help. To do so would be foolhardy. We will graciously take Christopher's proffer of assistance as long as he is able to give it."

Christopher bowed his head in deference before spinning on his heels and continuing on his way.

Mitchell did likewise, but not before I glimpsed the hurt in his eyes. I hoped he'd soon see reason and put his anger toward Christopher aside as I had. There was no sense hanging on to the past hurts, especially not when we needed each other so much now.

Tall John had moved to follow Christopher. "Saddle a horse for Sister Katherine," I called after the faithful steward.

"No," Sister Katherine said. "I am not going with you."

"Of course you are. You must stay with us, and we shall protect you."

"I will only slow you down—"

"That does not matter."

Sister Katherine shook her head. "No, Your Majesty." Her face was lined with a fierceness that told me she wouldn't go unless I physically picked her up and made her.

"What will you do?"

"I will do whatever God asks."

Before she could protest, I bent forward and wrapped the frail woman into a hug. Her body was broken, but I could sense her spirit was not.

She resisted the embrace for only a moment before sliding her arms around me and holding me tightly.

"You will one day be a great queen," she whispered in my ear. "Not because of what you accomplish, but because of who you will become as a woman of God."

With that, she released me and took a halting step back.

I had so many questions I wanted to ask about my parents, my sisters, the hidden treasure, and how I could possibly defeat King Ethelwulf. But our time was short. She needed to leave now, too, if she had any hope of evading recapture.

I could only pray one day soon our paths would cross again.

"God go with you, Your Majesty." She lifted her hood over her disfigured head and limped away.

Chapter 7

CHRISTOPHER

"WE MUST MAKE HASTE," I said to Adelaide as she conversed with an older peasant man and his sons inside the thatched cottage.

Adelaide nodded then pressed the coins into the older man's hand.

The only light in the one room hovel was from the low hearth fire, which showed the few ragged belongings of this poor family—nothing more than a few pallets, stools, and blackened pots.

For once, Mitchell and I had agreed on the need to ride directly away from Langley. But Adelaide had insisted on first stopping at a trusted elder's home and giving him a few coins that he could use to aid the peasants on Langley land until she returned. She'd charged him with buying supplies and distributing them.

I'd learned she and Mitchell had won the gold in a jousting tournament. From what I'd gathered in the argument between the two, Adelaide had been largely responsible for the winnings due to her participation in the tournament disguised as Mitchell.

Upon hearing the news of Adelaide's involvement in the joust, I'd wanted to thrash my younger brother for allowing Adelaide to do something so dangerous. Not only had she put her life in peril but her reputation as a noblewoman.

And as the queen.

I studied her features again, awe still mingling with surprise at the news the haggard old nun had delivered. The girl I'd grown up with, the one I'd wrestled and played with, was one of the lost princesses, the true queen of Mercia.

I'd been but a lad of five when Adelaide came to us, yet I recalled the secretive nature of her delivery by a nun. I also remembered my parents' whispered conversations, especially in those early days, and then how drastically my father had changed. He'd gone from a man who'd loved the previous king—King Francis—to a man who pledged his loyalty and life to Ethelwulf. I'd eventually despised him for the way he'd chosen to serve the new king with such fervor and devotion.

When I'd grown old enough to see the full effects of Ethelwulf's reign, the terror and cruelty with which he ruled his subjects as well as the exorbitant taxes he demanded from rich and poor alike, I'd questioned my father even more. How could he bow his knee to such a man?

Until this moment, it hadn't occurred to me that perhaps he'd only been playing a part. For surely Sister Katherine would have taken extreme care to place Adelaide with a family loyal to King Francis. Did that mean Father hadn't been as devoted to Ethelwulf as I'd assumed? That perhaps he'd remained a loyalist all along?

Outside a short distance away, Mitchell motioned at me from where he stood with Tall John by the horses, holding the reins of Adelaide's mount. He hadn't wanted Adelaide to give away any of the winnings, had asked her to save the gold for supplies we might need on our journey. I had agreed with him, and his unease matched mine.

Sister Katherine had indicated we had two hours and already we'd taken up the better part of one in readying to leave. Although I admired Adelaide's desire to ensure the well-being of the tenants who relied upon her, we were wasting precious time.

My lips started to form Adelaide's name. But I stalled. As the oldest of the three lost princesses and as the queen of Mercia, I could no longer simply address her as a young noblewoman. I had to give her the proper respect due her station.

"Your Majesty," I said with a bow. "Shall we be on our way?"

Her eyes flashed to mine and filled with censure for revealing who she was.

"Your Majesty?" said the elder, his eyes widening.

If Adelaide had any chance of regaining the throne from Ethelwulf, she could no longer hide who she was. She had to reveal she was queen, especially to those who loved her. She would need their aid.

"Shall I tell them or will you?" I asked Adelaide.

"I do not know if this is the proper place—"

"You must do this now everywhere we go." I was overstepping my bounds, but I was unable to stop myself from being straightforward with her as I'd always been. "You will give people hope for a better future, and in so doing will rally their support."

She contemplated my words only a moment before nodding. "You are right, my lord. You may tell them the truth." She didn't wait for me to speak but instead ducked past me out into the darkness of the night.

I made brief work of explaining that Adelaide was the queen of Mercia, the oldest daughter of King Francis and Queen Dierdal. Then we were on our way before the elder and his sons could ask questions or even pay their proper respects.

"We must find a safe place to hide," I called out once we were riding away from the village. I positioned myself alongside Adelaide while Mitchell and Tall John led the way. A sliver of moonlight provided ample guidance, although on Langley land, we could find our way well enough without it.

"Where do you suggest?" She was riding low, her cloak flowing behind her, covering her armor. Gone was the gown she'd worn earlier in the evening, the one that had taunted me with how grown up and beautiful she'd become.

Even so, I couldn't keep from picturing her again, so regal and dignified, already so queenly. Though I'd had no right to react to her, my heart betrayed me with a desire for her I couldn't explain.

"We could ride into Norland," I said, forcing myself to remain objective. "You would find sanctuary there. King Draybane is a kind and noble ruler, one who would welcome you and support your quest to regain the throne."

Ethelwulf had made a certain enemy of King Draybane, especially after plaguing Norland for years with attempted invasions. While Ethelwulf hadn't been able to penetrate the mountainous Highlands on their shared border or Norland's rocky cliffs along the shoreline, he'd resorted to terrorizing Norland's ships through blockading and pirating. In fact, Ethelwulf had attacked Norland for so many years that King Draybane would welcome anyone who might be able to bring an end to the greedy king's reign. At least I hoped so.

The pounding of our horses' hooves filling the night air nearly drowned out Adelaide's question. "Is it my quest to regain the throne, Christopher? Sister Katherine believes so. But is it really possible for me to prevail against King Ethelwulf?"

Was it? I didn't know. There was no denying Ethelwulf was powerful and always had been. I'd been only a young child when he'd conquered Mercia. All I'd ever known was the lawlessness, danger, and poverty his reign had wrought in both Mercia and Warwick. Although I hadn't liked it, I'd tolerated it like most people.

Until one of my trips with Father to Delsworth shortly after turning seventeen.

We'd happened to ride into the capital city after several noble families had been accused of disloyalty to the king—disloyalty for once having sons in King Francis's elite guard unit. As we'd ridden through town, we hadn't been able to avoid passing by an entire noble family hanging from poles that lined the main thoroughfare, from the nobleman all the way down to his infant grandchild. I'd been sickened by the sight of the bodies swaying lifelessly, rotting under the hot summer sun, the ravens already pecking the decaying flesh.

When another of the accused families had been paraded on the city street before their hanging, I'd pleaded with Father to stop the brutality and the injustice. How could Ethelwulf punish these families for something their sons had done years earlier?

But Father had hardened his face and looked the other way. He hadn't raised even the slightest breath of protest.

My youthful anger had taken control of me. I'd called my father a coward for his unwillingness to defend the family. I'd believed Father was wrong for not taking a stand against Ethelwulf and had let him know exactly how I felt about him.

I'd left Mercia shortly after that. I'd wanted to do something about the injustice, to raise an army of other discontents to fight against Ethelwulf. But I'd known I would need the assistance of someone greater than myself if I was to have any chance at succeeding. So I'd gone to King Draybane of Norland and offered him my services. Over the past five years, I'd not only defended Norland against Ethelwulf, but I'd organized concerted raids against Ethelwulf's ships.

Meanwhile, I'd bided my time, hoping and praying one day I could form an army from those who'd fled from Mercia—an army who, with the help of the king of Norland, would be able to surround Ethelwulf and force him into surrendering his hold on the country.

While I'd made progress in uniting other exiles into the beginning of a formidable foe, we'd never gained the momentum we needed. Was our failure because we'd lacked a true leader, someone worthy and capable, someone the people would love? Ultimately, someone they'd be willing to die for?

Could Adelaide be that person? I glanced at her riding next to me, her fortitude evident in the set of her shoulders. She'd always been a strong and determined girl but was even more so now that she was a woman.

More important, her kindness and compassion toward

the people who made their home in Langley knew no bounds. She'd also continued in Father's footsteps, taking care of all the laborers at the Everly iron smelter. If she had already shown herself to be just and merciful and fair here, she'd surely have compassion for the rest of her kingdom.

Yes, I could see the potential in her. She still had much growing to do before she'd be ready to rule. But she was of royal lineage, with more rights to Mercia's throne than Ethelwulf. Was it possible to bring the exiles, rebels, and other discontents to Adelaide's side? What about the many who still lived in Mercia but despised Ethelwulf?

Adelaide glanced at me, but it was too dark for me to gauge her expression. "You have nothing to say, my lord? You think because I am a woman I cannot match King Ethelwulf?"

"Far from it," I replied. "I was just thinking that perhaps you are exactly what the people need."

"In what way?"

"I believe many have resented Ethelwulf's rule. He has brought much pain and heartache to Mercia. Maybe not all have been as openly defiant as I have been, but they dislike the king's presence nonetheless and will be ready to embrace you as a kind, good, and benevolent queen."

"You have more faith in me than I have in myself."

"I see now what I never saw before—that Mother and Father trained you to be more than ordinary." I'd assumed they'd allowed Adelaide to participate in our tutoring, fighting, and leadership lessons because she hadn't wanted to be left out. But by including her on so many aspects of running the estate, they'd been preparing her for the role she would one day assume in running the kingdom.

"What you lack," I said, "you will easily learn."

"I pray you are correct."

"Then I shall take you to Norland to King Draybane."

"You have no right to make the decision on where we will go." Mitchell maneuvered his steed alongside Adelaide and now joined our conversation. "The nun said we must seek out Adelaide's sisters, that together they will find the treasure."

"Of what treasure does the nun speak?" I asked. If Adelaide had access to even a small supply, we would have the possibility of hiring mercenaries to aid our rebellion.

"King Solomon's treasure," Mitchell replied.

I couldn't contain a laugh at Mitchell's mention of the legendary fortune that all kings had sought but none had found.

"'Tis no laughing matter," Mitchell retorted. "Mother gave Adelaide a key to the treasure, one she'd held secretly all these years. And I believe the other two princesses may each have one of the other keys."

I had read the account of King Solomon's wealth, but I'd never heard of keys and had always assumed the stories about an ensuing treasure were myths. After all, how could remnants of Solomon's vast wealth, including chests of gold, survive the ages? If the legend was true, surely the riches had been found long ago. Or perhaps it was simply impossible to find. "What do you think, Adelaide? Do you believe such a treasure still exists?"

I expected her to scoff at Mitchell with me or at the very least to join in my skepticism. But she did neither and instead spoke in a low voice I could hardly hear above the clatter of our beasts. "Already I have had to believe things I never thought possible. Why not this too?"

Ahead our trail narrowed as it began a slow descent into the river valley and level plains. Adelaide nudged her horse forward to take the lead next to Tall John. I sensed our conversation was ending, that she no longer wished to discuss the matter of the queenship or elusive treasures. I could only imagine the shock she'd experienced when she'd learned her true identity as not merely one of the lost princesses but the heir to the throne. It would take time for her to accept the truth and all it entailed. We would need to be patient with her.

"We must follow Sister Katherine's instructions," Mitchell insisted. "First we need to find Emmeline in Inglewood Forest and Maribel at St. Anne's in the Highlands."

I shook my head. "We would do better to ride to safety in Norland and come up with a strategy—"

"Who placed you in command?" Mitchell's voice contained the same bitterness I'd heard earlier over dinner. Long gone was the younger brother who'd followed me around with admiration, and in his place was a man I hardly knew. I clearly had much work to do in repairing our relationship.

Before I could formulate a response. I sensed a rumbling through the earth below us. The slight tremor in the ground was followed by the heavy thundering of horses.

Our pursuers had found us.

Chapter 8

CHRISTOPHER

My senses went into warrior mode. Apparently, Sister Katherine had miscalculated our lead. Either that or Ethelwulf's men were faster than she'd anticipated. If they were a part of his elite guard of specially trained knights, they'd not only be swift but would excel at tracking.

Mentally I berated myself for not hiding our tracks better. I'd expected that once we left Langley land we'd follow Finham Brook as far north as it led. But I hadn't thought we'd need to be careful so soon.

I attempted to gauge the size of the band on our trail. At the same time, my mind scrambled to find a way to elude them. I was a strong soldier and could fight off many men. But I didn't want to take any chances around Adelaide.

"Ethelwulf's men are already upon us," I called.

"Can you tell how many?" Tall John asked glancing over his shoulder at the darkness behind us. The severity of his tone told me he'd sensed the pursuers the same as I had.

"My guess is less than a dozen." Too many would slow down their chase and bring them unwanted attention. Rather Ethelwulf would work secretively, hoping to catch Adelaide before she could flee too far or gain help.

"Can we outride them?" Tall John asked.

"No," I responded. "At least not for long. We need to take cover."

"There is no place nearby that will afford us cover," Adelaide responded, kicking her steed into a gallop. "We shall have to fight them."

My insides protested the very prospect, especially with Adelaide involved.

"They may outnumber us," she called, "but together we are stronger."

"The gorge ahead," Mitchell shouted, urging his horse to stay with Adelaide. "We can cut them off."

I knew the narrowed path of which he spoke. It would only allow one horse and rider through at a time. Mayhap such a strategy would slow the enemy down and give us an advantage. I'd have to pray so.

As we charged forward, my body still protested the prospect of Adelaide joining the skirmish. She might be a fighter, but she was no match for Ethelwulf's elite guard. Even if she hadn't just revealed her true identity to me, I wouldn't have wanted her to join the battle. Now I wanted it less.

On the other side of the gorge, we circled our steeds so that we were facing the ravine. Through the black of night, I attempted to scan the landscape around us, hoping to gain my bearings after so many years away, even as I loosened my bow from the saddle and slung it over my shoulder in readiness. Oncoming torchlight rent the darkness. The lights flickered up and down, bouncing along with their riders. My horse whinnied, sensing the peril every bit as much as I did. "Adelaide, this is too dangerous—"

"Do not underestimate me." The rasp of metal against metal told me she'd unsheathed her sword. "I have never cowered from danger, and I shall not start now."

I wanted to chastise her for being reckless and naïve. This was not the time for heroics. Yet once Adelaide made up her mind to do something, she was too strong-willed to be swayed.

I could not bear the thought of her getting hurt, and my blood pumped hard with the compulsion to protect her. The country needed her. The rebel band in Norland needed her.

Did I need her too?

It was an unbidden question I didn't have time to answer.

She charged back toward the ravine before I could stop her. Mitchell and Tall John spurred their horses after her.

"If the battle does not go in our favor," I called out, "one of you must take Adelaide away, even if you have to drag her."

"I shall protect her with my life." The fear in Mitchell's voice told me he knew as well as I did the stakes were high—too high.

Even as the first of Ethelwulf's men charged through the gorge, I broke off the path and wound my horse toward a large outcropping of boulders to my left. Behind me, the clamor of battle rose in the air—the shouts of men and the clash of swords.

Using the horse's momentum, I jumped onto the boulder and began to scramble upward, climbing the loose rocks until I stood at the top of the gorge. I positioned my bow with one hand and with the other slipped an arrow from the quiver at my belt.

A wounded cry echoed in the opening ahead.

"Saint's blood, Adelaide." My pulse accelerated at the realization the scream could have come from her.

From my height and by the light of the torches of two squires who'd reined well away from the gorge, I took aim at the black-cloaked knight making his way through the ravine opening. I sighted the weak spot in his armor at his neck and then released the arrow. Without waiting to see if it hit its target, I had another arrow nocked and took aim at the soldier directly behind him.

Shouting from the others in the gorge told me I'd lost my advantage, and I ducked in time to avoid a volley of return arrows. Rapidly I crawled backward and descended until I had aim of the knights who'd already made it through and were fighting.

With anxiety roaring in my veins, I honed in on the guard closest to Adelaide. She swung her flail expertly but the knight was twice her size and strength. As he swept his sword toward her, I located the defenseless area in his throat and let my arrow fly.

He collapsed, but immediately two different knights converged from the ravine upon Adelaide. Mitchell intercepted one. The other raised his dagger and swiftly lunged toward Adelaide.

I released an arrow, this time sending it through the soldier's leather glove, piercing his hand, and stopping his momentum. Adelaide had already swiveled to fend another attacker, heedless of how close she'd come to harm.

My fingers fumbled to fit another arrow, needing to

stop the injured knight before he could alert others to my presence. But I wasn't quick enough. He called out a warning to his companions, nodding in my direction.

One started toward me, but I quickly brought him down. From the corner of my eye, I could see that Tall John was in trouble, and so I took aim at the knight he was fighting. My arrow punctured the open spot in the chain mail at his armpit and his heart.

"Extinguish the torches," one of the assassins shouted to the squires, finally realizing I had an advantage in my high location and would continue to pick them off.

I studied the position of the remaining opponents. Before the squires could douse their torches, I took out one more soldier. As the blackness of the night fell upon the battle, I visualized my next target and took aim. Through the scant starlight, I did it twice more until the commander of Ethelwulf's band shouted a call to retreat.

Only then, did I whistle for my steed. At her snort, I sprang upon her and started after the few remaining soldiers. I rode low and fast, drawing my horse closer and at the same time unsheathing my sword and dagger. One by one, I eliminated the danger until finally only a lone squire was left. With my blade at his throat, I pierced the first layer of his skin.

He shuddered against my brutal hold, his rasping breath matching mine.

"Return to your king with the news that the true queen of Mercia will not rest until she has ascended to her rightful place on the throne."

I didn't give him the opportunity to answer but instead booted his horse to send him on his way. He wasted no time in riding off.

To my right flank in the dark came the crackle of

brush and the snort of a horse.

"Christopher?" Adelaide called my name in a half whisper.

"Here." I shifted in my saddle, assessing the area. We were safe. At least for now. Once Ethelwulf realized we'd decimated his small army, he'd soon be after us again.

"How do you fare?" she asked, drawing nearer.

I dismounted at the same time she did. Except for a few minor cuts and scrapes, I was fine. "I am unharmed. And you?" I found myself holding my breath until she stood next to me and answered.

"I fare well. And so do the others. They are checking the deceased." I could sense the forced bravado in her tone. Had she been hurt after all?

I reached for her hand, needing to assure myself she was well. She didn't resist but allowed me to enfold her hand in mine. I tried to examine her in the dark, but her cloak and the shadows of night veiled her too much for me to assess her true condition.

"You were not hurt, were you?" I asked.

She was silent, giving way to the clatter of the branches overhead swaying with the wind, filling the air around us with the strong fragrance of freshly bloomed meadowsweet. My muscles tightened in sudden fear of her answer, and my mind flashed with the image of a mortal wound, of blood pouring forth, of her life ebbing away at this very moment.

"No, my lord," she whispered, as though sensing my anxiety. "But I would have certainly perished if not for your quick thinking and your skill with the bow."

"True. You were reckless to ride into battle with no heed for the size or strength of your enemy. You let pride in your skills cloud your judgment."

She stiffened and tried to release her hand from mine, my words apparently not what she'd wanted to hear. Surely, she knew I'd tell her the truth whether she liked what I had to say or not. I'd always been honest with her, and I would not change who I was because I'd learned she was royalty. In fact, perhaps now more than ever she'd need someone who remained candid.

"You think me a fool?" she asked almost angrily.

"You are brave and determined," I answered. "But also inexperienced in the ways of warfare."

She didn't respond right away, but she'd at least stopped fighting my hold on her hand.

"You are a decent fighter, Adelaide," I said. "There are no other women—or many men—who can fight even half so well as you. But Ethelwulf's knights are superior warriors, experts, and vicious. We must not underestimate them."

At my chastisement, I thought she'd attempt to wrest free again. Instead, she released her breath in a slow exhale. "You are right. As usual."

I wanted to jest with her as we used to do when we were children. But the gravity of all that had just happened lay heavy upon me. I'd killed almost a dozen men. Even though they were Ethelwulf's soldiers who would have slain me if given the slightest chance, I never relished taking the life of another human.

"I have fought in melees in many tournaments and have jousted and won," she spoke again, this time her voice small like that of the girl she'd been when I'd seen her last. "I did not realize—did not expect—did not know this kind of combat would be so different, so difficult."

Her hand in mine trembled just a little, enough for me to realize how sheltered she'd been all these years.

"Killing, even in war, is never easy," I replied. "But when we are battling against evil for the greater good of many, there will always be a cost."

Her soft breathing filled the space between us.

"We are fighting for a better Mercia," I continued, "a place where fair laws are upheld, where justice prevails, and where people can reside peacefully and raise families in safety. No, life will not always be easy. But the citizens should be able to live with hope and not fear."

"You are wise and experienced and strong in ways that I am not. Perchance you should become the next ruler of Mercia."

I shook my head. "No—"

"What is so important about me that I should become queen? A royal signet ring and an ancient key are not enough to transform a person into a good ruler."

"You have more than that," I insisted. "You are a part of a royal line, a family who has ruled wisely and mercifully for centuries. You have royal blood running through you—"

"Why does royal blood matter? I should think strengths such as yours would be coveted."

"No, Adelaide. With your heritage and bloodline, you are set apart from the rest of us. God has chosen and sanctioned your family's leadership. And that is what the people want—a king or queen who is different from them, someone they can look up to and revere, someone set apart. Not someone ordinary like me."

"You do not know for certain—"

"I do know. I have tried to rally Mercia's outcasts into a rebellion. While they have respected my leadership, they need a ruler who represents everything they love and have lost, a special person they would be willing to die for."

"Therein you think I am that person?"

I couldn't see her features clearly, but I glimpsed enough to acknowledge how commanding her presence was. She had the bearing and appearance of a queen. And she would soon learn how to lead like one.

I lowered myself onto one knee, tossed back my mail coif, and bowed my bare head before her. "Yes, Your Majesty. You are that person. And I pledge you my fealty in both life and death."

Was this then my purpose? I'd floundered in recent years, trying to understand what I needed to do and how I could truly help my country. Mayhap this was what God had been preparing me for all along.

Of the many loyalists in Mercia, Sister Katherine had chosen my family for Adelaide. If my parents had been willing to risk their lives for her, surely God wanted me to do the same. Why else would He have orchestrated my return to Mercia to coincide with Adelaide's twentieth birthday and Sister Katherine's visit? God wanted me at her side to guide and protect her.

Who better than me? A nobleman in the thick of the rebellion? A nobleman with connections to the king of Norland? A nobleman who'd already fought in many battles and was seasoned in strategy and warfare?

She removed her glove and placed her hand upon my head. "Oh, Christopher," she whispered. "I thank you. You are a good man, and I pray I shall be found worthy of your fealty."

Her hand rested lightly upon my hair, but even so slight a touch burned into me. I had the sudden wish she would stroke my head in the tenderness of affection. How might it feel for her to comb back my hair?

The unspoken question took me off guard, and to end

the distraction, I gently captured her hand. As any nobleman would do to a lady, I brought her fingers to my lips and placed a kiss there.

If I thought having her fingers upon my head was distracting, having them against my lips was even more so, reminding me of earlier in the evening when I'd closed my mouth around those fingers as she fed me the piece of gingerbread. I knew I ought to drop her hand. But the softness of her skin against my lips was tantalizing. The slenderness of her fingers was mesmerizing. The gentle curves of her knuckles were enticing.

I tightened my grip and pressed my lips more firmly against her hand, breathing her in. She made no move to break the contact. Almost imperceptibly, her fingers tightened within mine, as though she welcomed my touch—though I could not think why she would.

"Adelaide!" Mitchell's anxious call penetrated our moment alone.

Adelaide stepped away from me, rapidly withdrawing her hand and tucking it behind her back as if to hide evidence of our closeness from Mitchell.

"I am here and safe," she replied in a slightly breathless voice that made me wonder if my kiss had affected her as much as it had me.

The crunch of brush signaled Mitchell's arrival along with Tall John. A moment later as I stood, I glimpsed their approaching outlines.

"You should not have rushed off without me," Mitchell said rebuking Adelaide as he slid from his mount.

"I only thought to aid Christopher in vanquishing the remainder of our foe."

"From now on, I would like you to stay with one of us at all times." Mitchell's request came out sounding more like a plea. While I agreed with him regarding Adelaide's proximity, I would have commanded Adelaide and not begged.

"Thanks to Christopher, we are saved," she said.

Mitchell sniffed derisively, tension radiating from his muscles. "Thanks to Christopher's slaughter of the entire regiment, we will face severe repercussions."

"We will face severe repercussions no matter what we do," I said.

"You could have allowed a remnant to live," Mitchell replied. "Now not only will the king be angry at losing Adelaide, but he will be sorely embarrassed at the defeat and will find a way to punish us most severely."

"He needed to know Adelaide is strong and not easily conquered."

"And he will show us in return that he will not tolerate our rebellion."

"So be it."

We had declared war against Ethelwulf. And I, for one, was more than ready for it.

Chapter 9

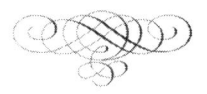

Adelaide

I leaned wearily back against the cave wall, not caring my hair had come loose and now hung in messy tangles over my shoulders.

"I'll take the first watch." Christopher knelt outside the narrow opening. His gaze swept over Tall John, who'd fallen into an exhausted slumber the moment he'd sprawled out on the cave floor. Then his sights moved to me. "Try to sleep."

"I shall take the second watch." I tried unsuccessfully to stifle a yawn.

"Before Mitchell left to hunt for game, he said he would take the next watch."

I nodded, too tired to protest. We'd ridden all night as fast as we could. By dawn, we'd had to stop and rest our mounts. Besides, Christopher had insisted we would be safer if we traveled under the cover of darkness rather than by daylight.

Closing my eyes, I breathed in the damp mustiness of the cave and hugged my cloak tighter about me to ward off the chill that permeated the craggy walls. Though still in the rocky heathland south of Langley, we were several days of riding from the wild woods of Inglewood Forest. Permeated with oak, beech, pine, and birch, the thickly forested land spread across the southern region of Mercia.

The rising crags and dense woods provided not only a rich resource of timber and charcoal for Mercia but had also been a shield to protect against King Ethelwulf's Warwick, which lay directly south of Mercia. Many years ago, King Ethelwulf had wisely chosen to invade Mercia from the East Sea with the help of the Danes, who'd perfected sea warfare. He'd attacked several coastal cities, the most important of which had been Delsworth, the capital and royal residence of King Francis and Queen Dierdal.

My parents.

I still couldn't reconcile the idea that the former king and queen were truly my parents. Although King Ethelwulf forbade speaking and teaching about the previous leaders, our tutor had educated us about the royal lineage anyway. Since Aunt Susanna's death, I'd been attempting to recall all the details the wise old scholar had shared.

Mostly, I remembered his tales of how the king and queen had died. When King Ethelwulf and his army had surrounded Delsworth, King Francis had participated in the defense of the city and had fought bravely alongside his elite guard of trained warriors. He'd been gravely wounded in the fighting but had clung to life.

Due to the stress of the siege and war, the queen had gone into labor and had delivered twin daughters. Shortly after the birth, she'd died, but not before asking one of her ladies-in-waiting to escape from the castle and take the newborn babes to safety.

When King Francis had learned of his wife's death, he'd succumbed to his injury and given up his tenuous grip on life. With both the king and queen dead and King Ethelwulf surrounding the city and royal residence, Mercia's army had surrendered.

Apparently, King Ethelwulf had ordered the execution of all the king's elite guards. He'd also put to death King Francis's closest advisors. Most shocking of all, he'd hung the dead bodies of King Francis and Queen Dierdal on the castle wall, swiftly punishing any citizen who protested.

In the dark of night, one small band of rebels had overpowered the gatekeepers and had stolen the bodies in order to give them a proper burial. The rebels and the bodies had never been located, though it was rumored King Ethelwulf had spent a great deal of time hunting them down.

I'd always been curious regarding the band who had so bravely defied King Ethelwulf and stolen the queen and king off the castle wall. I'd also admired their loyalty to the deceased couple—which had told me more about the previous king and queen than anything my tutor had taught me. The king and queen had been well loved and revered by the people of Mercia, so much that people had been willing to risk their lives for the couple even after they were dead.

Princess Constance had been only three years old at the time King Ethelwulf had taken the throne. Apparently, at the threat of attack on Delsworth, the princess had been evacuated along with most of the court to the city of Everly, which was situated among the foothills of the Iron Hills.

When King Ethelwulf's troops arrived in Everly, the nobility had already fled, Princess Constance was gone, and her old crippled nursemaid had been found dead in the nursery—stabbed in the chest with what had appeared to be a self-inflicted wound. She'd killed herself and had taken to the grave the whereabouts of Princess Constance. Since then, no one had known what had become of the princess.

Until now . . .

Now King Ethelwulf knew I was still alive. And after word reached him of the slaughter of his guard, he'd also know I would not be easily subdued. That, in fact, I planned to reclaim the throne. At least I tentatively planned that, though I knew not how I'd manage such a feat.

I shifted against the rocky wall, trying to find a more comfortable position. As tired as I was, sleep eluded me, bullied away by my ever-growing anxiety regarding the future, especially whether I'd made the right decision on where to go next.

Christopher wanted to take me to Norland, to King Draybane, assuring me the king would support my cause. It was doubtful he would lend his soldiers to our fight, but at the very least, he would give me refuge while we strategized. Christopher believed there were enough Mercians living in exile in Norland who were ready to rise up against King Ethelwulf.

Mitchell, on the other hand, insisted we go south and follow Sister Katherine's instructions to locate my sisters. He was determined to look for the illusive hidden treasure with the hope it would bring success to our campaign. After more heated debate last night,

I'd come to the conclusion we'd fare best if we adhered to Sister Katherine's directive. I took to heart her cryptic, almost prophetic words: *You are not alone. You must find your sisters. Together you will discover the treasure that will enable you to destroy the evil that has blighted this land.*

If all went as planned, by the end of the week I'd meet one of my sisters—Emmeline of Inglewood Forest. Once we explained her identity, would she embrace me? I couldn't deny I hoped so.

Yet my misgivings unsettled my stomach. What if she didn't like me? Even worse, what if we couldn't find her? How would we know where to begin our search among the vast miles and miles of woodland? Sister Katherine had said Emmeline was in the forest being raised by a charcoal burner and his wife. But how did we know that was still true, that they had remained in the woods, that they hadn't moved elsewhere over the years?

In addition, there were probably several dozen charcoal burners with official licenses living in the forests, but many more who operated independently and illegally. How would we narrow our search? And how would we evade Ethelwulf's soldiers? Though we were attempting to mask our tracks and scent, surely his best knights would continue to hunt me.

I moved again, trying to get comfortable, but to no avail. At the scuffle of footsteps outside the cave, I opened my eyes.

"Are you still awake?" Mitchell whispered as he crawled through the cave entrance, hidden by roots and moss from several of the trees growing above.

"I wish I could so easily forget the worries of the

day like Tall John," I whispered with a glance to our faithful manservant, whose soft snores drifted in the quiet of the cave.

"Have no fear." Mitchell unstrapped his belt with its assortment of weapons before lowering himself to the cave floor next to me. "We shall find Emmeline soon enough."

At the very least, my decision to search for Emmeline had satisfied Mitchell and had assured him I valued his advice as much as Christopher's. If only the two would make peace with each other.

"Before King Ethelwulf finds us? I fear next time he attacks, his men will be more prepared." My mind filled with images from the battle last night, how overwhelmed I'd felt when the king's men surrounded us on all sides. If not for my chain mail and armor, I would have been dead. And if not for Christopher's exceptional aim with his arrows, we would have been defeated.

That thought had plagued me all throughout the long night—the realization I wasn't as infallible or as strong as I'd believed. Christopher's rebuke still chafed me. *You were reckless to ride into battle with no heed for the size or strength of your enemy. You let pride in your skills cloud your judgment.*

Though I hadn't wanted to hear it, he'd been right. Henceforth, all I could do was learn from my mistake and pray the next time I faced King Ethelwulf's soldiers, I'd do so with more wisdom and skill.

"Do not trouble yourself," Mitchell said in the soothing tone he oft used with me. "Once we find the treasure, we shall have the wealth and power to do whatever we wish."

"*If* we find it."

"We shall. Sister Katherine has assured us that after you are reunited with your sisters, you will locate the treasure." His shoulder brushed against mine, and he smiled at me warmly. "You do still have the key, do you not?"

I fumbled for the leather pouch strapped to my side underneath the chain mail and my tunic. I loosened the strings and dug inside, grazing the signet ring King Francis had once worn. And then my fingers closed around the key. "I have it."

"May I see it again?" His eyes lit with excitement I couldn't resist. While Mitchell shared the same brown eyes and dark hair coloring as Christopher, that's where the similarities ended. Mitchell's angular face was more serious and aristocratic compared to Christopher's chiseled yet dashing countenance.

I'd never really considered whether Mitchell was handsome, not when I'd always secretly been enamored with Christopher. But now that the two brothers were together, I realized Mitchell had turned into a fine-looking man, too, though strangely, neither his appearance nor his aura appealed to me the way Christopher's did.

The remembrance of Christopher's kiss upon my knuckles caused sparks in my midsection like flint against wood. His mouth had been soft and warm, his kiss so tender. The strange sensation had filled me with confusion and a longing I still didn't understand and needed to put from my mind straight away.

I placed the key in Mitchell's outstretched hand. The sunlight streaming in through the cave opening past the tangle of roots gave him enough light to examine it. The pure gold glistened as he turned it over, studying the pomegranate pattern on the bit. "It is not as heavy as one would expect for being solid gold."

"Perhaps it is hollow." He cradled the thick shank in his palm, weighing it. "I think you may be right." He twisted the oval bow at the top. When it didn't budge, he attempted to rotate the elegant collar at the pin. It didn't move either.

"Do you believe the key somehow comes apart?" I asked.

"I can only conjecture from the rumors I have heard. Most speculators believe each key somehow contains a clue pointing to the whereabouts of the treasure."

I reached over and rubbed my thumb across the engraving on the bit. "Perhaps the picture is the clue, like hieroglyphs that communicate words through images."

"In ancient times, the pomegranate represented wisdom and learning. But such a symbol is much too vague to lead to the treasure." He fell silent as he again carefully examined the relic.

"Maybe one needs all three keys to make sense of the clues," I offered.

He released a disappointed sigh and returned the key to me. "You are correct, which is probably why Sister Katherine said you would have to work with your sisters."

I ran my fingers along the shank. Upon reaching the thin band that separated the shank from the collar, I stuck my fingernail into the narrow groove. When I tried removing it, the key's grip held fast. I wiggled the tip of my finger, hoping to loosen the hold, only to find that I'd somehow pressed in deeper.

"Look what I have done," I said to Mitchell with a smile. "I have been captured by the key."

He leaned forward and, seeing my predicament, gave a low whistle. "Adelaide, you *have* done it."

"I am only jesting."

"No, you have indeed discovered something more about the key." He peered closer at my fingernail wedged in the key. "I need a pin. Might you have one I could use?"

I plucked a hairpin from the mess of my tangled locks.

Eagerly he took it and poked the sharp end into the slit near my fingernail. He loosened the grip just enough for me to free myself then proceeded to wiggle the pin and prick the key, pressing all the way around the thin band. At a sudden click, the shank separated from the pin.

I sucked in my breath and waited as he worked carefully and slowly to finish prying the two pieces apart. When the shank finally came loose, Mitchell grinned and held up a narrow, empty tube.

"You were right." His voice hummed with renewed excitement. "It is hollow."

I reached for the shank, curious to see if it contained anything. Mitchell reluctantly released it, and I proceeded to peer inside and tip it over to no avail.

Mitchell handed me the hairpin. "There may be something wedged inside."

I slipped the pin into the hollow area and began a meticulous search along the edges, hoping to discover a note or item that might indicate more about the hidden treasure. "It is empty," I said. "If the shank ever held a clue, it no longer does."

"Did you reach the very tip, up near the bow?" His expression urged me to continue to try, not to give up yet.

I slipped the pin in farther and pressed against something. I wasn't sure if I'd simply touched the end or not, so I handed the shank and pin to Mitchell. "Maybe you should try."

Biting his lower lip as was his habit when concentrating, Mitchell gently probed until he finally grinned. "I have pried it loose."

"What loose?"

He tipped the shank upside down and tapped at the sides. Seconds later, a wad as small as a pea fell into his palm.

For a minute, we could only stare at the crumpled item. Finally, he lifted his hand toward me, deferring to me again.

I unraveled the scrap of parchment. It was leathery and wrinkled and worn with time. One side was blank, but on the other were two tiny block letters *H. W.* and the word *Fortress*.

"H. W. Fortress," I read.

He nodded at the parchment scrap. "May I?"

I handed it to him and waited as he examined the neat writing.

"This is no ancient language or message," I said, confused to find the print readable. "Not what I had expected for King Solomon's treasure."

Mitchell scrutinized the parchment, his expression intense, his eyes narrowed. "Perhaps a recent king, maybe King Alfred the Peacemaker or one of his forefathers, found the treasure and relocated it for better safekeeping. Or at the very least, took the initiative to hide clues to its whereabouts."

"Then you think H. W. Fortress is the location of the treasure?"

He shook his head. "No. That would be too easy. But this fortress is clearly someplace we need to go in order to uncover additional information."

"H. W. Fortress. I can recall no place in Mercia with that name. Can you?"

"My guess is that if this clue was written decades or even a century ago, the fortress may no longer exist."

I tried to picture the old drawing of Mercia we'd once studied during our geography lessons, a map from when Mercia and Warwick had been united under King Alfred and had simply been known as Bryttania. As I attempted to recreate the diagram in my mind, I couldn't remember anything labeled *H. W. Fortress*.

I leaned back against the cave wall again and closed my eyes. The excitement of finding something in the key faded with the realization it was likely only the first of many puzzles we must solve to find the location of the treasure. Even if we eventually found the site, it appeared a previous king had already discovered it. Would anything remain? Was it even worth pursuing? Especially when so much was at stake?

As I fell into a restless sleep, doubts crept in and left me more confused than ever.

Chapter 10

CHRISTOPHER

The skin at the back of my neck prickled with unease. I glanced over my shoulder into the dense woods we'd traversed. But I could see nothing that should alarm me. Only the lush green of the heavy underbrush that covered the forest floor and impeded our travels.

After one night of navigating Inglewood Forest in the dark, I'd realized the foolishness of my plan to ride by night and sleep by day. That had worked on Langley land and on the heathland we'd crossed with only boulders, gorse, heather, and a few silver birches. However, once we'd entered the thick vegetation of the forest, we'd circled aimlessly, going nowhere. We'd lost precious time and would find no charcoal burners' houses in the dark.

Halfway through the first night, we'd made camp, slept, and resumed our journey by light of day. Yesterday we hadn't seen a single soul. Today we'd glimpsed evidence of smoke rising a distance off to our west. But after riding for hours, we still hadn't encountered a charcoal burner's fire or home.

Now, near dusk, I was beginning to believe we were being followed. I didn't think our pursuers could be Ethelwulf's men. Though we'd traveled nigh five days since the night we'd battled his elite guard, the lone squire I'd released would have needed two days of hard travel to reach Delsworth to the east. Even if Ethelwulf had sent more guards after us right away, his men couldn't catch up to us so quickly. I guessed we had at least a day's lead.

Nevertheless, the prickle on my neck crept up to my scalp, and I tugged my chain mail hood forward. I wanted to move directly behind Adelaide so I'd be in a position to protect her better. But she'd stayed close to Mitchell over the past couple of days.

I hadn't agreed with her decision to attempt to locate her sisters first. I'd wanted to ride directly to Norland where King Draybane would counsel us wisely on how to proceed. He'd become like a father to me and would do all he could to come to my aid.

However, Mitchell had persuaded Adelaide we should pursue the other princesses and the treasure before doing anything else. I suspected he was enamored with the treasure hunt more than finding the princesses, especially after discovering the slip of parchment inside the key. He'd talked of little else since.

I couldn't fault Adelaide for her desire to seek out her sisters or the treasure. We'd be stronger with both. Yet I was apprehensive to remain in Mercia now that Ethelwulf knew about Adelaide.

A sudden flap of wings in the high branches overhead startled me. Through the canopy of leaves, a dozen or more blackbirds rose into the gray sky, the sign danger was rapidly approaching.

My steed tossed his head and snorted as if adding his warning.

"We've got company," I called to the others.

Ahead, Tall John unsheathed his sword and scanned the woodland. "Which direction, my lord?"

I reined my horse and stopped to listen. The others did likewise.

Except for the angry squawk of the blackbirds flying away, the forest was strangely silent. Only the faint rustle of the afternoon breeze among the leaves mingled with the soft buzz of cicadas.

Whoever was following us knew the forest well enough to stay undercover.

I surveyed the low-lying brush, taking in each twig and leaf. At the pair of golden eyes staring through a narrow parting of leaves, I froze.

"Mitchell," I said quietly. "You and Adelaide climb up the tall oak next to you."

I scoured the dense, low greenery and counted five more pairs of golden eyes for a total of six. And each was locked on Adelaide. My blood turned to ice and spurted forward in painful, sharp bursts.

"John," I continued as calmly as I could manage. "Take our horses due south. Tie them there and hasten back. We shall have need of every hand for the fight."

We couldn't risk losing our horses, and they'd spook, cause more chaos, only getting in the way of the battle. I slid off my mount and handed the reins to Tall John. He took them without question.

Of course, Adelaide was not so compliant. She remained on her steed and slanted a demanding gaze at me. "I am better at fighting upon a horse."

"To the tree, Adelaide." My voice turned urgent. And

when the first pair of golden eyes pushed through the brush to reveal a narrow black snout, sharp fangs, and pointed ears, my veins converged into a pool of panic at the center of my chest. "Now."

"You do not know me well enough to make such a decision for me," she responded, her tone growing haughty.

"For the love of the saints, Adelaide." I took out my first arrow, nocked and aimed it at the enormous black wolf crouched less than two dozen paces away. "I beg you to obey me for once."

After the battle the other night and retrieving the arrows I could reuse, I had only five left in my quiver. I couldn't afford to miss a single shot. Even then, I would find myself one arrow short of what I needed.

Though I stood in closer proximity to the wolf, its golden eyes were fixed upon Adelaide's back. From its size and strength, I surmised this pack wasn't ordinary. Rather they were Highland black wolves. Ethelwulf used special animal trainers known as Fera Agmen to communicate with wild animals and control their behavior.

Such creatures were deadly. They'd stop at nothing until they fulfilled the wishes of their Fera Agmen. I had no doubt these wolves had been ordered to kill Adelaide.

"Come, Adelaide," Mitchell said, his voice edged with fear. He'd noticed the wolves now, too, and recognized the danger she was in. He motioned toward the oak towering above us. "I shall race you up into the highest part of the tree and see which of us can get there the fastest."

Before Adelaide could respond with more stubbornness, the wolf released a feral growl. She twisted in her saddle. At the sight of the beast, she screamed, terror rippling across her face and turning it ashen.

The noise, along with the panic in her expression, hit me so forcefully my fingers nearly slipped from the taut bowstring. For an instant, fear tore into me as viciously as fangs tearing into flesh.

Just as quickly, I pushed aside all emotion and released the arrow. With a whistling whir, it ripped through the air and impaled the wolf through the head. Two more slinked out of the thick brush and began to creep toward Adelaide from the front. A third emerged from the rear.

How could I take out all three before any one of them made it to Adelaide?

Her horse snorted, nostrils flaring, eyes rounded and wild.

"Leap into the tree, Adelaide," Mitchell pleaded, dropping from his horse and slapping its rear so that it bolted in the direction where Tall John had disappeared. "We need to get up the tree."

Another wolf sprang from the woods and charged directly at Adelaide's horse.

My arrow flashed forward, hitting the target and stopping the creature so that it fell motionless to the ground.

With the dead wolf at its feet, the horse reared onto its hind legs, neighing in alarm. Adelaide clutched after the reins, but she was too late. They slipped out of her reach, and the horse's motion sent her toppling backward.

She screamed again, and instead of landing on her feet as I'd seen her do plenty of times in the past, she plummeted to the ground on her backside.

"Get up, Adelaide." Mitchell attempted to hoist her to her feet. But she resisted him and scrambled away, her dagger out and ready.

"Watch behind!" I called.

Catching sight of the wolves creeping in on all sides, Adelaide released another terrified shriek.

Mitchell already had his sword out along with his flail. But he was staring helplessly at Adelaide and not on high alert as he needed to be in order to fend off the remaining pack.

I fitted another arrow into my bow and sighted the creature that seemed the most menacing. Out of the corner of my eye, I caught the movement of another closing in on the right. They'd surrounded us. If only I could keep them from attacking until Tall John returned.

However, I had the terrible foreboding they planned to lunge for Adelaide at the same time. If they did, I wouldn't be able to hold them off. I might kill two or three before they reached Adelaide, but not all four, not even if I had a full quiver.

"Mitchell," I called. "You have to act now in order to protect Adelaide. I need you to eliminate the wolf to the left. And I shall take out the others."

He lifted his stricken attention away from Adelaide. Our gazes collided for an instant, long enough for me to see once again how much he cared for her, that he loved her deeply and couldn't bear the thought of losing her.

"Fight, Mitchell," I admonished. "You must fight."

My words seemed to rouse him. He crouched and faced the wolf, flail swinging and sword at the ready. In that instant, I saw him for the strong and competent man he'd become. He was no longer the little brother who'd trailed after me, attempting to keep up with all my escapades. I had a momentary pang of regret. If we didn't survive, I wouldn't get the chance to bridge the gap between us.

All the more reason to prevail. I focused on an imaginary target upon the closest wolf's head. I would have preferred to pierce its heart, but it stooped too low for me to manage the shot. Since I didn't have any arrows I could waste, I had to make the kill now.

The instant my arrow left my bow, the remaining wolves took that as their cue. All of them lunged in a coordinated attack that only confirmed these animals had been trained for battle by Fera Agmen.

My arrow stuck deep into my target's forehead between its eyes, dropping it to the ground. Immediately I released another shot, sending it into the heart of the next creature. The yelp and ensuing silence told me I'd made the kill. Without time to aim, I released the fifth and final arrow. It pierced the wolf's chest, but not in the heart.

Tossing aside my now useless bow, I reached for both my dagger and sword and leapt to place myself between the injured wolf and Adelaide. Already it was crouching and preparing to spring at Adelaide again.

Yelps came from the wolf Mitchell was still fighting. I prayed he would be able to keep it at bay until I could spin around to help him.

The golden eyes of the beast before me fixed upon Adelaide. The thick black fur near the impaled arrow had turned wet and slick with blood. But he bared his teeth in a low, menacing growl, and then sprang with a deft and powerful leap in spite of his injury.

I lifted my sword to finish him, but from the corner of my eye, I caught the shadowy black outline of a seventh alpha wolf flying through the air—this one, the largest of the pack, had kept himself hidden in order to orchestrate a surprise attack once his companions had distracted us.

Sickening bile swelled into my throat. I was too late to help Adelaide. Even as I frantically slashed my sword across the injured wolf's neck and pivoted, I knew I couldn't stop the alpha from landing upon Adelaide.

Silently, I willed Adelaide to overcome her fear and fight. She might not be able to kill the beast, but she could at least put up a measure of defense. However, she didn't seem to notice the newest threat. Her attention was fixed upon the dead creature in front of her, her breath coming in wheezing gasps, her expression still one of terror.

I drew back my arm and flung my dagger at the alpha wolf. At best, I could only hope to hit its spine and slow it down. For a long agonizing heartbeat, I watched helplessly as the beast leapt in a high arc above Adelaide, its sharp claws outstretched and long fangs open.

"No!" I dove at it, intending to wrestle it with only my brute strength if need be.

My knife lodged into the beast's back at the same time another knife soared through the air end over end. The blade sliced directly into the wolf's heart. A second later, the creature knocked into Adelaide, throwing her backward and its full weight landing on her.

Her scream came to an abrupt halt, as did my heartbeat. I rushed to her. All I could picture were fangs piercing the vein in her throat and her lifeblood slipping away.

As I shoved the alpha wolf off her, Tall John broke through the brush, and I knew then his knife had brought the massive creature down. With his sword drawn, he ran to aid Mitchell, who was still fending off his wolf.

I heaved to free Adelaide, throwing the alpha wolf aside. It fell limply away. Gasping for breath, I dropped to my knees beside her. Bright crimson coated her chain mail. Frantically, I wiped at the blood and attempted to assess her injuries. From what I could tell, thankfully, the blood was from the wolf. She appeared unscathed.

I released a tense exhale, relief swelling up and making my hands shake even as I tossed aside my gloves and checked the pulse in her neck.

Behind me, the forest grew quiet, and a moment later Mitchell knelt on the opposite side of Adelaide. Perspiration ran down his face along with blood. I counted several scratches on his face, but they weren't deep or life-threatening.

"Adelaide?" he gently shook her.

"She took a hard fall." I lifted Adelaide's head, pushed off her mail coif, and probed her scalp for injuries. I felt nothing but the silkiness of her hair. As though my touch had beckoned her from oblivion, her long lashes fluttered up. Her impossibly blue eyes peered at me, first in confusion and then with fear.

"Christopher, save me," she murmured before her eyelids closed again.

I thought maybe she'd fallen into an unconscious state once more, but with Mitchell there to take over her care, I started to rise, knowing I needed to assess our situation and determine if Ethelwulf had sent any more danger our way. Before I could move away, one of her gloved hands darted out and clasped mine.

"Do not leave me," she whispered, opening her eyes again.

"You are safe now," I reassured her, surprised at how shaky my voice came out.

"Please. I beg you." Panic settled into her features again. I'd never seen Adelaide so frightened. Usually, when she was afraid, like the other night after we'd battled Ethelwulf's knights, she remained composed. This was a side I didn't know how to handle.

I glanced at Mitchell for his guidance. If anyone should be offering Adelaide comfort, he needed to be the one. Adelaide shifted her sights to Mitchell too.

"We killed the wolves," he said tenderly, reaching down to stroke back a messy strand of her hair.

She lifted her head slightly and attempted to look at the carnage around us. As her gaze jerked from one dead wolf to the next, her hand in mine began to tremble until her entire body was shaking. She closed her eyes, her face as pale as death.

"We must be on our way, Adelaide," I said quietly but with the firmness our situation demanded. We were still in danger and needed to find a safe campsite.

She nodded but didn't stop trembling.

"You will ride with Mitchell until your fears are put to rest," I suggested. Mitchell nodded as eagerly as I'd expected. I moved to leave, the matter settled.

She clung to my hand with unexpected strength. "No, my lord. I shall ride with you." She looked at me with such vulnerability, I didn't know how I could resist.

I shot Mitchell another glance, and hurt filled his eyes. My gut told me I should insist that her place was with my brother. She'd been fine without me all these years. She'd always had Mitchell to turn to with her concerns, and I needed to encourage her to continue going to him. But with her beautiful eyes pleading with me and her hand so tightly holding mine, I could not deny her.

"Very well." I refused to meet Mitchell's gaze. "Can you stand?"

She started to sit up, caught sight of the dead wolves, and then fell back, shaking again. Without wasting further time, I slipped my arms underneath her and scooped her up like a babe. In turn, she wrapped her arms around my neck and leaned her head against my shoulder.

Silently, Mitchell rose and began retrieving our weapons. Tall John moved to assist him, but not before pointing the way to our horses, which he'd led a short distance away. When I reached them, I lifted Adelaide toward my saddle, but she clung to me. Her grip around my neck held firm, and she burrowed her face in the exposed area of my throat that my chain mail didn't cover. Her nose was warm, and her breath bathed my skin, rendering me immobile. If a wolf had decided at that moment to attack, I would have been helpless.

When she nestled in farther and her lips inadvertently brushed my flesh, I closed my eyes at the pleasure of holding her. For a few seconds, I basked in the sensation of her body in my arms, of feeling her pulse moving in time with mine, of knowing she'd wanted to be with me.

"Adelaide," I murmured. "We must make haste." I chastised her as much as myself and yet couldn't stop from pressing my nose into her hair and breathing in her essence and the faint scent of lilac.

The strange longing I'd had since the first time I'd seen her upon my return rushed back in a wave that left me weak. My relief at her safety, that she was still alive, that the wolves hadn't accomplished their mission to obliterate her, overwhelmed me so that I pressed my lips against her hair and breathed her in once more.

At the same moment, she shifted her nose and mouth, brushing my throat again, making me sharply aware of her lips, how close they were, and how easy it would be to bend down and touch mine to hers.

The second I considered it, I rapidly berated myself

and pulled back. "Adelaide," I said, this time hoping I sounded more in control. "I must put you on the horse."

"Then stay with me." Her words were warm and breathy against my neck.

I clenched my jaw, determined to bridle my emotions. I couldn't explain this new power Adelaide held over me, a power that made me want to capitulate to her every whim and do whatever she asked. Always in the past, I'd been the one bending her and Mitchell to my devices, cajoling them to my antics. Why could I not continue to see her as my cousin and playmate? Such a view was much easier.

Yet after the past days of riding and talking with her, I couldn't go back to seeing her as simply a childhood companion. I'd come to realize even more how much we'd both grown up, especially the extent to which she'd changed in five years. Not only had she turned into a stunning woman with the ability to take my breath away, but she was interesting, engaging, and someone I thoroughly enjoyed being with.

Nevertheless, I was a strong man who'd always resisted temptations, who'd never fallen prey to any woman. I wouldn't start now, especially not with Adelaide. Though I'd always sensed her admiration when we'd been children and even now over the past week of being together again, I couldn't encourage it. Maybe under different circumstances if I wasn't an outlaw and a danger to everyone who knew me. Maybe if I'd never run away from home and could offer her a title and land.

Even then, even if everything was perfect, deep down I knew nothing could ever happen between us, no matter how strong the pull. Not now that she was the queen of Mercia.

"Christopher," she whispered, her fingers brushing the nape of my neck. "Please."

Just my name falling from her lips was enough to weaken me. I closed my eyes and fought against the strong feelings tightening within my chest for only a moment longer before giving way to them. Even with an inner warning urging me to oppose her wish, I told myself this was different, that she needed my comfort, and that I'd be careful.

"Just for a little while," I whispered.

Only then did she loosen her arms and allow me to lift her into the saddle. Once astride, she glanced around with wide, frightened eyes, her hands trembling against the reins. Clearly, she was still afraid of the wolves, almost unnaturally so. Now was not the time to question her about it. But after we were on our way, I would pry into her strange reaction.

When I climbed up behind her, the tight confines of the saddle squeezed us together much closer than I'd anticipated. Far from being uncomfortable with our closeness, my presence seemed to calm her.

As I reached for the reins and surrounded her with my arms, she melded against me as though she belonged there. A protective surge rose from within, and I was surprised by the depth of my feelings and the desire to keep Adelaide in my arms evermore.

Such feelings would bring trouble, and I desperately needed to keep a barrier between us so that I remained only a friend and her loyal subject. I had to make myself do it, no matter how hard it would be.

Chapter 11

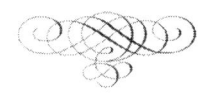

Adelaide

"*If we continue the search for Emmeline,*" I said as I rested against Christopher, "we shall likely take King Ethelwulf directly to her."

Darkness was beginning to fall and with it a sprinkling of rain. Christopher hadn't yet suggested I return to my horse. I knew I couldn't ride with him indefinitely, as my extra weight would tire his steed, but I wasn't ready to be away from the safety I felt in his embrace.

Ahead, Mitchell led the way on Roland. Tall John rode behind, guiding my horse by a lead rope. I'd thanked the faithful manservant for the knife throw that had saved my life, but my words had somehow seemed inadequate. I wished I could do more to show my appreciation to him, to all of them. But in the hours since the attack, I couldn't seem to find the right way to express my gratitude.

We'd ridden mostly in silence. Mitchell held himself stiffly, the sure sign I'd offended him when I'd decided to ride with Christopher instead of him. I couldn't explain what had prompted my decision. I'd speculated that in my moment of unexpected weakness I'd needed Christopher's strength and steadiness. Even now, his calmness and certainty soothed my still-frayed nerves.

Whatever the case, Mitchell wouldn't harbor his annoyance with me for long. He never did. By the time we made camp, he'd forgive me, and we would be steadfast friends again. At least I hoped so.

Thankfully, my outward shaking had diminished even though my heart quavered. "I shall wait to seek Emmeline until we can do so covertly or else we have more forces to withstand anything King Ethelwulf might send our way next."

"I think that is a wise decision, Your Majesty," Christopher responded.

Something in his tone irritated me. Was it the formality? The distance? The way he was holding himself back? I was enclosed in his arms, and I reclined into his chest. But more than just our armor separated us. And I didn't like it.

There were times I sensed a connection between us that went beyond our childhood ties, like when he'd held me in his arms after the battle with the wolves. But then, at other times, I felt a thick stone wall I couldn't penetrate, a barrier I didn't understand.

I wanted to demand he explain himself, but was afraid I might not like his answer. After all, Christopher was sometimes painfully honest with me. I didn't know how I could bear his telling me he didn't share the same affection. I'd be entirely mortified if he learned that my girlhood infatuation—which I'd thought I'd successfully squelched—had blossomed again upon his return. In fact, it was stronger than ever, but he was just as oblivious as always.

"You need not call me 'Your Majesty,'" I said testily.

"I must give you the respect due the queen of Mercia," he said evenly. "And you must demand it of everyone."

His counsel was correct. Even so, I couldn't help wishing for more than guidance from him. "We are still friends, my lord. Surely we can behave as we always have toward each other."

"No, things must change—have already changed. You are my queen and I am your servant. We must accept the new roles God has given us."

I bit back another testy response. I loved Christopher's integrity and honor. He was a wise advisor and a valuable man of strength to have on my side. Yet could I find a subtle way to communicate my attraction and learn if he'd ever reciprocate?

Perhaps under different circumstances, I might have made an impression on him. After all, his eyes had lit with appreciation when I'd donned a gown for dinner the night Sister Katherine had come.

Was there any other way to impress Christopher and in doing so cause him to harbor affection for me in return? Or would this wall always exist between us?

I swallowed a sigh. If only love came more easily. But then, love wouldn't mean as much if one could gain it without any cost whatsoever.

"You are right about our new roles, Christopher," I said. "I will try to accept the many changes. However, I have one request of you."

"Yes, Your Majesty?"

"When we are alone together like this, you must address me as 'Adelaide.'" He started to protest but I continued. "I may have to live my public life by new standards. But in private, I want to know I am still loved by my family for who I am as a person."

For a moment, Christopher was silent and the sounds of the coming night settled around us—the soft chirping of crickets and the faint clicking of a bat. Finally, he shifted in the saddle, drawing forward and pressing his face into the back of my head.

At his touch, my blood pulsed with warmth. I closed my eyes and leaned into him, relishing this brief breach in the wall and that he was letting me into his heart—even if only for a few seconds.

I could feel the hard press of his lips against my hair before he shifted to whisper in my ear. "My dear Adelaide, I will always enjoy knowing I once wrestled with the queen of Mercia and pinned her to the ground."

At the humor in his voice, I smiled. "If I remember correctly, I was the one with my blade at your throat."

"Only because I let you."

Laughter bubbled up. "That is why you still harbor a wound on your neck from where I cut you?"

"'Tis but a nick."

"And would have been much deeper if I had willed it."

It was his turn to laugh, which served only to widen my smile—until I caught sight of the glare Mitchell cast over his shoulder. The dark look was aimed at Christopher. Even so, I felt the sting of it.

Suddenly, I dreaded the news I had to tell Mitchell:

that we would shift our course away from finding my sisters, at least temporarily. He'd be disappointed as he was so intent on helping me uncover the hidden treasure. But after what had occurred with the wolves, I couldn't willfully put either of my sisters into such grave danger. They wouldn't be able to fend off Ethelwulf's forces the way we could.

At the remembrance of the wolves, I shuddered again.

Christopher's thick arms pressed me closer. "What happened back there, Adelaide?" he asked softly.

I knew he was referring to the wolf attack. I didn't quite understand what had happened yet myself. But now that my heart had returned to its normal speed and fear had released its claws from my body, I supposed I had to try to make sense of the attack.

"I was afraid," I admitted, though it embarrassed me to say it. I'd been unable to move or fight. Facing the wolves had filled me with terror, almost as if I was reliving a nightmare.

"You were more than afraid," Christopher said.

Somewhere in the far recesses of my memory, I could picture Aunt Susanna soothing me in the dark of night, the echoes of my screams surrounding us, her cool hands caressing my face. "I used to have nightmares."

"Yes, I remember," Christopher replied. "For many years. Until they grew less frequent and finally stopped."

"I did not realize you had heard me," I said.

"We all did."

"I am sorry. I can only imagine how disruptive my cries were to everyone's sleep."

"Mother somehow had the ability to make everything seem less of a problem than it was."

I nodded, a lump forming in my throat at the remembrance of the woman who'd raised me like her own and loved me without hesitation—even though I'd posed so much danger to her and the rest of her family.

"Did you have nightmares about wolves?" Christopher asked, his voice once again gentle.

I delved into the far corners of my memories, searching for the blackness that had haunted my dreams so long ago. But I'd apparently blocked all recollections of whatever had caused my nightmares. Had I been haunted by wolves? And if so, why?

"Mayhap something happened before you came to live with us?" Christopher suggested. "Mayhap you and Sister Katherine were attacked by wolves as she brought you to Langley."

My mind flashed with a sudden image of a cave and a wolf lunging at me. I shuddered again. "You must be right, my lord."

"That would explain your nightmares as well as your fear of the wolves we encountered."

"Even so, I am mortified I neglected to fight them alongside you. Next time, I shall rise up valiantly." Although I prayed there would never be a next time.

"Yes, you will," he said. "You must face the demons of your past so that you can force yourself to finally walk beyond them."

"Of course I should not expect you to tell me I have nothing to worry about, that you will be there by my side to fight them off for me again."

"Of course not." A hint of humor returned to his

voice. He surprised me by reining his steed and halting. "From the imaginary daggers Mitchell has been shooting at me, I think it is past time for you to take a turn riding with him. If I hold you much longer, I am afraid his daggers will become real."

Ahead, Mitchell ducked under a low branch. "He is acting like a petulant child, and I have no wish to stoop to his level."

"Put yourself in his situation, Adelaide. He is used to having your attention all to himself and not having to share you. After his being there for you all these years when I was not, I can understand how it galls him that you turned to me for comfort and not him."

My heart sank at the realization of how I'd slighted Mitchell. "You are right. I must make amends."

"And you must tell him we are no longer looking for Emmeline."

I nodded, although reluctantly at the thought of bearing the bad news. But Mitchell would take the change of plans better if it came from me rather than Christopher.

Christopher gave a short whistle that stopped Mitchell and Tall John. Then he slid from his saddle and stretched out his hand to help me down. I didn't need his assistance, but I took it anyway, embarrassed with myself at how much I liked the pressure of his hands at my waist before he set me on the ground.

I rode with Mitchell until we made camp for the night. I slept in spurts, too frightened to close my eyes for long. When we set off again at dawn, I resumed riding my own steed. Though the fears lingered, I pushed myself onward as we veered in a new direction, working our way out of the forest to the east where we would make our way to the coast. While Mitchell wasn't supportive of abandoning the search for my sisters and the treasure, he acquiesced without complaint—at least to me.

As with the journey into Inglewood Forest, the trek out was as taxing. By the end of the day, the overgrown woodland finally began to thin. Even then, exhaustion nearly toppled me from my saddle as we traversed several particularly challenging ravines.

From behind, I'd felt Christopher watching me closely. After the last near-fall, he glanced overhead. "Since rain is fast approaching, we shall attempt to find the old ruins of Wellmont Castle on the eastern border of Inglewood Forest and rest there for a spell."

Ahead, Tall John nodded his agreement. "I know of the place and can take the lead."

"Very well," I said, knowing Christopher hadn't wanted to stop until we reached the coast and located a ship that could take us to Norland. He was kind to consider my needs, although once again, I hated to admit to my weakness. "We shall slumber only for a few hours before resuming our journey."

"We shall slumber as long as you need," Mitchell added, tossing Christopher a dark look that dared him to contradict.

"Of course without the cover of the forest we shall be more easily detected than here in Inglewood," Christopher replied. "But with Huntingdon Rocks acting as an extra line of defense, we should be sheltered enough."

At the mention of Huntingdon Rocks, I jerked on my reins and put a hand to the pouch at my side containing the ancient key with its cryptic message: *H. W. Fortress.*

Huntingdon and Wellmont, both in the same area. Surely that wasn't coincidence. I glanced at Mitchell beside me. "Did Wellmont Castle have another name at one point?"

Mitchell cocked his head. "Wellmont Castle? No. Not that I am aware of."

"Something having to do with Huntingdon Rocks?" Mitchell and I had already had many such conversations as we'd continued to unravel the clue we'd discovered inside the key. Even with Christopher and Tall John's input, we'd had no success in deciphering the meaning and had been scratching at the dregs left at the bottom of the barrel of possibilities, like I was now.

"Long ago," Tall John started, clearing his throat and shifting in his saddle.

I nodded at him to continue.

"Wellmont and Huntingdon Rocks were covered in forest just like what we're in now," he said slowly in his deep voice. "My grandfather said the area was so thick with game, the locals called it Huntwell because they could kill two prey with one stone."

Mitchell's lips curved into a grin, the first one of his I'd seen in many days. "I had forgotten about that legend, but you are correct. The area was called Huntwell, which could mean the fortress at one time also went by that name."

"Then you think the ruins of Wellmont could be

our mysterious H. W. Fortress?" I asked.

"It is possible. It is certainly the closest answer we have had thus far."

"Thank you, Tall John," I said as he resumed his lead. I nudged my horse back into motion and prayed we were one step closer to discovering the treasure but somehow sensed we were still only at the beginning of our journey.

Chapter 12

CHRISTOPHER

I PEERED OUT INTO THE BLACK NOTHINGNESS OF THE HEATHLAND. From the highest point of Wellmont ruins, I'd hoped to have an advantage of plenty of advance notice if Ethelwulf decided to march against us, especially if his knights rode out of Inglewood Forest and crossed the barren plain toward the ruins.

But under the moonless night, I could see nothing in the darkness surrounding the rocky crags, even from the remains of the tallest turret. I could only pray we still had a day's advantage on Ethelwulf's men, for I had no doubt he'd sent more than wolves after us.

His soldiers would easily find our trail now that we were out in the open without the windfall or numerous creeks to cover our tracks. I'd debated not stopping at all and continuing toward the coast without a break. But I'd pushed Adelaide too hard already, and she must have some rest before the hard ride ahead.

I pulled my cloak tighter against the rain and cold and kept my feet moving from one crumbling crenellation to the next, my sights constantly assessing the darkness for any flicker of light that might give an enemy position away.

"Tall John said you wanted to speak with me." Mitchell's voice came from the stairwell doorway.

"Yes, I did." I didn't pause in my guard duties. I walked several rounds but couldn't find the words I needed, words that could bring healing between us instead of hurt.

"If you will say your piece, then I shall be on my way," Mitchell said irritably. "After all, you did inform us we would not be able to stay long, and I have much to do in searching for the treasure before you force us to move onward."

"I am not *forcing* anyone." I realized I was taking his bait, the bait he'd dropped in order to start a fight. But if we needed to battle it out, now was as good a time as any, the first time we'd been alone since my return. "Adelaide saw the wisdom in protecting her sisters and not endangering their locations yet, not until she's able to strengthen her position and numbers."

"She saw the wisdom in following Sister Katherine's advice until you convinced her otherwise."

"No one convinces Adelaide to do anything she does not wish. You know that as well as I do."

"I've seen the way you have tried to charm her this past week of traveling—"

"I have not charmed." My tone rose in spite of my desire to keep our conversation amicable. "We have talked and enjoyed each other's company no more or less than any friend would."

"You would have provided more if the opportunity presented itself." Mitchell's voice rang with accusation and bitterness that went much deeper than the happenings of the past few days. The current situation was just the simmering top layer of a pot left to boil too long. "I have seen the way you look at her. And you cannot fool me with your noble talk of friendship."

"How exactly do I look at her?" That I may have given the impression of more than friendship troubled me, especially if Adelaide had sensed it.

"You look at her as if you already possess her—"

"Already possess?" His words halted my calculated steps, and I turned my attention from the dark landscape to the equally dark doorway. I couldn't see Mitchell there, but I could hear his short bursts of breath.

"She is not yours," Mitchell responded in a low, almost menacing tone.

"She is not anyone's." My tone was just as low and hung in the air between us.

I sighed and then resumed my duty, scanning the horizon again for any signs of movement or light. "I did not call you up here to argue over Adelaide. I asked you to come so I might apologize for the hurt my leaving Langley caused you. I have no wish for the gulf that exists between us and desire to find a way to bridge it."

For long moments, the silence was punctuated only by the patter of rain. I'd almost believed Mitchell had gone when he responded. "What is done is done," he said more quietly, the anger in his voice flat, replaced by a sad, almost defeated tone.

"I can be here for you and Adelaide now—"

"Now that you know she is the queen?" Frustration crept back into Mitchell's voice. "Now that you have something to gain by staying?"

I wanted to deny my brother's accusation. But the

truth was that I would have left Langley and my family once again if not for Sister Katherine's revelation regarding Adelaide's true identity. I would have returned to Norland and continued with my life there. Of course, I'd thought I was being honorable by coming home and giving Mitchell my title and inheritance. I'd assumed by finding Adelaide a husband I'd be helping secure her future too.

But had I simply been selfish and calloused all along? Had I ever stopped to think about what they might want or need?

"I understand it may appear I am staying for what I may gain from Adelaide as queen. But you must know my discontent with Ethelwulf drove me from Mercia. Now it is my anticipation over seeing him removed from power that drives me to return."

"So you will use her now to aid your efforts?"

"No, of course not." But something in his words pricked me. "No matter what you may think of me, I would not use Adelaide as a pawn in a game for the throne."

"Then you swear you have honorable intentions with her, that you are not making plans to manipulate her affection and loyalty?"

"I swear it. She is and will always remain a friend and queen. Nothing more. My whole purpose in staying is to protect her and help her regain the throne."

The steady ping of rain settled around us once again. Finally, Mitchell spoke. "Very well. I have no choice but to trust you."

"Thank you."

"Adelaide is the world to me. If you hurt her, you will wish you never returned." The fading thump of his bootsteps in the stairwell told me this time he had indeed left. And for a reason I couldn't explain, our conversation hadn't made me feel better. It had only made things worse.

※

I poked at the glowing embers and low, flickering flames left in our fire, stirring them for more warmth. Inside the old walls of Wellmont ruins, we had shelter from the rain but no refuge from the damp chill permeating the stone structure.

The stairs nearby spiraled up one of the four castle towers where I'd already taken first watch. Tall John had relieved me a short while ago. I needed to get a couple hours of sleep before we were on our way again, but I was too tense with the premonition we were in danger.

Only an arm's reach away, Adelaide tossed in her sleep. I was tempted to wake her and leave. At Wellmont, we were a full day's ride from the sea. I'd decided that once we reached the coast, I would attempt to locate a merchant who was loyal to Mercia's true heir, someone who would be willing to sail us north to Norland. Although we could traverse by horse across country as I'd done on my ride home to Langley, by sea we'd be able to move more swiftly and I'd be able to keep Adelaide safer.

But I hesitated in waking Adelaide. After hearing her tossing restlessly last night, I knew she hadn't slept much and now needed the rest. Besides, Mitchell wouldn't be ready to go. Even now, instead of sleeping, he was exploring the ruins, searching for the ancient treasure. I'd warned him to stay inside the old bailey so that if

Ethelwulf's forces were nearby, they wouldn't see his torch.

Our conversation earlier had played through my mind over and over. Mitchell needn't worry about me having aspirations toward Adelaide. Even if I couldn't deny my growing fascination with her, I'd resigned myself to remaining nothing more than her friend and loyal subject.

I'd had plenty of time to ponder my changing feelings toward her during the past day of riding, and I'd come to the conclusion that since she was Mercia's queen, neither Mitchell nor I was worthy of her. While we were noblemen, our father had never amassed a fortune or land that would make us marriage candidates for a queen. Not many would be worthy of the queen, and most likely Adelaide would need to marry royalty.

Once she ascended to Mercia's throne, she'd have no shortage of suitors. Kings from all the surrounding nations would send their sons, princes who would fight over her. Her closest advisors would encourage her to make a match that would benefit her kingdom.

The truth was, no matter how much Mitchell adored Adelaide, he must put away any thought of a future with her. He wouldn't be able to marry her any more than I would—not that I wanted to or had considered it. Just because I thought Adelaide was beautiful and my body had betrayed me a time or two in reacting to her didn't mean I was thinking of wedding her. Far from it.

If I wanted to get married, I'd have to consider King Draybane's offer of his daughter. The Princess Violet was sweet-tempered and lovely. Even as the youngest of King Draybane's many children, she was more than I deserved since I wasn't a prince or a wealthy nobleman. The king had made the proposition out of obligation, to repay me for my service to Norland because my leadership and skills had driven Ethelwulf's pirate ships away. I'd not only protected the coastal cities, but I'd also raided his ships and increased King Draybane's coffers as a result.

In addition, during the recent drought, I'd helped keep his population from starvation. I'd led the organization of hungry field laborers to become teams of fishermen, which had allowed the country to sustain its own people. Our fishing efforts had been so successful we'd had enough left to trade for other food stores from countries to the south that hadn't been affected by the drought.

I respected King Draybane and had earned his respect in return. However, we both knew if I accepted his proposal of marriage to Violet, I'd essentially bind myself in service to him for the rest of my life. And mayhap he'd made the offer with that ulterior motive. He had no wish for me to return to Mercia. I was too useful to him.

While I'd been flattered, I hadn't been sure I wanted to relinquish all ties to Mercia, and I'd requested time to contemplate his generous gift. Now that I was here, now that the wheels of revolt had been set into motion with Adelaide's claim to the throne, I realized I couldn't marry Violet. My heart belonged to Mercia and always had. More than anything, I longed to restore my country to a land where peace and justice reigned hand in hand, where I could set the wrongs to right, where innocent people wouldn't be hanged in the streets and left to rot for the birds.

Though the challenge of freeing Mercia from Ethelwulf's grip wouldn't be easy, I relished the prospect of working toward that goal. Restoring Mercia to a just and peaceful land had been a burning desire for as long as I could remember. Now that the possibility was within my sights, I couldn't walk away.

Most of all, I'd already pledged my fealty in life or death to Adelaide. Even if I'd made the promise in a moment of heated emotion, I wanted to be by her side, not only to help her but to ensure her safety. I didn't trust many others to protect her the way I could.

Mitchell's premonition that I would use her was wrong. I cared more about her than the cause, didn't I?

I glanced down at her sleeping face, the low firelight illuminating her exquisite features. With her hair unbound and cascading over her shoulders in silky waves, she had an almost ethereal quality about her.

Tenderness pooled in my chest. I prayed one day God would bring a worthy man into her life, someone who would appreciate her strengths but at the same time refuse to bow to her whims. She needed a husband who wouldn't be intimidated by her status and could stand on his own next to her but who wouldn't attempt to dominate her.

I shifted the embers again, causing sparks to rise into the blackened stone chimney—the only one remaining of the dozens that had once graced this fortress. A stone roof overhead shielded the room, which had likely been a private chamber for the master of the house. The remains of the great hall stood outside our shelter, but the high ceiling was gone, allowing moss, vines, and other foliage to grow in abundance.

From our brief exploration upon arrival, I'd noted a set of stone steps leading down from the great hall into caverns underneath the castle, to storage rooms as well as former dungeons. I'd heard rebels speak of taking refuge among the Wellmont ruins in their efforts to flee from Ethelwulf's men.

I hoped I hadn't been unwise in using the small private chamber on the main floor rather than staying underground. The room was barren except for dust and animal droppings and a lone rabbit carcass, likely left by another rebel taking shelter from the elements. We'd covered the window to better keep out the rain and cold as well as to prevent the hearth fire from attracting undue attention.

"No!" Adelaide cried out. "No!"

At the fear in her voice, my blood turned as cold as it had been during the wolf attack. Even though I'd shed my armor, my dagger was still strapped to my belt. My sword, my bow, and the arrows I'd retrieved from the wolves were by my side. I had my dagger out in an instant, my body tense, my senses attempting to gauge the danger.

Adelaide kicked at the coverlet and whimpered.

I scanned the room and watched the open door that led to the great hall. The blackness of the night was all that greeted me along with the steady patter of rain.

"No!" Adelaide shouted, this time louder. She tossed about in agitation, then released a scream—the terrified scream she'd elicited earlier, the kind that still haunted me.

"Adelaide," I said, putting my dagger away and positioning myself next to her. "Wake up. You are dreaming."

Her scream only grew louder.

I suspected she was having a nightmare, perhaps about the wolves. Even if I was sympathetic to her fear, I had to keep her quiet. I couldn't let her screams rise into the night and chance anyone nearby hearing them and guessing our location.

I cupped my hand over her mouth in an attempt to

mute her noise. At the pressure, her eyes opened. She flailed, trying to free herself, groping for the knife at her side.

"Adelaide," I said sternly, hoping my voice would break through her terror before she loosened her knife and plunged it into my heart. "It is I, Christopher. Have no fear."

Her screams continued as did her fumbling for her dagger. With my one hand over her mouth, I attempted with my free hand to prevent her from unsheathing her knife, but the move made her thrash harder. Her eyes were wide open, but she seemed not to see or hear me. She was shaking and crying and screaming all at once, though the sound was muted by my hold over her mouth.

I bent in and pressed a kiss against her forehead. "Adelaide," I commanded more firmly. "Wake up and you will see you are safe with me."

Her strength took me off guard. Fear had apparently lent her its aid. She had her dagger halfway out of its sheath in spite of my efforts to keep it there.

Needing both hands to subdue her, I reluctantly released her mouth. Once again her screams filled the air. I quickly pinned her arms to her sides, and then, not knowing what else to do to silence her, I bent down and covered her lips with mine.

Chapter 13

Adelaide

My scream couldn't find release. Instead, warm, soft pressure fitted against my lips, making me forget about the need to scream. In that moment, I realized I was awake and shaking. My eyes were already open, and through the dim firelight, I could see Christopher was holding me down. His fingers shackled my wrists.

Had I tried to stab him?

And why had he pressed his lips to mine? Had he intended to distract me with a kiss?

If so, it had worked. My nightmare, whatever it had been, was gone. Suddenly, I was filled with the realization Christopher was kissing me—or at least was covering my mouth with his.

Every other thought fled, and I could think of nothing save the tenderness of his lips. I'd never before experienced a kiss, and I likely wouldn't have welcomed the intimacy from anyone else. But this was Christopher, the man I'd adored for so long. And whether he'd meant to kiss me or merely silence me didn't matter. His lips touching mine provided an invitation too welcoming to resist. Although I didn't know how to kiss a man, I returned the pressure, letting my lips stroke his.

He froze, as though he hadn't been expecting my reaction. His honey-brown eyes flew to mine, wide with surprise.

Without breaking our gaze, I again caressed him.

"Adelaide," he whispered, breaking the contact and starting to back away. "I am sorry—"

Freeing my arms from his imprisonment, I wound them around his neck, trapping him into place above me, preventing him from going away. I pulled him down until his lips once more met mine. At the soft contact, I closed my eyes and breathed a sigh of deep contentment. I loved his nearness and the safety I felt in his presence. More than that, this gentle brush of our mouths made my entire body tingle with a rush of sweet energy.

Once again, he did little more than let his lips rest against mine. I could feel tension growing in his shoulders and in his back, and I sensed his discomfort with our predicament.

Mortification spilled through me. I'd clearly made more of the situation than he'd intended. Apparently, my infatuation had clouded my judgment, and I'd allowed myself to get carried away.

"Christopher," I whispered, starting to release him. How would I ever be able to look him in the eyes again? Now he knew my longing for him. And we'd both know he hadn't reciprocated. "I was mistaken. I thought you wanted to—that you desired—that you meant more . . ."

He released a shaky breath.

My insides swirled with growing embarrassment, and I rolled to free myself from him entirely. But before I could escape, he planted his arms on either side of me. Between one second and the next, he bent and touched his lips to mine, fusing us together in a moment in which the world fell away and all I could think about was him. And how much I adored him and had my entire life.

Was it possible I was falling in love? These past days of denying my feelings were futile, and I gave myself up to the sensations now enveloping me.

His kiss was powerful and decisive and breathtaking and exactly the kind of kiss I would have expected from a strong man like him. His hand moved into my hair at the same time I slipped my arms around him and tugged him closer—

"What are you doing?" came a harsh voice nearby.

Christopher jerked away from me at the same time I did him. He scrambled to his feet while I pushed myself to my knees.

There, standing in the doorway, his hair and clothes dripping wet, eyes round with shock, was Mitchell. For a moment, the two brothers stared at each other, Mitchell's face tightening with anger and Christopher's flickering with guilt.

"I thought I heard Adelaide screaming, and I came as fast as I could." Mitchell's sword was out as if he'd expected to ward off an attack. Instead, he'd found the two of us locked into a passionate kiss.

I felt my cheeks heating and didn't dare meet his gaze. I could only imagine what he must be thinking.

"You swore you had honorable intentions with

Adelaide." Mitchell's voice was bitter.

"I do—"

"You swore you would not manipulate her affection or use her." Mitchell stepped farther into the room, lifting his sword and pointing it at Christopher.

He wouldn't dare go after Christopher, would he? My limbs quavered at the thought. "He was not manipulating or using me," I cut in, unable to stay quiet. "Christopher meant to comfort me from a nightmare."

"Comfort?" Mitchell's tone rose a notch.

"It may have started as a calming effort," Christopher interjected. "But it did not end that way."

To hear him say such words swirled the lingering heat in my belly. I slanted a glance at him, too embarrassed to look at him fully. He held his chin high, clearly planning to tell the truth just as he always did.

"Then you admit to using her?" Mitchell asked, taking another step into the room.

"I did not start out with the goal of kissing her."

"But you let it happen nevertheless?"

Christopher didn't respond except to glare back in that unrelenting way he had about him. The two looked as if they were on opposite ends of the jousting lists, about to charge toward each other.

My body stiffened. I would not let my favorite people left in the world fight each other. If necessary, I'd raise my own weapon and beat them back to their corners.

"This is my fault," I said, wishing I could find a way to facilitate peace between them. "I made more of the moment than Christopher intended—"

"I shall not allow you to take responsibility,

Adelaide," Christopher interrupted. "I was fully aware of what I was doing. I could have walked away, but I chose not to." For an instant, his gaze collided with mine, revealing something I couldn't name but that made my heart beat faster.

Whatever it was, Mitchell must have seen it too. His eyes sparked with hurt. "I thought I could trust you, but it looks like I was wrong, that you are just as selfish as always."

With that, Mitchell spun and exited the chamber, disappearing into the rain and darkness. Part of me wanted to shout after Mitchell and tell him to stop being petulant again. Yes, maybe seeing me kiss Christopher was a shock. And yes, maybe my relationship with Christopher since his return had moved quickly. But what right did Mitchell have to react so strongly against us?

Christopher stared out the open doorway, the muscles in his jaw rippling. When he finally moved, he spun toward the fire, grabbed a stick, and began to stir the embers.

I wanted to stand, walk to him, and wrap my arms around him. But I held myself back. Just because we'd shared a kiss didn't mean he would welcome my embrace. And I wouldn't be able to bear him pushing me away, not after what had transpired. Even if he hadn't meant the moment to deepen, it had, and now he couldn't deny something special existed between us. Surely, he felt it as much as I did.

"Do not fret," I finally said tentatively. "I shall talk with Mitchell tomorrow and make him understand."

"What will you make him understand?" Christopher asked without turning.

I wasn't exactly sure. I loved Christopher, didn't I? But he hadn't given me any indication he felt likewise. "What would you like me to tell him?" I asked, hoping Christopher would declare his love for me—or at the very least, his affection.

Christopher added a handful of gorse to the fire before responding. "You may tell him that although I am indeed besotted with the queen of Mercia, I have no intention of overstepping the boundaries again."

I couldn't contain a smile. So he was besotted with me? I rose and crossed to him, waiting for him to circle around and smile at me in return. He continued to poke at the now flaming gorse as though heedless of my presence. But he was too seasoned a soldier not to have heard my tread behind him.

Finally, I touched his arm. "I am gladdened to know you are besotted."

He broke from me, as though the merest contact burned him, and strode toward the door, widening the gap between us.

My smile faded, particularly when I saw the granite lines of his profile. It was the same expression he'd worn the day he'd left home five years ago—the deep scowl, the determined set of his chin and lips, and a hardness in his eyes that said he would not be swayed.

A stone dropped in my chest and almost knocked me to my knees. Christopher wouldn't leave me. Surely not. "Though you freely admit to caring for me, I am yet undesirable after all?"

He stopped in the doorway and stood a full minute before pivoting to face me. As previously, something flickered in his eyes that made my pulse patter faster again. "You are desirable, Adelaide. Too desirable. And it would appear I am a weaker man than I thought in allowing myself to kiss you."

"What is so wrong with kissing me, my lord?"

His sights lingered on my lips as if reliving the kiss we'd shared. It was a kiss I'd never forget. It was the kind I'd only dreamed of and never imagined possible. "Nothing is wrong with you, Adelaide. But everything is with me."

"You speak in riddles."

"There can never be anything between us. You are the queen of Mercia. You belong to the royal House of Mercia. And someday you must unite with a man who is worthy of your bloodline, a prince who is also of a royal lineage."

His words were blunt and to the point. And though his frankness regarding my union with a prince was embarrassing, I was equally indignant. "Someday, as you point out, I must unite with a man. But that man will be of my choosing, someone I love—"

"You will have little choice, Adelaide. Not as the queen."

"As the queen, as the ruler, I shall make my own choices. I can decide whatever I wish."

"Not if you hope to keep the peace with your advisors and the nobility who will expect you to form an advantageous marriage. They will likely suggest an alliance with the Franks, Queen Dierdal's family, mayhap to a cousin."

His somber words settled around me like the damp chill of the night. I hadn't considered tradition and what would be expected of me in marriage. But Christopher was right, as usual. My betrothal and marriage would be a public act, just as my parents' union had been.

Our tutor had explained that King Francis had picked his bride to form an alliance with the Franks. Princess Dierdal had been the oldest daughter of the king of the Franks. The union had brought about the security and help of the Franks during a troublesome time when Ethelwulf had just begun attacking the southern borders of Mercia.

Fortunately, the match had ended as a happy one. Stories abounded of the love King Francis and Queen Dierdal had shared. However, equal stories abounded of other royal marriages that did not share such love.

If only Queen Dierdal's family had sent aid more quickly when they'd learned King Ethelwulf had started attacking Mercia's eastern coast. But apparently, the queen's missives for help had been intercepted, and the Franks hadn't realized what was happening until too late. Didn't that prove marriage alliances weren't trustworthy and shouldn't be the basis for a union?

"I wish there was another way," Christopher said. "But there is not."

I couldn't speak past the emotion in my throat.

"We will both have to make many sacrifices in the days and years to come for the greater good of Mercia and her people. Can you do that, Adelaide?"

Could I sacrifice my fledgling desire to be with Christopher? I didn't want to. But if God had ordained me to be the queen of this land, then I must obey His purposes above my own personal desires. "I shall pray for strength to do whatever God requires of me."

Only then, did Christopher smile, but it was sad and tired and didn't reach his eyes. "You already have proven yourself to be the best queen Mercia could ask for."

Although I was glad my answer had satisfied him, I was too disheartened to manage a smile. When he stepped away from the door and back into the chamber, I hugged my arms across my tunic and fought off a wave of chills.

"You should try to sleep a little longer," he said quietly.

I returned to my spot on my pallet, wrapping myself into my cloak and coverlet. Although I closed my eyes, I was no longer tired. My mind swirled with how I would explain to Mitchell that what he'd witnessed meant nothing now.

But how could it mean nothing? Hadn't Christopher also experienced the intensity and beauty and power and connection of our kiss? My emotions had been so strong, so heady, that I'd thought I loved him. Had the feelings come only from the heat of the moment? Was I still allowing my childish attraction to influence me? Or was my love for him real?

I gave myself a mental shake. It didn't matter if my love was real or not. It was forbidden for both of us. And Christopher was a man of such integrity he would never do anything that went against principle. He was willing to go to great lengths for what he believed. After all, he'd left his family and country to stand up for what was just and true. He'd been ready to sacrifice his title, lands, and rights for principle.

I wished he wasn't willing to sacrifice me too. He'd done it once when he'd ridden away from me as his cousin and friend. And I knew he was sacrificing me again, this time as a woman he could possibly care about if he allowed himself.

Although I shouldn't compare this situation to the past, I couldn't keep from feeling the same hollow ache I'd experienced the day he'd ridden out of my life the first time. In some ways, he was rejecting me now the same way he had then.

My eyes stung, and my throat ached.

I swallowed hard. I wouldn't cry. Not here. Not in his presence. Besides, he was still with me. I could console myself that even if I could never love him the way I longed to, he would be a part of my life.

At least I hoped so. He hadn't ridden off again. Not yet. But would he someday?

"Christopher?" I pushed up on my elbows.

"Go to sleep, Adelaide," he whispered as he poked at the embers.

"Promise you will not make plans to leave? Promise you will stay with me and always be my closest advisor?"

He faced the flames, back stiff and shoulders erect. When he didn't answer right away, anxiety pushed me up further. Was he already contemplating leaving? Was that why he wasn't answering?

"Christopher? Please?" I asked, not caring that I was begging.

He audibly exhaled. "I promise to stay with you for as long as I am able."

I knew what he was saying. He would stay with me now, but he refused to vow he would forever. It wasn't the answer I'd wanted. But it would have to do.

Chapter 14

CHRISTOPHER

I ASCENDED FROM THE DANKNESS OF THE DUNGEONS AND SILENTLY berated Mitchell. I'd searched all over the castle ruins for him to no avail. I knew not whether he was off somewhere seeking the so-called hidden treasure or if he was still angry at me for kissing Adelaide.

I had a feeling it was both.

"This is not the time to act like a child, Mitchell," I whispered with mounting frustration. As I'd searched, I couldn't shake the foreboding that our enemy was drawing nearer. The heathland was too quiet, containing the calm which came before an attack.

After ascending the steep stairway, I located Adelaide and Tall John waiting in the shelter of an arched doorway near the crumbling front of the keep. "Have you had any luck locating him?"

Tall John shook his head, his narrow face taut with anxiety. "No, my lord."

Donned in armor, Adelaide wore her surcoat over the metal plates and chain mail. Her hood was up against the cool drizzle and shadowed her. Even so, by the flickering light of Tall John's torch, her face was pale and drawn.

Over the past two hours she hadn't fallen asleep again, at least not while I'd remained with her. Though I'd felt her gaze upon me from time to time, she'd kept silent. Part of me had wanted her to fight me and demand she have her own way—like the Adelaide of my childhood would have done. But she'd clearly taken my rebuff to heart and had too much pride to try to persuade me otherwise.

More than once, I'd wanted to spin around and apologize. I couldn't tell her I was sorry for kissing her, because that would have been a lie. The moment she'd initiated pressure against me, I'd been lost. The desires I'd barely been able to keep in check had come crashing out at full speed. And after releasing them, I hadn't wanted to stop, which scared me.

Nevertheless, I could have apologized for hurting her, for making our relationship more complicated, and for not being able to give her what she'd yearned for. No matter how much either of us might want to pursue these feelings that had somehow developed between us, we weren't free to do so.

Moreover, at this moment, other things demanded our attention. Like finding Mitchell and riding on our way before the break of dawn.

"Do you have any idea where he might be looking for the treasure?" I directed my question to Adelaide. While riding the last of the journey to Wellmont, the two had speculated on the clue, the key, what might be hidden, and how to find it.

Adelaide rested her hand on the hilt of her sword. "I suspect he is searching for a keyhole in a place that relates to the pomegranate engraving on the key, anything that signifies wisdom or learning."

Wellmont no longer contained doors and thus no keyholes, except for in the dungeons. A few of the thick iron doors still remained in some of the cells, and a set of keys covered in spider webs hung at the base of the dungeons, rusted and aged with time and disuse. Other tunnels and caverns had been carved out underneath the old ruins over the decades. But I'd seen no sign of additional keyholes or portals wherein treasure might lie.

I glanced at the dark eastern horizon, attempting to gauge how much time we had before dawn's appearance. "We may have to start without him."

"No," Adelaide said almost defiantly. "I shall not leave him behind, not under these circumstances."

I knew she was referring to his anger over witnessing our kiss. Mitchell had every right to be angry with me. I'd sworn to him that Adelaide was nothing more than a friend, and then in the next hour he'd found me locked in a heated kiss with her.

Now after pushing him further away, I would need to fall on my knees before him and apologize. It was the least I could do, along with vowing to him I would never touch Adelaide again. I'd already vowed it to myself when she'd asked me to stay. Part of me had wanted to ride away as fast and hard as I could. She was a temptation I wasn't sure I could resist. But the other part of me demanded I remain and see her to the throne. I'd only be able to do so if I kept her at arm's length.

"We must wait for Mitchell," Adelaide said. "I shall only hurt him all the more if I abandon him now."

I wanted to release a frustrated growl. Even if Mitchell had every right to be upset and to run off to lick his wounds, he was putting Adelaide in danger with his escapade. As fast as we were, I had no doubt our lead had diminished substantially, especially since the encounter with the wolves had slowed us down. If a company of Ethelwulf's elite guard was anywhere nearby, they'd surely pick up our trail now.

"A few more minutes," I said. "That is all the longer we can afford to wait."

Adelaide didn't object, and I took that as her assent.

I pulled up the hood on my cloak. "In the meantime, I shall search for him again." Perhaps his treasure hunting had led him to the ruins of outbuildings on the edge of the old fortress wall.

"Would you like me to search as well, my lord?" Tall John asked, shifting the torch and scanning the crumbled pillars and the stone walls.

"I would prefer you stay with Adelaide."

"I can take care of myself," she retorted in the same aloof and angry tone she'd used with me when I'd first arrived at Langley.

"Stay with John," I replied, stepping over rocks and passing through the broken arched doorway. "I do not wish to begin a hunt for you too."

I didn't wait for another of her belligerent answers but descended a short stairway and crossed through damp overgrown grass into what was likely once the gardens until I reached the far edges of the keep.

"Where are you, Mitchell?" I asked into the breeze that had picked up over the past hour. Instead of the steady rain from the night, the wind brought a mist. I could only pray the heavy mantle of cloud cover would prevent Ethelwulf's forces from progressing too quickly, although I feared nothing would slow them.

Holding out my torch, I ducked into the remains of what I assumed had once been a brewery. "Mitchell?" I called softly, to no avail. The urgency prodded me to a jog as I checked the last few buildings before I circled the keep and ended where I started at the inner bailey. I drew back in surprise at Mitchell's appearance seemingly out of nowhere.

In his haste, he stumbled and nearly fell into my path.

"Where have you been?" I asked, my voice sharper than I intended.

He didn't immediately respond. With his hood pulled low over his forehead, he flashed me a brief look, one reflecting bitterness.

"We need to leave straightaway," I said. "I had hoped to be far from here before the break of dawn."

I strode ahead of him to where Adelaide and Tall John stood with our horses.

"Mitchell." Adelaide reached toward him, but he passed by without sparing her a glance.

The hopefulness in her expression fell away, and she tucked her hand back into her surcoat.

Instead of nearing his horse, Mitchell veered toward the steps and the arched door of the keep. "Christopher, I need to speak with you in private."

"We must be on our way," I insisted as I stopped in front of my mount.

"I will not go until I say my piece." He took the steps two at a time and disappeared into the keep, giving me no choice but to follow him.

Mayhap letting him speak his mind was for the best. He'd had the past couple of hours to ruminate on what had happened with Adelaide. And now, he apparently needed to give voice to his frustrations.

I raced to catch up and found him waiting at the top of the dungeon stairwell. At my appearance, he started down the steep flight of stone steps.

"We can talk up here," I called after him.

He kept going, descending into the blackness of the underground cavern.

I held my torch high and illuminated the narrow passageway lined with moss and debris. Mitchell had already reached the bottom and was veering into one of the tunnels.

"Mitchell, stop!" I rushed down after him, my frustration building. We didn't have time for this. If he needed to berate me, why lead me into the dungeons?

A sickening sense of dread halted me on the bottom step, and I unsheathed my dagger. In his anger, Mitchell wouldn't consider hurting me, would he? As soon as the thought came, I shoved my dagger back into its case and let shame blanket me. Just because we'd fought over Adelaide didn't mean we were mortal enemies. We'd had a disagreement, and we would work through it like two grown men.

The mustiness of damp stone and earth along with the chill of the darkness seemed to warn me to retreat. But my torchlight revealed Mitchell's cloak-covered form ahead in the passageway containing rows of identical dungeon cells. He was turning an old rusty key in each of the doors without success, until finally, one clicked open with a squeal.

He flung the iron gate wide and then stood back to wait for me. Hidden by the folds of his hood, I couldn't gauge his expression, but from the stiff set of his shoulders, I sensed his anger as if it was a living dragon about to rip me from limb to limb.

I stopped in front of him, clenching my fists to keep myself from reaching for my sword and dagger. Even if he pulled his weapon on me first, I didn't want to battle him. "I hope we can work out our problems without our weapons."

"I hope we can too." He waved toward the cell. "You first."

"Can you not say what you must here?"

"In there."

I exhaled an exasperated breath and walked inside. "This is absurd, Mitchell." I crossed to the far end and held up the torch to examine our surroundings, noting the slimy, mold-covered walls. "We have already wasted time waiting for your return, and now this?"

He didn't respond. Instead, the door squealed closed, and the key clicked in the lock.

I spun to see that Mitchell was still standing outside in the passageway. He hadn't followed me inside. In fact, he took a step back as though he had every intention of leaving.

I bolted across the cell and grabbed the bars on the door. "What are you doing, Mitchell?"

He threw back his hood. Only then did I see that his nose was bleeding and his lip cut. Bruises were forming under one of his eyes. "What happened to you?"

"Captain Theobald bade me welcome."

"Captain Theobald." My gut churned.

"The head of King Ethelwulf's elite guard."

"I know who he is." Although I'd heard plenty about the captain, even in Norland, I'd only seen Theobald once, that fateful day when I'd visited Delsworth with Father. Theobald had led the procession of the noble family to their hanging. I remembered the calm, almost emotionless expression he'd worn, as though he were taking a leisurely stroll rather than marching an innocent family to their deaths.

Mitchell took another step back. "He is waiting past the gatehouse for me to return with Adelaide."

"No!" Fear slammed into my stomach at the same moment I slammed my palm into the bars. "You cannot hand Adelaide over to that man. You must not."

"It is for the best—"

"Take me to Theobald in her stead." I stretched through the bars, grabbing Mitchell's arm.

He jerked free and put enough distance between us so I couldn't reach him.

"Kill me, behead me, do whatever you must to appease him. But do not give him Adelaide."

Mitchell pulled himself to his full height, which was still a head shorter than me. "It is too late."

"No—"

"I already struck a bargain." Mitchell lifted his chin even as he wiped away the blood trickling off his busted lip.

"Let me go and we shall fight against him together."

Mitchell hesitated, which birthed hope in me.

"Please, Mitchell. At the very least, we can hide down here in the tunnels."

He shook his head. "I have seen Theobald's forces, and we are far too outnumbered and wouldn't make it out of the tunnels alive. We are safer if we surrender."

Suddenly, I understood. Ethelwulf's men had likely just arrived when Mitchell had stumbled upon them. Why hadn't Theobald killed Mitchell on sight? The only explanation was that the cruel captain was under orders from Ethelwulf to bring us to him alive. For what purpose?

So he could execute all of us publicly, including Adelaide, and in so doing demoralize and deter any other rebels?

"Better to fight together than to capitulate." I lunged as far as I could in a last effort to wrest the key ring from him. But he was too far away now. "Release me and we shall vanquish Theobald."

"He has vowed that if I give him the key to King Solomon's treasure, I may take Adelaide back to Langley. Once there the king may yet allow me to marry her."

"Surely, you did not tell Theobald Adelaide has the key."

Mitchell paused which was answer enough. "The key is all King Ethelwulf and his kin have ever wanted. Theobald assures me if we hand it over peacefully, the king will allow us to go free."

"Even with the key, Ethelwulf will never allow a true heir to remain alive. He would not risk any threat to his kingship."

"Unlike you, I have worked hard to cultivate a steadfast and worthy reputation with the king. He trusts me as he did our father. On my last visit to Delsworth, the king agreed to my taking the earldom as well as marrying Adelaide—"

"That was before he knew who Adelaide was. He will never agree to it now." I wasn't surprised Mitchell had already gained permission to marry Adelaide. But I did wonder how he'd planned to inform and convince Adelaide—not that it mattered anymore.

Mitchell started toward the stairwell.

I had to make him see reason. "Theobald is known for being a liar and a brute. You cannot trust anything that comes out of his mouth."

Without glancing back at me, Mitchell paused to hang

the rusty keys back on the nail at the base of the steps, too far away to be of any use to me.

"Once Theobald has the key," I called, "he will kill you and Adelaide both."

Mitchell started up the stairs.

"For the love of the saints! You cannot do this! If not your own life, then think of Adelaide. You will lead her to her death."

Mitchell paused several steps up, his shoulders slumped and his head bowed. "Fighting Theobald and his guards is suicide. Even if he is lying, at least now we have a chance of survival."

"If we cannot fight them, then we will outrun them."

"Believe it or not, I am saving your life by locking you up down here."

"I do not need you to save my life. I would rather die than give in to Theobald."

"Stop trying to be the hero again, Christopher," Mitchell retorted, his voice stretching thin with anger. "It irks you that this time I shall save Adelaide and that she will want to fall into my arms instead of yours."

"I have no intention of being a hero." My only thought was how to make Mitchell release me from my cell so I could keep him from his foolish bargain with Theobald.

He resumed his ascent up the stairs. I was losing him. I pressed against the bars as if in so doing I could stop him. "I was wrong to kiss her! I beg you to forgive me!"

Mitchell's feet disappeared from sight.

"I know you love her! That you want to marry her! If you release me, I vow I will help bring about your union to her." I didn't know how I'd fulfill such a promise, but I was desperate to save Adelaide's life, and I would say or do anything.

The scrape of wood was followed by a slam that echoed down into the dungeons, telling me with a sickening finality, he'd closed the door and walked away.

Chapter 15

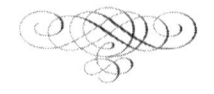

Adelaide

The mist and fog swirled around us as we rode down the rocky slope of the ruins, the faint light from Tall John's torch guiding the way.

"I think we should wait for Christopher." I reined my horse and forced Mitchell behind me to halt.

"He insisted we ride ahead." Mitchell nudged Roland with the heel of his boot. The beast snorted in displeasure but began moving again, urging mine to do the same. "With the break of dawn, he did not want us to waste any more time."

"'Tis strange since he was so anxious to be off."

"He wanted to climb the tower and see if he could gauge our lead against King Ethelwulf."

"Then he believes the king's forces are nearby?"

"Yes."

Something in Mitchell's tone hinted at nervousness. Was the situation more volatile than he was telling me? Was that why he'd spoken with Christopher in private? So he could inform him of our dire situation without worrying me?

"Whatever you revealed to Christopher you may also reveal to me." I jolted in my saddle with each rocky step my horse took, and I leaned into him to lessen the impact.

When Mitchell didn't respond, a new sense of dread bored a hole in my chest. We were in danger. I just prayed this time we wouldn't face wolves. "If it pleases the Almighty," I whispered. "No more wolves."

At the bottom of the embankment, Tall John slowed. "Which way, my lord?"

"Straight ahead," Mitchell responded.

The blackness of night was beginning to fade, but the fog hung heavily, making our flight difficult, even with Tall John's torch.

"Will Christopher be able to find us?" Once my question was out, I knew how silly I sounded. Christopher was a seasoned knight, a skilled hunter, and an expert warrior. Even in our childhood, I'd watched him track prey with a precision that had put both Mitchell's and my skills to shame.

Thankfully, Mitchell didn't berate me for my ignorant question. Instead, we rode silently until Tall John's steed came to an abrupt halt and shied sideways, whinnying a protest.

"Is something amiss?" I asked.

His horse backtracked several paces until it bumped into mine. Tall John leaned in and spoke soothingly to the animal.

Mitchell urged Roland forward and passed both of us. At the front of our procession, he, too, stopped short. He sat upon his mount silently, unmoving, as though waiting for someone or something.

I opened my mouth to speak again, but just then the fog lifted to expose a sight that chilled my flesh down to the bone. Knights in black armor. I didn't have to see the emblem upon their standards to know they were from King Ethelwulf's elite guard.

My sword and dagger were unsheathed before I could take full stock of our situation. All I knew was that we would have to fight. I could afford no fear or hesitation.

I dug my heels into my mount to spur him forward, but at the sound of my movement, Mitchell reared his horse into my path. "No, Adelaide! Put away your weapons. They come in peace."

Roland shifted with a snort of protest, and at the same time, I scanned the surrounding area. Through the rolling fog and the light mist, I caught a glimpse of the dark shapes of dozens of knights and their flickering torches. As if they'd been waiting there just for us, they surrounded us in a circle that left no room for escape, even in the direction we'd just come.

Their ready presence, Mitchell's nervousness, Christopher's absence. It all made sense now. Somehow, Mitchell had communicated with King Ethelwulf's soldiers and had betrayed us.

Swift anger bubbled up. "What have you done? And where is Christopher?" I turned on Mitchell. But as I spoke, several knights broke away from their ranks and rode toward us.

"Speak no more of him," Mitchell said harshly.

The guards closed in, their weapons drawn. I lifted my sword and braced myself for battle.

"Captain." Mitchell bowed his head to the knight on the largest warhorse. The royal standard upon the banner covering the horse contained two golden lions facing each other in the salient, or leaping, position on an ebony background. Mercia's standard was nearly identical with two golden lions in rampant, or standing, against a ruby background. When King Ethelwulf had united the kingdoms, he'd taken Warwick's emblem and added a ruby border. Otherwise, Warwick's original standard remained unchanged.

I'd always wondered if King Ethelwulf thought his leaping lions were superior to standing lions. Maybe he believed physical prowess drove a kingdom. I was of the mind people flourished better when they were treated with kindness and respect.

The knight didn't respond to Mitchell but instead stared directly at me with narrowed eyes as cold and sharp as ice floes in the East Sea. His chain mail hood surrounded his face, but I could see the three warrior braids, the traditional hairstyle of the king's elite guard. A deep scar ran the length of his cheek, starting just below his eye and disappearing into a long pointed beard in the style of King Ethelwulf. The captain held himself rigidly, his gloved fingers tight against the hilt of his sword as if he expected some resistance.

I burned with the need to ask Mitchell where Christopher was and why he wasn't with us. But I held my tongue. It was possible this captain didn't know yet about Christopher's presence. And it was possible Christopher was somewhere nearby waiting for the right moment to attack and take the knights by surprise.

"The Princess Constance," the captain said almost derisively.

"*Queen* Constance." I lifted my chin and refused to

let this man intimidate me. I had the feeling I should know who he was, but my sheltered existence had kept me from court and political life. "Who are you, sir?"

His cool eyes assessed me too intimately. "The resemblance to your mother is striking."

I bristled at his blatant disregard for my query of introduction, but I forced myself to remain composed. "Then you met Queen Dierdal?"

"Not formally, unfortunately." His voice turned soft and contradicted the hardness of his eyes. "But I feel as though I grew quite familiar with her since I was the one who hanged her body from the castle wall at Delsworth."

Revulsion swelled in my throat. I didn't know what this man wanted from me or what Mitchell hoped to accomplish with his betrayal, but I had the premonition I wouldn't live long to find out.

My face must have reflected my disgust, for his lips curled into a semblance of a smile revealing he was the sort of twisted man who found pleasure at the expense of others. I'd do well not to show my true emotions, which would deprive him of the pleasure he sought.

I gave him what I hoped was my haughtiest look. "I am surprised, sir, that King Ethelwulf did not hang you in her place after her body was stolen away by her beloved followers."

The captain's tight smile faded, and he assessed me more keenly. "Perhaps I will have the satisfaction of getting to know you the same way I got to know your mother."

His insinuation made me want to shudder, but I squared my shoulders and didn't back away. "You shall soon discover I am not like my mother." I didn't realize my voice contained a challenge until he unsheathed his dagger halfway and shifted his attention to my neck, a deadly glint in his expression.

Behind me, I heard the rasp of metal against metal as Tall John and Mitchell unsheathed their swords.

I had no doubt the captain was accustomed to unquestioning obedience and was quick to cut down anyone who opposed him in the slightest. I waited for him to strike. I would most certainly fight back. Instead of lashing out as he likely would have done with anyone else, he slowly pushed his dagger back into his belt.

Only then did I realize how tightly I gripped the hilt of my sword. I loosened my hold but didn't let go completely. What was stopping him from hurting— even killing—me as he clearly longed to do? I was King Ethelwulf's enemy. Surely, the king wanted me dead and would have given orders to kill me upon sight.

"Hand over the key." The captain held out his hand to Mitchell.

Mitchell stuffed his sword back into his belt and nudged Roland next to me. His eyes pleaded with me to understand and forgive him. "If we give Captain Theobald the key to the treasure, he will permit us to return to Langley."

My brows shot up. This was the notorious Captain Theobald? I should have guessed his identity. He certainly looked the part of the heartless captain who had caused Mercia so much grief over the years.

For a brief instant, I considered making the first move against him. I longed to take him unaware and rid Mercia of so merciless a leader. But I sensed he was as quick as I was and would deflect my blow if I struck him.

Instead, I met the captain's gaze squarely. "I do believe you are as dishonest as they say. The king most certainly would not allow me to return to Langley." If I did, what would stop me from attempting to rise up again, especially after I'd had time and opportunity to rally rebels and loyalists to my side? The king would never chance it.

"King Ethelwulf only wants the ancient key to King Solomon's treasure," Mitchell said. "That is all he has coveted."

Captain Theobald didn't respond to either of us. I suspected he'd take the ancient key from me whether I gave it peacefully or not. He may have convinced Mitchell he was negotiating, but from the stories I'd heard about Captain Theobald, he was a man who took whatever he desired any way he wanted.

"Please, Adelaide," Mitchell whispered. "Give him the key. Then we can return home."

The captain didn't release me from his sights. He watched me with a strange, narrowed anticipation, as though he hoped I would refuse so he could forcibly remove the key from me.

Keeping my expression emotionless, I reached for my leather pouch underneath my cloak and chain mail. I loosened the drawstring and fingered the heirloom. Did I dare to part with it? Sister Katherine had said I'd need the treasure to rid the land of evil. If I handed the key over to the king, would I be handing over my chances at finding the treasure? Dare I fight to keep it?

I glanced at the shadowy outlines of the knights surrounding us. Where was Christopher? He should be shooting his arrows by now. Without his aid, we wouldn't be able to fight this many men. If I initiated,

I'd bring death not only to myself but to Mitchell and Tall John.

My fingers brushed against the signet ring, the one Aunt Susanna had kept hidden for me all these years. In bringing me into her home and caring for me, she'd exhibited both courage and caution. Her example was one I needed to follow. And this situation demanded caution.

I pushed aside the signet ring and reluctantly tugged the key out of the pouch. Then I held it out to Mitchell. I refused to personally give it to Captain Theobald.

Mitchell completed the deed. The captain examined the relic before tucking it away.

"Now that you have the key," Mitchell said, "we shall be on our way to Langley."

"First we ride to Delsworth." Captain Theobald motioned to the several knights who accompanied him. Before Mitchell or Tall John could react, the knights drew alongside me, one on each side and the other behind.

"Captain," Mitchell called, "you gave me your word we would be safe, that you would not harm Adelaide or my manservant, and that we could leave peaceably."

"We are leaving peaceably." The captain urged his horse around, his spurs jangling. "As long as you do not resist, I have been ordered to bring you to the king alive."

"You have no need for Adelaide now," Mitchell insisted, the fog and darkness of the morning swallowing him and making him disappear from my sight. "I shall return with her to Langley."

"First the king would like to hear any additional

information you have about the other princesses and treasure."

"I know nothing more."

"And of course, he'll want to discuss your family's loyalty to him."

"I have provided the key to the treasure. I had no reason to tell you about it other than to prove my loyalty."

Captain Theobald released a mirthless laugh. "You must know by now the king will require much more than that to prove your faithfulness."

I wanted to believe Mitchell had made the deal with the captain in order to protect me. But perhaps he also worried for his own life now that the king realized his father—the former Earl of Langley, his once trusted and loyal advisor—had betrayed him by harboring me for so many years. King Ethelwulf would certainly now call into question Mitchell's loyalty and would seek retribution.

"I have already done much to demonstrate my allegiance to the king," Mitchell said. "Whatever he has asked of me, I have done it."

"So did your father."

"I am not my father," Mitchell said angrily. "I told you I would lock away and leave for dead my traitorous brother, and I have."

Leave for dead my traitorous brother? The words pierced my chest like arrows. I halted my steed, forcing the black knights around me to stop. The world turned dizzy and tipped upside down, and I had the sudden overwhelming need to vomit. Instead, I unsheathed my dagger and lunged toward Mitchell. Before anyone could stop me, I had the knife at the tender spot in his throat.

"You're leaving Christopher behind to die?" My voice was like iron.

Mitchell didn't move.

"Then you are a murderer."

"His grand plans were for naught, Adelaide, and you know it. He could never succeed against King Ethelwulf."

"If you'd like," Captain Theobald said, "I can send one of my men down to the dungeons to retrieve him. Perhaps you'd prefer to watch as I slay him before your very eyes instead of letting him waste away slowly and painfully."

For a moment, I considered the possibility that if the captain brought Christopher out, he might be able to overcome his captor and escape. But even if he freed himself, I knew in my heart he'd never leave me behind. He'd attack Captain Theobald's army and fight for my freedom. And in doing, I had to admit, he'd likely die, especially if Mitchell refused to join the battle against Captain Theobald and his men.

For now, I had to resign myself to Christopher remaining locked in the dungeons. In the meantime, I'd figure out a way to free myself or find someone who was willing to return to the Wellmont ruins and free him.

"Leave him," Mitchell said disdainfully. "He deserves a slow and painful death."

"I'm glad you agree," Captain Theobald said still watching my face. "To ensure no one finds him or comes back to free him, I'll have my men fill the stairwell opening with stones."

I could only stare at Mitchell. A thousand thoughts

ran through my mind, thoughts of my childhood with Mitchell, of playing in the rivers and woods around Langley, of riding and hunting and training together, of the skinned knees and elbows, of nettles in our hair and bee stings on our bare feet. We'd been companions for as long as I could remember.

I couldn't believe Mitchell was capable of such treachery, much less murder. Then again, I'd never seen him as angry as I had last night when he'd walked away after witnessing me kiss Christopher. Was it possible he'd reacted in a moment of fury he'd later regret?

He swallowed hard, his Adam's apple rubbing against the tip of my dagger. "Christopher was a danger to you. So I did what I needed to keep you safe."

"And am I safe?" I waved my hand to the heavy cavalry of knights watching our interaction with interest.

"When the king is assured of my loyalty, he will allow me to return to Langley. He already gave me permission to marry you when I last traveled to Delsworth. We will wed and in doing so assure him you are no threat."

"We will wed?" My voice rose with incredulity. "I shall never marry you."

Mitchell's countenance hardened, and he shoved my dagger away. "You might not have a choice this time, Adelaide."

Christopher's words about how I'd slighted Mitchell came back to me. Ignoring him after the wolf attack had hurt him deeply. And I'd also hurt him by finding comfort in Christopher's arms and kisses. Even so, I'd never considered the possibility Mitchell had intentions that went beyond friendship. Was there a chance he'd been secretly infatuated with me the same way I had been with Christopher? Perchance such feelings had only made his conflict with Christopher worse.

"So you're destroying Christopher because you didn't want me to get closer to him than you? How could you?"

"He had no right to have you—"

"Enough," Captain Theobald interrupted. "We must be on our way."

"I shall marry whomever I choose." I ignored the captain. "And it will not be a murderer."

Mitchell flinched but refused to back down. "If the king decides it, you will do it."

I started to rebut him, but the captain cut us both off with a vicious growl. "The king has already decided Princess Constance will marry Prince Ethelrex. They are to wed immediately upon our arrival at Delsworth."

Captain Theobald's news rendered me speechless. The king had made plans for me to marry his oldest son, the crown prince? From the shock rippling over Mitchell's features, I guessed he hadn't expected to hear that any more than I had.

"Then why did he send the wolves after me?" I asked, finding my voice.

"They were commanded to capture and trap you until I arrived with my men."

A shudder crawled up my back at the remembrance of the wolves surrounding me. If the ferocious beasts had truly wanted to kill me, they probably could have, even with Christopher and Mitchell fending them off.

Now I understood why the captain hadn't abused and killed me yet, why he'd sought a peaceful negotiation rather than attempt a battle against me. He had instructions to bring me in alive and unharmed in order to unite the House of Mercia with the House of Warwick. Such a move would silence any remaining opposition to the king's rule and cut off the rebellion that had been brewing for years. How could anyone fight against King Ethelwulf if he legitimized his family's claim to the throne through his son's marriage to me?

The captain watched my reaction, his lips once again twisting in pleasure at my horror. He knew as well as King Ethelwulf that my marriage to the crown prince would appease those who were discontent but would ultimately render me powerless. Instead of becoming a ruler in my own right, I'd merely be a pawn in a dangerous game. Nothing would change in the kingdom. Injustice and lawlessness would continue.

Captain Theobald's grin inched higher. "Since your groom is anxiously awaiting your return, we must not keep him waiting. Would you not agree, Princess?"

He gave me no more chance to respond but instead spun and urged his horse into a trot. The knights surrounding me took that as their cue to move, giving me no choice but to do the same.

My body reacted woodenly, my movements like a puppet on a string. More than the news of my fate, the truth of Christopher's predicament drained the lifeblood from me. He was trapped in a barren ruin and would soon be buried there alive.

Even after he'd ridden away from Mercia, I'd

always harbored hope that he'd return, that I'd see him again, and that he'd learn to love me. Even after he'd rejected me in the Wellmont ruins this past night, somewhere deep inside a flame had still flickered—though weakly—that perhaps I could someday change his mind about me.

But now he was gone. There was no hope for him. He was all but dead. And inside I was dead too.

Chapter 16

Adelaide

By midday, the fog had dissipated. However, rain continued to fall nigh into the evening, drenching us and making us miserable in spite of our oiled cloaks—although I didn't know how I could get any more miserable with thoughts of Christopher's death haunting me at every turn.

During the long hours of riding, I'd counted three dozen elite guards and three unit commanders. With Captain Theobald, that brought the total number of soldiers to forty. As much as I wanted to fight my way free, I reminded myself as I had earlier that any attempt to battle them would be suicide.

Had Mitchell realized that as well? From his black eye and split lip, I suspected he'd crossed paths with Captain Theobald's group by accident during his search for the treasure. Maybe upon seeing how outnumbered we were, Mitchell had realized the impossibility of winning a fight. He always had been more reasonable and logical than I had.

He'd clearly expected that in eliminating Christopher, a sworn enemy of the crown, and in giving Captain Theobald the ancient key, he'd prove his loyalty, secure my release, and take me back to Langley.

I wanted to shake Mitchell for his foolishness. He should have known the king would never free me. I was too dangerous. Perhaps Mitchell had known but had hoped to spare our lives. Whatever the case, what neither of us had expected was that the king would use me to his advantage through marriage to his son.

In the waning daylight, Mitchell plodded behind me, Tall John riding at his side. I'd considered urging Tall John to sneak away and return to Wellmont ruins to free Christopher. But I knew he wouldn't get far before the knights recaptured him, likely killing him on the spot.

At times, I could feel Mitchell's gaze boring into my back. I sensed he longed to explain himself. But I was too angry and hurt and devastated to spare him more than a passing glance.

Ahead, I caught sight of the faint wisps of smoke curling into the air, which meant we were coming upon a village. My stomach growled, a reminder I hadn't eaten all day. The captain had sent several of his men out to hunt, but since we'd veered east to the coastal road and a more populated area, the soldiers came back empty-handed. Like so many other places, the land had been overhunted in the past year by hungry locals.

All day everywhere we traveled, I'd witnessed the overwhelming poverty of the bondsmen. Although I'd previously seen the oppression on trips with my uncle to Everly, this time I saw the hardships with new eyes. This time I saw the plight of the people through the eyes of a queen, and it only strengthened my resolve to do for Mercia what I'd done for the people of Langley and Everly. I vowed to myself that I would serve them, care for them, and sacrifice my own desires and needs for them.

When Captain Theobald broke away from the rest of us and rode ahead with a unit of soldiers, I contemplated attempting to escape. But I was still surrounded by two dozen of the country's fittest, strongest, and biggest knights. Even though I counted myself skilled with the sword, I wouldn't be a match against these men. I'd learned that lesson well enough during the battle our first night.

Thankfully, the knights had all treated me with the utmost respect, none daring to speak to me, much less lay a hand upon me. They never looked directly in my eyes, obeying the law that required them to avert their gazes in the presence of one more prominent than themselves.

I'd noticed Captain Theobald had no trouble making eye contact during his interactions. However, other than a few sharp commands for his men to unarm me of my weapons, he'd left me to myself most of the day.

At a flurry of shouts and screams, I sat up straighter in my saddle and peered over the shoulders and helmets of the guards in front. Ahead, the thatched roofs of a dozen or more wattle-and-daub homes came into view, simple huts much like those of the peasants who lived on Langley land. Along the waterfront, only a few dilapidated fishing boats bobbed in the waves, and I surmised that most of the men were still out at sea filling their nets with the cod, haddock, and whiting they'd sell at markets further inland.

I could see that many of the homes had enclosed gardens, which were starting to flourish with the first vegetables of the summer. After the year of drought, the vibrant greens and overflowing herb beds were a welcome sight.

The screaming and crying and shouting, however, were very unwelcome, and only grew louder the closer we drew, as did the shattering of pottery and other vessels.

"I demand to know what is happening," I said.

The closest knight, an enormous man with arms the width of an oak, was staring ahead and frowning. So far on the journey, the guards hadn't shown any emotion. They were trained not to display their feelings and to remain impassive and uninvolved, so the slight infraction was unusual.

"I will string up anyone else who resists," came a shout from Captain Theobald. I caught sight of him at the center of the main thoroughfare. He had his sword pointed against something hanging from a tall post.

The guards at my front parted enough for me to see more clearly. Only then did I realize the something was a woman, and she was upside down. A rope had been strung about her ankles and looped over the pole so that her skirt and shift fell away to reveal her bare legs. In addition to the degradation of baring her body for everyone to see, red welts formed where the rope was digging into the flesh at her ankles.

I realized then the muffled screaming was coming from underneath the layer of skirts that had fallen across the woman's face. She flailed about with her arms, but each move only caused the rope to dig deeper into her flesh.

Next to her, Captain Theobald waved his sword impatiently as his knights brought forth another woman who screamed and writhed in resistance. All around, weeping children clung to their mothers' skirts, hampering frantic efforts to give their meager stores of food to the soldiers who were traveling from house to house. Instead of simply taking the food, the knights had begun to ransack each home, tearing apart feather mattresses, emptying chests, and smashing bins into the muddy street.

Fury rose in my chest with the force of a fire on a dry summer day. The kindling had already been smoldering, and it now exploded. As Captain Theobald commanded his soldiers to tie a rope around the ankles of the second woman, I could not stand back and watch a moment longer.

"Hand me your sword," I said to the guard with the oak-tree arms.

His frown had disappeared, replaced by impassivity, but something dark smoldered in his eyes. "I'm sorry, Your Highness—"

"Give it to me now!" Without waiting for his permission, I kicked my horse forward, reached for his sword, and unsheathed it on my own. I expected at least a word of protest, perhaps even a small effort to prevent me from taking it. But the guard said and did nothing.

Heedless of anyone in my path, I galloped toward the center of the street to the peasant woman hanging upside down. When I rode past, I slashed at the rope holding her in place and sliced it in half, freeing her so that she dropped to the ground.

A short distance away, I circled my steed back. This time my sights focused on the knights with the cord half tied around the ankles of the other woman. I charged again, the warm moist air blowing against me, reminding me of a jousting tournament, except this time my aim wasn't the breastplate of the knight riding toward me. It was the rope.

Before I could reach my target, the two guards dropped the twine and stumbled back, likely fearing I would slice them. In an easy motion, I looped the rope, cut it, and let it fall to the ground at the woman's feet.

She stopped screaming and stared up at me, her eyes wild with fright. The desperation and fear there only fanned the flames in my chest into scorching walls of fire.

I reared my horse and found Captain Theobald. "What is the meaning of this?" I waved my sword toward the tortured woman and then to the destruction all around.

At my sharp question, the captain bristled, lifting his chin so the scar running the length of his face was fully visible. He seemed to be waging an inner war of whether to answer my question or drag me off my horse and string me up by my feet in the woman's stead.

His knights had ceased their ransacking and stood mutely, watching our interaction. Mitchell and Tall John had urged their horses near mine, likely in an effort to protect me, and now watched me with trepidation. The townspeople, too, had quieted, with an occasional muffled sob still punctuating the silence.

I leveled my gaze at the captain, refusing to look away until he answered my question.

He finally dropped his head into a semblance of a bow, as though paying me homage. "Your Royal Highness, Princess Constance," he said in a placating tone. "I would not see you or my men go hungry."

At the captain's declaration of who I was, whispers and murmurs passed through the crowd. Thin, haggard faces peered up at me, faces that testified of their hardships, particularly over the past year. Although the fishing industry had kept them from the same starvation-like conditions others in the land had faced, they had little enough to spare for me or the soldiers.

I lifted my chin. "I shall remain hungry rather than watch these people suffer at my expense."

"You may not need nourishment, Your Highness," Captain Theobald replied. "But my men must eat. Since we can find no game, it is a common practice for the people to provide for us."

I took in the state of the guards, their heavy armor, the punishing conditions under which they worked. The size of their bodies most certainly matched the size of their appetites, and I couldn't begrudge them a meal.

From the slight smile Captain Theobald gave me, he understood my dilemma and reveled in it. We could feed the soldiers and starve the townspeople. Or we could allow the townspeople to keep their food and make the soldiers suffer. Either way, someone would be dissatisfied with me.

"Continue the confiscation of food," the captain shouted to his men.

The guards moved more slowly to obey as if they

were waiting for me to come up with a solution.

A solution?

The ancient King Solomon had prayed for wisdom, and God had bestowed it upon him. I could now understand why the king had treasured such a gift. It was difficult to rule justly and fairly.

If God offered me riches, health, and wisdom, I knew without hesitation what I would choose. Like Solomon, I'd rather have the wisdom to rule my people properly than have wealth and long life.

God, I pray that You will give Your servant a discerning heart, I silently prayed the same words King Solomon had used in ages past. *I need Your wisdom to govern the people and distinguish right from wrong.*

In that moment, I sensed God was pleased with my prayer, as He had been with Solomon's. With confidence, I scanned the town, the small huts, a cooper's shop, a blacksmith, and a warehouse for storing dried and salted fish. What would help these people survive after this destruction? And what would be fair to the hungry knights?

I patted the pouch at my side underneath my chain mail. The remainder of the jousting tournament winnings. It was still a substantial amount, even after paying the physician and giving some to the elder before leaving Langley land.

"Captain," I called. "You may have your men continue to gather enough food for one meal and no more. And they shall do so peaceably henceforth."

From the stiffening of Captain Theobald's shoulders, I sensed my authority maddened him, that he'd much rather roll in the nearby pile of dung than listen to me. But I was counting upon the king's plan to marry me to his son to protect me. The captain wouldn't harm me in any way, knowing the king had use of me.

I dug the pouch out from beneath my layers of garments. I held the bag in my hands, relishing the weight. "You will also have your men bestow a gold coin to each person in payment for whatever you take."

My announcement was followed by complete silence. This time no sobs, not even a sniffle could be heard. The soldiers, as well as the townspeople, stared at me in disbelief. My offer was too generous since several pieces of gold would suffice to pay the entire town for all the food.

I opened the pouch and bounced the coins, knowing most of these paupers had never seen or held real gold, that one coin alone would provide for their needs for several months.

The captain eyed my small bag. "There is no need to waste gold—"

"Captain," I interrupted. "I am the queen, and the gold belongs to me. I shall do with it as I please."

Again, silence fell over the gathering. I held Captain Theobald's gaze. I'd outwitted him, and the angry glint in his eyes told me he knew it.

The guard with the oak-tree arms slid from his mount and kneeled before me. When he arose, he kept his gaze trained on the ground. Even so, I sensed the respect in his stance and expression. "Your Highness, you can trust me to fairly distribute the payment for the food."

I'd laid his sword across my lap and now touched

the hilt. He'd allowed me to take his weapon and in doing so had likely earned himself the captain's censure if not severe discipline. What was one more act of defiance against his superior?

"Tell me your name, sir." For his act of courage, I would see he was protected from the captain's wrath and repaid with kindness once we reached Delsworth.

"Firmin, Your Highness." He bowed his head again.

I handed him the bag of gold coins. "Very well, Firmin. I give you leave to pay each household for the food we must collect."

"Yes, Your Highness." He took the bag, set his shoulders with determination, and then strode to the closest cottage, to a gaunt woman who stood in her doorway, a child on either side of her. She cowered under Firmin's intimidating presence and rapidly handed him a loaf of bread and a string of fish. She began to retreat but stopped when Firmin pulled a single gold coin from the pouch and held it out to her.

She reached for it but hesitated to touch it. Firmin nodded his encouragement and held it closer. Tentatively she took it.

Firmin wasted no time in moving to the next cottage, but my gaze lingered upon the gaunt woman and her intense fascination with the coin in her palm. When she finally looked at me, her eyes glistened with tears, several of which spilled over and ran down her cheeks. Gratitude and love seemed to pour out as well.

I nodded at her, hoping I silently conveyed my apologies for the trouble these men had caused her and this village.

She proceeded to lower herself to her knees,

bowing her head before me in a move of respect and subservience. In that single act, she'd spoken louder than words ever could. She'd acknowledged me as her true queen.

Chapter 17

CHRISTOPHER

MY VOICE WAS HOARSE FROM YELLING, MY PALMS BLOODY FROM beating them against the bars, and my fingernails ragged from prying at the crack in the door. Over the past hours, I'd tried everything to free myself from the dungeon. I'd used my torch to try and melt the metal, attempted to pick the lock, and fought to bend the bars.

Nothing had worked and eventually my torch had spluttered out. Even so, I rammed my shoulder into the bars, needing to find some way of escape. Anxiety ate away at my stomach and nearly doubled me over with pain. I had to reach Adelaide and protect her. My determination hadn't diminished throughout the long day. In fact, the need to free her only burned hotter, like a smelter stove after the bellows had been pumped.

It didn't matter that Theobald's men had filled the stairwell with rocks and boulders—at least from the scraping and crashing, I gathered that's what they'd done. I'd decided if I freed myself from the dungeon, I wouldn't let the stones stop me from going after Adelaide. I'd roll each one out of the way with my bare hands if need be.

However, after the passing of so many hours, I suspected I was running out of time to save her. If I didn't rescue her before Theobald reached Delsworth, I feared the torture he'd inflict upon her there. The very thought of her suffering stirred my anguish. How could I have failed her so miserably?

I'd assumed God brought us together for me to be her guide, protector, and champion. I'd believed I possessed many advantages that could successfully lead her back to the throne. Had I been wrong?

"Father in Heaven," I prayed into the darkness. "What did I do wrong?"

Somehow, I'd allowed my guard down and hadn't anticipated Mitchell's treachery. I'd wanted to believe the best about him, that we could reconcile. But his love for Adelaide went deeper than I'd realized, and the kiss had been too much.

At the thought of her sweet lips pressed against mine, I groaned and buried my face into my bloodied hands. In that moment, she'd been more than just my queen, my charge, my duty. She'd simply been a woman. A very desirable woman—and not only because of how beautiful she was, although she was breathtakingly so. No, she was more desirable to me than any woman I'd ever known because of all the things I loved about her, including her strength, her need to do what was right no matter the cost, her zeal for helping the less fortunate, her depth of insight, and so much more.

Was it possible I was falling in love with Adelaide?

"Adelaide," I whispered. "What have you done to me?"

I sagged against the bars and slid to my knees, my legs unable to hold the weight of my body. Though I'd fought valiantly against the attraction, I could no more ignore it than I could my own beating heart. I'd been as helpless to walk away from her earlier after kissing her as I was to thrust away this pulsing need for her now.

No doubt she felt this growing magnetism too. Why else would she have wound her arms around my neck and kissed me back? And why else afterward would she have hinted that she wanted more in a relationship with me than a queen and her knight.

Had I pushed her away too quickly? Should I have given us a chance? After all, she wasn't queen yet. No one was dictating what she could and couldn't do. At least not yet.

"What do You want me to do, God?" I whispered. What if Providence had planned for more in our relationship? What if He wanted us to be together as man and wife, knowing we'd be even stronger that way? Stronger than any political ties she could form in an arranged marriage?

The prospect pulsed through my blood with a rush of anticipation but just as quickly fizzled to despair.

Mitchell had handed her over to Theobald. My only hope was that somehow Ethelwulf had resolved to keep her alive—at least until he had the chance to see her and determine her worth.

"Adelaide," I whispered into the dank air. "Stay alive. You have to survive. And I will come for you."

I lifted my head and grabbed the rusty bars again. The torn flesh of my palms burned. But I pulled anyway. I had to find a way to free myself. Not because of the very real possibility of starving to death in the dungeons without food or water, but because I needed to reach Adelaide before it was too late.

Adelaide

The smoke of campfires and roasted venison wafted into my tent, as did the laughter of the knights standing around the fire pit. After riding all day in the rigid orderliness and silence required of the king's elite guard, the laughter was jarring and added to my despondency.

I turned over on my pallet and pulled my coverlet around me to ward off the chill. Though the rain had ceased, the air was still damp. The darkness of the night had only made it more so.

I was surprised the captain had the decency to provide me a tent, especially after I'd defied him in the coastal village. My only guess was that he realized the implications of his actions for the future. If I married Prince Ethelrex, I would one day be his queen. Even if I wasn't the sole ruler, I'd still be able to exert a great deal of influence, and the captain would be wise not to anger me overly much lest I conspire against him.

I'd allow him to believe his generosity to me now would work to his favor. But the truth was when I became queen, I'd do everything in my power to expel him from Mercia. I knew not how, but I was determined he would not only pay for the crimes he'd committed against the people of Mercia, he'd also pay for hanging Queen Dierdal and King Francis on the castle wall. Perhaps I'd have him hanged in the same place. Along with Mitchell.

I sighed and flipped to my back, staring up at the shadows of firelight flickering against the canvas. Mitchell had sentenced Christopher to his death. I shuddered with a fresh wave of despair. I grieved not only the loss of Christopher but Mitchell too. I'd lost two friends today, not just one.

The hot trail of tears slipped down my temples, and I angrily swiped them away as I had the other times they'd escaped. I wouldn't cry. At least not for Mitchell.

I thought I'd known him, hadn't believed he'd ever be capable of murdering—especially a family member. Uncle Whelan and Aunt Susanna had taught us to live with high standards of godliness and love. They'd modeled it in the way they treated the people who worked their land. And Uncle had always shown it likewise, in the Everly smelters with the men and families who relied upon his business.

I'd assumed Mitchell and I shared the same values and philosophies. Perhaps his had not taken root so deeply as mine. Or perhaps Christopher's rebellion and leaving had left a bigger wound in Mitchell than any of us had realized.

Whatever the case, I could never forgive Mitchell.

Outside the tent flap, Mitchell addressed the guard. "I would like to speak to Queen Adelaide."

"She said she has no wish to be disturbed."

Four knights had been posted, one on each side of my lodgings. I guessed the captain wasn't taking any chances of me attempting to escape during the night.

Though I'd considered fleeing to Wellmont, I could never slip past these knights. They were too vigilant and hadn't let me out of their sights all day. My best hope for saving Christopher was to pay someone with the little gold I had left to go to Wellmont and free him.

But other than the interaction with the woman in the coastal village, I'd had no opportunities to speak to anyone else. Even if I managed to somehow rescue Christopher, I'd resigned myself to marrying Prince Ethelrex. Such a move was preferable than dying. After all, what good would I be to my people in the grave? As Ethelrex's queen, I'd be able to have some impact—at least I hoped so.

I didn't know much about the future king, only the occasional gossip since he'd recently arrived in Delsworth after spending most of his life thus far at the royal residence in Warwick. I'd heard he was a skilled fighter and tough warrior, renowned for his strength. In a recent tournament, Mitchell had boasted that the prince had taken down three giant Danes single-handedly.

"Please," Mitchell said. "I shall not be able to rest until I make amends."

He'd already tried to speak to me on several occasions throughout the day, and every time I'd only nudged my horse away from his.

"You will not be able to make amends, Mitchell," I called.

"I beg you to let me try."

The laughter of the soldiers around the campfire died away as they awaited my verdict. Part of me never wanted to see or speak to him again. But another part longed to know why he'd stooped so low. I needed an explanation to help make sense of what he'd done.

I sat up on my thin mat. I'd shed my armor but remained in my cloak and garments for the warmth they could provide. But even now, I shivered more from the misery of all that had happened than the cold.

"You may never forgive me," Mitchell spoke in almost a whisper, apparently realizing we now had an audience. "But I implore you to allow me the chance to explain."

Outside, a log in the fire pit popped and sent a spray of sparks into the air—just like my life, volatile and dangerous.

"Very well," I said. "You may explain. But I shall give you only five minutes."

The guard lifted the canvas away from the opening, and Mitchell ducked inside. The guard held a torch inside and glanced around. The tent was conical in shape and spacious. I had but a few possessions to take up room, certainly nothing to cause my captor alarm. He bowed in my direction then backed out and closed the flap.

Mitchell knelt upon the damp grass floor and lowered his head.

For a long moment, neither of us spoke. I was painfully aware of the quiet outside, which meant the soldiers were still listening and that our moment of privacy was public to the entire camp. Hopefully, Captain Theobald in his tent on the opposite side of the fire wasn't paying any heed to the conversation.

"Why did you plot against Christopher?" I finally asked, unable to keep the hurt and accusation from my voice.

Mitchell didn't raise his head, but instead soundlessly slipped off his gauntlet gloves. "I was angry at him for earning your favor so easily."

"So you locked up your own brother and left him to die because you were jealous?" Jealousy and anger were a hazardous combination. I should have paid better attention to the favor I'd extended to Christopher. Maybe I could have prevented the situation from escalating.

Mitchell pushed the gloves toward me, nodding that I should put them on. Then he began unlacing his boots. "I hoped in removing him from your life you would trust and look to me for counsel again."

"I never stopped trusting you—until today." I tried to make sense of why Mitchell was shedding his shoes.

"I regret I betrayed your trust." He slid his boots toward me. Before I could think of an answer, he unpinned his surcoat. "I only hope I may one day regain it."

"I could never—"

"Remember all the jousting tournaments?" He removed his cloak. Then with a glance over his shoulder as though to ensure we were still alone, he began to inch his chain mail mantle over his head. Again he motioned for me to start putting on his discarded garments.

I picked up one of his gloves. Why did he want me to don his armor? Did he plan for us to fight our way free? But why give me his instead of putting my own back on?

"You were always braver and stronger than me." His voice turned soft so that I almost couldn't hear it. "Even when you were me." He laid the mantel next to me and motioned for me to hurry, taking my cloak and pointing from himself to the pallet.

My pulse lurched. Did Mitchell want me to dress in his armor and pretend to be him? Was he planning to lie down in the tent in my stead while I walked out as him?

It was a daring feat. But... we'd fooled many people in the past with our duplicity. Why not now?

I hesitated. Was it possible I could make it back to Wellmont and free Christopher after all? Was that what Mitchell was insinuating? But what would Theobald do to Mitchell if I left, especially after discovering his duplicity?

Even if I was angry with Mitchell, I couldn't put him in danger.

Mitchell shoved his cloak at me urgently.

Maybe this was more than just about freeing Christopher. Maybe this was another chance to fight back against King Ethelwulf, a chance I'd thought was gone.

Aunt Susanna's request upon her deathbed reverberated in my mind: *God saved your life, Adelaide. And now it is time for you to give it back in service to Him as the ruler you were born to be. Promise you will do so.*

I'd vowed to her that I would. After the sacrifices she'd made for me, how could I give up now?

The same with Sister Katherine. She'd endured years of horrible torture and had risked her life again and again for me. If she'd never compromised her quest to restore Mercia, how could I? If she'd never stopped believing in my rule as queen of Mercia, how could I?

I grabbed the garments and began to dress, making as little noise and movement as I could, all the while talking with Mitchell, each of us playing our part. By the time I was fully attired in his armor, surcoat, gloves, and boots, I couldn't recall the words I'd spoken to him in reply to his petitions for forgiveness, except that I'd continued the pretense of arguing so the guards outside my tent wouldn't suspect what we were doing.

"Please, Your Majesty," Mitchell said once more, bowing before me.

The five minutes I'd promised him had passed, and I sensed this was the moment of transition when he would take my place on the pallet and I would rise to become him. I lowered myself, placed an arm across his back, and then gave him the absolution he sought. "Though I can never forget what you did to Christopher, I shall ask God to help me forgive you."

"Thank you, Your Majesty."

We were side by side for just an instant, long enough for him to whisper in my ear. "John is forty paces south of camp. Free Christopher and get out of Mercia."

How had Tall John managed to get away without detection? And how would Mitchell save himself?

The questions begged for release. But Mitchell pressed something into my hand. "I found this locked in a stone bookshelf in the ruins of the scriptorium." He gave me a sharp nudge to be on my way.

I stuffed what seemed to be a torn piece of parchment into my pouch then rose, pulling my hood up just the way he'd worn his when he'd entered my tent. He likewise rolled onto my pallet and covered himself with my cloak and blanket, tucking them high enough that the guard wouldn't be able to see his face or hair.

I spun on my heels and pushed against the tent flap. Instantly, the guard lifted the canvas covering. I ducked outside into the darkness of the night and imitated Mitchell's stance. I could feel the stares of the soldiers around the campfire and tensed as I waited for them to call out in recognition.

The tent guard raised his torch inside again before backing out and closing the flap. Using Mitchell's gait, I started across the camp toward his bedroll, which he'd laid out near the southern edge underneath a low-lying hawthorn bush. At the sight of Tall John's long frame already slumbering on the bedroll next to Mitchell's, I narrowed my eyes in confusion. Perhaps Tall John hadn't made his escape yet after all.

With each step I took, my blood pounded a deafening tempo. I expected one of the soldiers around the campfire to demand that I turn around so he could examine my face. I tried to tell myself this was no different from other occasions when I'd pretended to be Mitchell. I'd perfected his stride and mannerisms. There had even been a couple of instances when I'd had to emulate his voice. I prayed I could escape without question this time. These guards were too well trained and would surely notice something amiss if I spoke.

By the time I reached the bedrolls, my stomach had cinched into a hangman's noose. I stepped over Tall John and threw myself onto the ground, acting the part of a despondent man. I turned away from prying eyes, praying the hawthorn bush would give me enough cover to keep up the charade until I had the chance to sneak away.

I couldn't wait too long. I had to make my escape

before anyone suspected we had switched places. At the same time, I knew I had to remain until the firelight dimmed and the soldiers retired for the night.

I wanted to speak to Tall John, but he was strangely silent. After long minutes, I realized he wasn't there, that somehow Mitchell had disguised Tall John's bedroll to appear as though he was sleeping. I would have to do the same to mine.

The minutes crawled by as I plotted my course of action. By the time the last of the soldiers around the fire dropped onto his pallet, I had enough windfall gathered into my bedroll to form the shape of my body underneath the blanket so that if one of the tent guards or other sentries on duty glanced my way, they wouldn't realize I was gone. At least hopefully not until morning when they kicked my blanket to awaken me and found the sticks instead.

On my belly, I slid like a serpent through the brush until the darkness consumed me.

Chapter 18

Adelaide

Twigs and branches scraped my face. The tangle of brush snagged at Mitchell's chain mail, slowing me down. But I pushed myself to keep going, fearing that at any second I'd hear shouts and commotion behind me as the soldiers recognized my absence.

With the continued silence, I finally rose and wished for some way to mask my trail, cover my boot prints, and smooth away the broken blades and leaves. But in the dark without the stars or moon, I had to use every sense to stay on course south of the camp, testing the position of the moss and the breeze.

Even so, I realized I'd veered off when after forty paces I hadn't come into contact with Tall John. I stopped and listened for the horses but heard nothing. Taking a chance, I risked a soft whistle, the one I used when we were hawking together and wanted to let him know my position.

I held my breath and waited for his answering whistle. When none came, the anxiety roiling through my chest squeezed at my lungs so that I could hardly manage another faint whistle.

A moment of silence passed with no response. If I couldn't find Tall John or if he'd been caught already, I'd have to return to Wellmont on my own. It was a full day's ride by horse to the ruins, even longer by foot.

I needed to make haste. Every minute of delay could affect Christopher's life. And every minute of delay could also put me in jeopardy. If I was very fortunate, I'd have until dawn to get a head start. If Captain Theobald discovered my absence sooner, I'd have even less time to outrun him and his elite guard.

I dropped my head in despondency, but then... A faint birdcall wafted on the breeze.

Tall John? I perked up and listened. Had it come from the east?

After several heartbeats, the soft trill came again. I started in the direction of the sound. It was most definitely east, which meant I'd gone farther off course than I'd realized. Thankfully, a short time later, I found myself hugging Tall John. I didn't wait to question how he'd managed to steal away his horse and Roland. And I didn't stop to inform him of how I'd made my getaway. Instead, we mounted our horses and silently moved out.

Once on our way, I still couldn't breathe normally. I could only think about the fact that if I was recaptured, I wouldn't be able to reach Christopher in time and that he'd surely perish.

We rode all night pushing our steeds hard. At the first light of dawn, we'd reached the craggy trail that cut through Huntingdon Rocks. As the crumbling structure of the old fortress came into view, I tossed a glance over my shoulder praying, as I had been all night, that Captain Theobald and his men weren't on our trail yet. The eastern sky lightened into a bloody crimson stain along the horizon behind us, but we were yet alone.

I kicked Roland into a trot across the uneven ground. Sensing my urgency, he moved with me, obliging me with the grace he always had.

"This way, Your Majesty," Tall John called, veering away from the ruins altogether.

"Do you really think we'll be able to find another entrance?"

"We need to try," said my faithful steward. His thin face radiated weariness and his shoulders were stooped, but he'd ridden all night just as tirelessly as I had.

During the long hours, Tall John had told me more legends regarding the Wellmont ruins from the days when it had been called Huntwell Fortress. Apparently, servants had hidden Queen Leandra's newborn babe, Princess Aurora, at Huntwell to keep her safe from Queen Margery, who had decided to try to take the kingdom away from the new heir.

Though I was familiar with the tales regarding King Alfred the Peacemaker's twin daughters, I was struck by the realization that Queen Leandra was my great-grandmother and Princess Aurora my grandmother. I was related to those strong women I'd always admired.

Tall John's grandfather had told him stories of hidden passageways underground that had been used for hiding the Princess Aurora, and how an opening had eventually been created leading into Inglewood

Forest so the princess could go out from time to time.

Of course now, after so much of the eastern forest had been cleared away for its timber, Tall John believed the secret entrance was somewhere among the rocky formations on western heathland. He also believed that after so many decades with the castle in ruins, the passageways were still useable since he'd heard rumors that loyalist rebels had used them to hide from King Ethelwulf, especially during the purging.

I was inclined to think Tall John was wasting precious time that could be better spent hauling rocks out of the dungeon stairwell. However, if we could find the opening, we'd have the cover we'd need to hide from Captain Theobald when he caught up to us. Thus, I'd agreed to the search and prayed the old fables were true.

With the growing light of dawn at our aid, I followed Tall John's lead. The further away from the ruins we went, the more I doubted we would find anything. Along a rise in the heathland, we circled around the largest of the rock outcroppings until they all began to look alike to me. As the sun rose steadily higher, I halted my steed and was about to call off the search, when Tall John motioned me toward a boulder smaller than the others we'd explored.

"Here!" His voice contained a note of excitement. "It's here!"

I dismounted next to Tall John and examined the high mound and the stone wedged into it. The place looked as ordinary as any other with a plain granite rock that contained no visible markings or signs.

"Are you certain?" I asked, watching him heave against the stone with his shoulder.

"Aye, here." He thrust aside a clump of gorse and pointed to grooves at the base of the stone. "It won't budge in my strength alone, but together we might be able to move it."

We shoved and struggled until finally it shifted enough to reveal what appeared to be a tunnel. With renewed enthusiasm, we doubled our efforts until at last the boulder gave way to a dark passage that sloped gradually downward in the direction of Wellmont ruins.

Our horses had to duck low and balked at entering until Tall John lit a torch from his pack. Once inside, we slid the entrance stone back into place with greater ease than we'd had in opening it. After two dozen paces, we came to a cavern that was spacious enough for our horses to rest while we navigated the remainder of the distance alone.

Though the earth was damp with puddles on the floor—likely from the recent rains—the tunnel was free of obstructions. Supported on the top and sides by wooden beams, some appeared newer than others, and I guessed Tall John's stories about rebels finding refuge under the ruins were truer than we'd realized.

Having to crouch, Tall John led the way with the torch. Other than a few rodents skittering away at our approach, we were eerily alone, the mustiness of wet soil and rock our only companion. With each step closer, my anticipation of seeing Christopher mounted.

"Mitchell was a fool to betray Christopher," I muttered.

"Sir Mitchell was merciful." Tall John's voice echoed in the hollow tunnel. "Lord Langley would be dead if Sir Mitchell hadn't locked him up."

I'd already come to the same conclusion that if Christopher had remained free to fight Captain Theobald's forces, he wouldn't have survived. I hadn't considered, however, that locking Christopher away had been an act of mercy on Mitchell's part rather than a jealous tantrum. Was that possible?

"In fact, we'd all be dead if not for Sir Mitchell making the deal with the captain," Tall John continued. "He knew we were surrounded and that the only way to survive was to turn you in with the key."

"Even if Mitchell believed he was doing the right thing by handing us over to Captain Theobald and refusing to fight, he should have been honest with us." As the words tumbled out, a niggling of guilt tugged at me. Perhaps Mitchell had felt he'd no other choice but to lie. If he'd told us, we'd have done as we pleased without any thought to his plans.

"He was only trying to save us," Tall John insisted, swiping at a cobweb that impeded our progress and showed the passageway hadn't been used in a while.

"You may be right. Nevertheless, he neglected to inform me he'd petitioned the king for permission to marry me."

"To save you from a match with Lord Mortimer."

"I had no intention of marrying Lord Mortimer." I stepped carefully through a particularly large section of water, my hood brushing against the dripping ceiling.

"Sir Mitchell got wind of a rumor that Lord Mortimer was planning to ride to Delsworth for the purpose of arranging a marriage to you."

My thoughts returned to my last encounter with Lord Mortimer who'd been on his way to Delsworth for that very reason. Was that why Mitchell had traveled to the capital city? So he could appeal to the king before Lord Mortimer did and purchase the official seal first? "Mitchell thought to do the honorable thing and marry me for himself?"

"Aye."

I swallowed hard against a sickening lump in my throat. I couldn't keep from thinking back to the way I'd rebuffed Mitchell all day. Had I rushed to judge him? Apparently so. Perhaps he'd harbored good intentions even if he'd gone about it the wrong way.

"I shall set things right with him when we next meet."

"Next? I highly doubt there will be a next time."

"Certainly the captain will show a measure of leniency. He said King Ethelwulf wanted to question Mitchell further."

"That captain will torture Sir Mitchell badly for aiding your escape." Tall John's voice turned hoarse with emotion.

The sick lump fell to my stomach. Of course. The captain was sure to be infuriated when the guards went into my tent and discovered Mitchell there in my stead. But I'd been so focused on saving Christopher, so determined to hold Mitchell responsible, that I hadn't given enough thought to what Captain Theobald would do after I escaped.

I tried to shut out the images of what would happen to Mitchell, but the visions swarmed into my head regardless—visions of him being dragged from the sleeping mat, pushed to his knees, and then beaten, perhaps even killed.

"Do you think the captain will spare Mitchell's

life?" I asked.

Tall John paused. The torchlight illuminated the straight path and a door ahead.

"He is a nobleman and a loyal follower of the king," I said, as if defending Mitchell to Tall John might actually save him. "The captain will punish him but surely will not kill him, not if the king desires to question him."

Tall John didn't respond. He didn't need to. I knew he was thinking the same thing as I. King Ethelwulf would be infuriated to discover Captain Theobald had had me within his grasp only to lose me. The captain would need to blame someone for his mistake, and Mitchell would provide an easy target and an easy way to deflect the king's anger.

I pressed a hand to my mouth to hold back my nausea. I wanted to halt, bend over, and give in to the need to be sick. But a new sense of urgency propelled me forward. When we finished freeing Christopher, I had to return for Mitchell. I couldn't let him suffer and die, especially at the hands of Captain Theobald.

As we reached the end of the tunnel and the doorway, I met Tall John's somber gaze and prayed we'd be able to rescue Mitchell before it was too late.

Christopher

The scrape of a distant door startled me awake. I sat forward, my knife out, my body tense. My limbs had grown stiff from the damp chill as well as from all the battering I'd done trying to free myself.

Had Mitchell finally realized the foolishness of his plan and come back? More likely Tall John had found a way to escape from Theobald and had returned to set me free.

The squealing of rusty hinges was followed by the glow of light coming from one of the many tunnels that branched out from the dungeons. Was this newcomer a friend or foe?

I scrambled to my feet and pressed against the bars, prepared to bargain for my freedom no matter who was coming.

"Christopher?"

My body tensed at the familiar voice. "Adelaide?"

Footsteps pounded nearer. "Where are you?"

"Here, in the third cell."

With the growing torchlight, I could see the bars again, as well as the passageway leading away from the cells.

"Are you hurt?" I strained to get my first glimpse of her.

"I am unharmed."

At the news, I released my breath, unaware I'd been holding it, and I whispered a prayer of gratitude heavenward.

Within seconds, she was standing in front of the cell door. If I hadn't heard her voice, I would have mistaken her for Mitchell since she was wearing his garments and chain mail. Behind her, Tall John held up a torch giving me a glimpse of her face. Her beautiful face, a face I'd thought I'd never see again.

More gratitude welled in my chest and clogged my throat so that for a moment I couldn't speak. I could only take her in and assure myself she truly was alive and untouched.

"The keys, my lord?" Tall John asked.

"Over there at the base of the stairway." As Tall John went after the keys, I knew I should be thankful Mitchell had left them behind and that they were still accessible amidst the rubble, but I was too frustrated with my brother to feel anything but ill will toward him.

"And you?" Adelaide said, examining me the same way I had her. "How do you fare?"

"Now that I know you are safe, I can die in peace."

"You will not die today, my lord. I shall not allow it." Though her voice was forceful, it wobbled on the last word, telling me more than anything else that our situation was still dire.

The lock was stubborn, and Tall John had to fight to twist the key. When it finally gave, I shoved at the door at the same time Adelaide tugged it open from the other side. I couldn't reach her fast enough and gathered her into my arms.

She didn't resist. In fact, she seemed as eager as I was to embrace. She wrapped her arms around me and squeezed tight. "I did not know if I would see you again."

I tugged off the hood of her surcoat and chain mail and then kissed the top of her head just like a father or cousin would do—at least that was my intention. But as my lips pressed against her silky hair, I couldn't make myself move back. My relief was so overwhelming that I closed my eyes, buried my nose in her hair, and breathed her in.

She was alive. At the moment, I never wanted to let her go or allow her out of my sight.

The warmth of her breath tickled my neck, and stirred longings within me I couldn't even name. All I knew was that I wanted to kiss her. Desperately. As if in kissing her, I could somehow ease the torture I'd experienced over the past twenty-four hours of not knowing whether she was dead or alive.

I didn't care that Tall John would witness the kiss. I didn't care that I was hungry and thirsty. And I didn't care that we were still in danger. I needed to taste her lips more than anything else.

Before I could shift and capture her, she released me and took a step back so I was left with no option but to let her go.

"We must be on our way," she said, nodding toward the passageway they'd used to find me.

I stepped from the cell, having had my fill of the dark dungeons, and I fought against my need to draw Adelaide back into my arms, to reassure myself she was safe and alive, to feel her warmth and the silk of her hair again.

The somberness in her expression stopped me.

"My lord." Tall John bowed his head, his countenance equally grave.

"What news do you have for me, John?"

Tall John looked to Adelaide, clearly deferring to her for leadership. She didn't wait for me to question her. "We need to return and rescue Mitchell." She spread her feet apart, as though prepared to fight me to have her way.

My mouth was parched, my body sore, and my eyes still adjusting to the torchlight after so many hours in complete darkness. And at the moment, I simply couldn't fathom exerting any energy to rescuing Mitchell. "Whatever trouble he is in, he has brought it upon himself and deserves the consequence."

"He sacrificed himself for me," Adelaide replied.

"He handed you over to that bloodthirsty fiend, Theobald. You are fortunate you remain in one piece and that the captain did not cut you apart one limb at a time."

"Mitchell believed he was saving us from bloodshed."

"He was a fool."

Adelaide's chin jutted stubbornly. "He may have been rash, but he acted in love."

I'd had plenty of time in my cell to vent my frustration over Mitchell. Though my anger toward him still burned low in my gut, I wouldn't speak ill of him now. Perhaps I'd betrayed him by kissing Adelaide, but his retaliation could have cost Adelaide her life. I wasn't sure I could ever forgive him for that.

"I intend to go back and free Mitchell," Adelaide said. "I welcome your assistance, but I will go whether you give it or not."

Chapter 19

Adelaide

We made quick work of backtracking to our horses. I didn't begrudge Christopher the time he needed to refresh himself with the little food and water remaining of our supplies. But I was anxious to be on our way, knowing the longer we delayed, the worse Mitchell would fare.

Even so, the moment we opened the stone door, we realized a contingent of Captain Theobald's men swarmed the ruins looking for us. He'd obviously discovered the duplicity shortly after I'd left and had been close behind.

While I'd wanted to rush out and fight the men, I held back and instead prayed for wisdom regarding my endeavor to reach Mitchell. In doing so, I realized that wisdom required taking into account the advice of others. With both Christopher and Tall John's admonition to wait in seclusion until the elite guards gave up their hunt, I settled against the cavern wall and slept for a few hours.

When we emerged at midday, the guards were gone. They apparently hadn't known about a secret opening that led under the castle ruins, or they wouldn't have given up the search.

With his own steed confiscated by Captain Theobald, Christopher climbed on Roland behind me, and we started on our way toward the coastal road. Tall John led us through secluded meadows and woodlands in an effort to avoid any of the captain's men who might still be searching the countryside for me.

While we rode, I explained to Christopher all that had transpired the previous day and night and how in the end Mitchell had been the one to set me free at his own expense. That even now, Captain Theobald was likely punishing and perhaps killing him for the deception.

"Then our mission is indeed futile and foolish," Christopher said. "The captain will have sent men to fetch you. By the time we evade them and reach Mitchell, he will be dead."

The June day had turned hot, with the sun's ray shimmering on the land. Where summer rains had fallen only yesterday and turned the fields green, today the withering heat was already at work to deplete the moisture.

Christopher's realism withered me the same way.

"Must you always stomp all hope?" I responded as anger and aggravation collided within my chest.

"No matter my personal frustrations with my brother," Christopher said, "I cannot offer you hope regarding his life when there is none."

"I realize you think we are wasting our time, and if

you do not wish to do this, I shall not hold you to it." My tone was irritable, but I was tired and discouraged.

"I have always been honest with you, Adelaide," Christopher said quietly. "Even when the truth is painful."

Normally, I could accept Christopher's forthrightness. But today, at this moment, I wanted—no, needed—to cling to the hope I could help Mitchell. "There are times when we need to hold out faith and hope even when the circumstances seem impossible."

I touched the place where my pouch contained the slip of paper Mitchell had handed me, the parchment he'd found in the scriptorium. Although I hadn't seen the scriptorium ruins, I guessed it had been among the outbuildings he'd explored, a place where monks had meticulously copied books by hand.

At one time, the building would have been filled with old texts and scrolls, all of them brimming with wisdom and knowledge, just as the pomegranate on the key suggested. I could only imagine Mitchell's excitement when he'd discovered the scriptorium and even more the remains of a stone bookshelf with the keyhole.

I hadn't studied the parchment long, but I'd realized it was a piece of a map. An unusual map, to be sure, one I assumed would lead to the hidden treasure when it was reunited with the missing part. Was that why Mitchell had been so willing to give Captain Theobald the key? Because he'd already found what we needed?

Maybe Christopher could make more sense of the map than I could.

"Mitchell found something at the ruins," I said,

slipping out the parchment.

Christopher leaned his head over my shoulder to study the paper. His breath against my cheek dispelled all other thoughts save his nearness. His chin brushed my tender skin, and the scratchiness of his unshaven stubble sent a tremor through my stomach.

I wanted to relax into him and let myself savor this closeness. But after our kiss and his pushing me away, I didn't know if I could handle further rejection—not today, not with everything in tumult.

As much as I cared for Christopher, I couldn't allow my feelings to run away and dictate my behavior. After all, emotions were fickle and never formed a solid foundation for any decision. I'd do well to heed Christopher's advice to sacrifice my personal desires for the greater good of Mercia and her people.

Even as Christopher pressed in closer, I sat rigidly until finally he finished studying the parchment. For some time we discussed the possibilities and came to the conclusion that it was indeed a part of a treasure map, but of where, we could not decipher. Certainly not any place within Mercia that we knew.

Though Christopher remained skeptical, I guessed that if a treasure did exist somewhere, we would still have need of the key to access the treasure and would now have to wrest it away from King Ethelwulf. But I could only pray I was wrong.

As we neared the coastal road, the land gradually gave way to rolling hills and fields. With no sign of Captain Theobald or his men, we rode well into the night until we finally came upon the campsite of the previous eve. The area was deserted except for several young shepherds resting with their sheep. A bonfire beckoned along with the scent of roasting meat, but Christopher bade me to remain in seclusion with Tall John in the depths of the wooded area while he spoke with the shepherds.

When he returned, he informed us that the king's soldiers had gone north on the coastal road toward Delsworth and were stopping and searching merchant vessels for the escaped Princess Constance.

Since we didn't know for certain whether some of King Ethelwulf's men were still searching for us in the countryside as well, we continued traveling, keeping to footpaths and deer trails. In the early hours of the morning, Christopher led the way to a manor home of a family he claimed had loyalist leanings who would be able to offer us a meal and shelter.

Once we arrived, news of my presence spread throughout the area so that nobility, tradesmen, and peasants alike gathered to get a glimpse of "Queen Adelaide Constance" as they called me. I was afraid all the attention would lead Captain Theobald and his men to the manor, but Christopher assured me the captain wouldn't attempt to recapture me amidst so many people, that he'd likely wait to draw me out and isolate me.

Christopher spent most of the day in meetings with locals, inviting me to join in after I'd rested. He again reassured me the support was a good sign, an indication the people were ready to oust King Ethelwulf and embrace me as their rightful ruler.

By the time we left the following morning, several knights offered to ride with us. Throughout the day, more continued to join us so that by eventide, we'd amassed a group of at least a dozen knights.

Christopher had borrowed a horse from our hosts, and all day I'd tried not to think about how much I missed his close presence behind me on Roland.

"Word of your bravery and generosity at Smithtide has spread," Christopher said, as he took Tall John's place next to me and allowed the manservant a chance to fall back.

Smithtide, I'd learned, was the coastal village where I'd defied Captain Theobald and paid for the soldiers' food in gold.

"The people cannot stop speaking of you," he continued. "You have won their hearts, just as I knew you would."

"That was not my intention," I replied. "I would have acted as I did with or without the praise of men."

"I know that." Christopher's voice contained pride that did strange things to my heart. "You are a compassionate and fair woman. And that is why you will make a noble queen."

I made the mistake at that moment of meeting his gaze. The golden brown was alight with his admiration and something else I couldn't name but that made my pulse lurch. I didn't trust myself to respond to him, so I nodded my thanks and stared ahead, unwilling for him to see that with only one look he could render me a quivering, lovesick girl once again.

Silently, I berated myself for thinking of him as anything other than my friend. He'd made clear his position, and his words from the night of his kiss still echoed in my mind. *We will both have to make many sacrifices in the days and years to come for the greater good of Mercia and her people. Can you do that, Adelaide?*

After the reverence and homage I'd received from the people we'd met and now those who rode with us, I was beginning to understand the significance of my role as the queen in a way I hadn't heretofore grasped. The position was one of great responsibility, one the people esteemed, one I could not treat lightly.

When darkness fell, the knights in our group led us to another fortress belonging to an old nobleman, Lord Chambers of Chapelhill, who had once been a loyal supporter of King Francis. His son had been on King Francis's council and had been among those slaughtered by King Ethelwulf, along with his wife and four out of five children. The youngest, a boy of four years at the time of the siege, hadn't been among those slain. Somehow he'd disappeared, and no inquiries or searching over the years had led to any discoveries of what had become of him.

Lord Chambers fed us and offered us beds for the night. While I was anxious to continue our travels and find Mitchell, Christopher reminded me of our need to build alliances.

At the break of dawn, the lord provisioned us with an abundance of supplies. As I thanked him for his hospitality, one of his servants helped him down to his knees. He bowed before me, his gray head bent.

"My lord," I said, feeling as though I ought to bow to him rather than the other way around. "I wish I could repay you for your kindness and generosity."

The group of men riding with me waited a discreet distance away, already armed and mounted. Many had brought their squires, who carried additional weapons and armor. And now, Lord Chambers was sending half a dozen of his retainers, the knights he'd hired to form a private army of his own. While I drew hope from the growing following, we would still be outnumbered when we faced Captain Theobald's elite guard.

"Your honored presence in my home has been payment enough." He looked up at me, his wise old eyes filling with tears. "I would give you my wealth, my land, my very life to avenge my son's death and see you on the throne in the place of the evil one."

A familiar lump swelled in my throat. Lord Chambers' story of sorrow and his pledge of loyalty were becoming all too familiar. So many had suffered under the rule of King Ethelwulf, and their tragic stories served only to strengthen my resolve to bring peace and justice to the land.

"I am most grateful for your support and loyalty," I replied, motioning to the servant to help his master rise. "I only pray God will give me a discerning heart to govern the people and distinguish right from wrong."

Since the incident at Smithtide, I'd started reciting King Solomon's prayer for wisdom oft. At my verbalization of the ancient words, Lord Chambers began to tremble. His eyes widened and fixed upon me with such intensity I wondered if I'd been sacrilegious to utter the prayer aloud.

Lord Chambers pushed the servant's offer of aid away and instead reached for my hand and kissed it. "Your Majesty, I believe you are the fulfillment of the age-old prophecy that foretells a young ruler filled with wisdom who will use the ancient treasure to rid the land of evil and usher in a time of peace like never before seen."

My rebuttal rose swiftly. I wasn't anyone special. Why would I be the fulfillment of an old prophecy?

As if sensing my denial, Lord Chambers spoke again before I could. "You have the humble heart of King Solomon himself. From what I have heard of your deeds, God has already granted you wisdom, and He will also bestow upon you untold treasure that will aid your quest to restore the land to peace and godliness."

I started to shake my head, but Christopher's touch at my elbow stopped me. As usual, he stood next to me, my personal guard and most trusted advisor. His eyes warned me to accept Lord Chambers' blessing gracefully.

I hesitated, but then bowed my head to the old nobleman, acknowledging his words and thanking him at the same time.

With Lord Chambers' blessing echoing in the morning air, I mounted and rode near the head of our assembly. Outwardly, I kept myself composed and tried to appear confident. But inwardly, I quavered at the responsibility of being the queen, the challenges that came with the role, and the question of whether I was worthy of such a task.

By midday, Christopher galloped ahead with another knight, the two of them acting as scouts. We were still in danger of an attack by Captain Theobald and his men. Thus, rather than being taken by surprise, Christopher decided to discover their whereabouts so that we might be able to plan a more secure route. I also asked him to do whatever he could to discover how Mitchell was faring.

As I waited for Christopher's return, I prayed as I had the past several days that Mitchell was still alive and unharmed and that we could find and liberate him before it was too late. By the time Christopher and the other knight rejoined us, we'd stopped for the night, making camp in an open area where we would be able to see any approaching danger.

"Theobald is as crafty as a serpent." Christopher took a trencher from the squire who'd helped to assemble a dinner of roasted pheasant and the rye bread Lord Chambers had sent with us. The darkness of the evening had already descended, and now light from the bonfire at the center of our camp illuminated the strong lines in his handsome face.

One of the younger knights, whose diminutive size reminded me of Mitchell, regarded Christopher with a look of both awe and fear. "Do you think the captain hopes to lure us close enough to the capital city so he can call upon reinforcements before battling us?"

"Theobald is playing a game of cat and mouse," Christopher replied, avoiding my gaze as he had since he'd ridden into camp.

All day my mind had been conjuring images of him captured by Captain Theobald. I wasn't sure I'd be able to live with myself if I lost Christopher in addition to Mitchell. So at the sight of him riding toward us, I'd wanted to run to him and throw my arms around him as I had in the dungeons.

As much as I'd longed to hug Christopher and reassure myself of his well-being, I'd refrained, knowing the other men wouldn't understand my relationship with him. They accepted his place as my most trusted advisor. But if I showed favoritism beyond that, even something as simple as a hug, I would surely cause undue gossip.

Christopher trained his sights upon the blazing fire. "I believe the captain hopes to lure in the queen so he can recapture her without a fight."

"And how will he lure the queen?" another asked.

The muscles in Christopher's jaw visibly flexed. Then he finally darted a glance at me. The stark sadness in his eyes pierced me. I stiffened ahead of the bad news he bore.

"Do not hold back, my lord," I admonished. "You must share your news."

He took a bite of the drumstick on his trencher and chewed but didn't swallow. Finally, he turned to his fellow scout and nodded.

The man cleared his throat and then bowed his head at me. "Your Majesty, we saw Sir Mitchell."

My stomach turned over in dread of what was to come. "And?"

"Captain Theobald is torturing him."

"Then he is yet alive?"

The scout glanced at Christopher with uncertainty. But Christopher chewed slowly and stared blankly into the fire.

"I give you permission to speak honestly, sir," I said.

He returned his attention to me. "Your Majesty, Sir Mitchell lives, but with what the captain is doing to him and the way he is suffering, he'd be better off dead."

Images of a hundred different torture methods rolled through my mind, and every single technique made my stomach roil. Which one was the captain administering to Mitchell? I stifled a shudder, but the thought of Mitchell's agony only drove a painful spike into my heart.

"So Captain Theobald believes I still care enough about Mitchell that I will attempt to set him free?" Despite my arguing and fighting with Mitchell in front of Captain Theobald, he'd obviously seen through the turmoil to the deep bond we shared.

"We believe so," the scout continued. "He leaves Sir Mitchell just outside of camp like bait. We've concluded that rather than seeking after you, he hopes to draw you to him instead."

It was a clever plan. The captain had learned very quickly I had a tender and merciful heart for those who suffered, and now he was using it against me. I had no doubt he would ensnare anyone who walked into the trap he'd set around Mitchell. Then he'd torture them, too, until I finally gave myself over to him.

"How many hours' ride ahead are they?" My mind was already spinning with a plan.

"We cannot attempt the rescue." Christopher spoke in a flat voice.

"Is there a way to end Sir Mitchell's suffering and evade capture?" someone else asked.

"We shall not even consider such an option," I retorted as I bent to retrieve my saddlebag so I could begin packing it.

"I would have done it already if I could have found the right angle for my arrow," Christopher said without meeting my gaze. "But Captain Theobald is too intelligent to allow us to kill the quarry."

"'Tis fortunate you were not able to kill him." I

straightened and glared at Christopher. "For I shall not abide murdering. We shall take him alive."

"If you saw the way he suffered, you would have pity on him."

"I shall have compassion on him by saving his life, not taking it."

At my sharp exchange with Christopher, the other men drew silent so that suddenly the crackling of the fire seemed louder. No one dared to look at either Christopher or me. Instead, they focused on their boots or the flames.

"How many hours' ride ahead are they?" I asked again.

Christopher didn't respond.

His fellow scout waited a moment, his eyes imploring Christopher. When no answer was forthcoming, the scout bowed his head. "Your Majesty, we can easily reach the enemy camp by dawn."

"Then let us prepare to leave." I folded a tunic and shoved it into my saddlebag. "Captain Theobald may hope to trap us. But what he will not expect is that we shall come after him with a trap of our own."

Chapter 20

Adelaide

The darkness of predawn obscured our view of Captain Theobald's camp and Mitchell. The sky was turning a faint pink in the east above the sea, and we would need to put into action our plans just as soon as we had enough light to see the enemy positions.

We crouched low on our bellies, hiding behind gorse and tall grass. The morning dew and the breeze cooled my face after the long night and contained the hint of damp sand and seaweed.

Next to me, I could hear Christopher's breathing. His shoulder brushed mine as he leaned into me. "I do not like the plan, Adelaide. You are taking too great a risk."

"I shall not change my mind," I replied. We had gone over every alternative as we'd ridden. And the safest option for everyone involved was for me to be the one to sneak to the edge of the camp.

Of course, Captain Theobald's soldiers would be ready. His sentries likely knew we were there.

However, they'd be expecting our entire company to attack rather than me approaching alone. And they certainly wouldn't harm me like they might Christopher or any of the other knights. Captain Theobald was under orders from King Ethelwulf to bring me to Delsworth alive. I was counting on that command to save my life. And Mitchell's.

"Adelaide, I beg of you." Christopher's whispered plea was warm against my ear. Something in his tone made me hesitate. When he bent closer, so that his nose brushed my cheek, I sucked in a breath.

I had no doubt he heard my intake, for in the next moment, he let his lips graze the same spot on my cheek. The touch was as light as a dewdrop, and yet it sent a shiver of pleasure up my spine.

He pulled back slightly so that once again only his warm breath touched me. "I cannot bear the thought of losing you."

I closed my eyes against his admission and the power it held over me. From his tone, I sensed the depth of his emotions. From his breath against my cheek, I sensed his desire. In this moment before battle, would he finally allow himself to care about me?

We'd been too busy and too surrounded by others to converse privately over the past few days of traveling. But from time to time, I'd sensed him watching me and wanting to say more. Had he changed his mind about us?

I remained rigid and unmoving, although his nearness beckoned me closer. Deep inside, I had to admit that if he but gave me the slightest indication of a change of heart, I'd put aside my reservations. Even now, I wanted nothing more than to turn my head and burrow my face into his neck.

"Mercia cannot lose you," he said softly.

At his statement, a draft of chilled air slapped me, and I stiffened. What was he saying? What had his kiss just now meant? I'd assumed he was admitting he cared for me as a woman. But was he thinking of me as the queen? Was he concerned only about the greater good of Mercia?

Apparently, I was fooling myself into believing Christopher could ever love me for who I was as a person. He loved me for what I could do for Mercia. As the queen. He was single-minded in his determination to see the wrongs in Mercia made right. I couldn't fault him for that. It was one of the qualities I loved about him.

Nevertheless, my disappointment stung. For a brief instant, I'd allowed myself to hope again for more when he hadn't meant to give me hope. I couldn't forget his words from the night of our kiss: *There can never be anything between us.*

I shifted to put distance between us and at the same time focused on the rear of the camp. Captain Theobald had situated Mitchell two dozen paces outside the ring of horses and tents. The scout had informed us the captain had stretched Mitchell out and secured him to a log that was towed at the rear of the entourage whenever they moved.

Of course, the ride would have been bumpy and painful, especially since the log rolled around. But surely Christopher and his fellow scout had exaggerated the severity of Mitchell's condition.

I'd sneak in, cut his bindings loose, and then drag him as far away as I could before I was caught. Most of our forces would then rush to defend me, which would draw out Captain Theobald's men. Once they were engaged, Christopher and another skilled bowman would begin taking out the soldiers one by one while those of us in the melee engaged in hand-to-hand combat.

I'd issued Tall John with the task of aiding Mitchell the final distance to safety. Even now the faithful manservant waited expectantly on my opposite side, having heard Christopher's impassioned declarations but wisely saying nothing.

The battle would indeed be difficult since we were outnumbered. But with Christopher and the other bowman shooting quickly, hopefully we wouldn't be at a disadvantage for long. They just needed enough light at dawn to sight their targets, but not enough that the elite guards would be able to locate their positions.

Not only would we free Mitchell, but we'd also show King Ethelwulf we were a strong force, would not cower, and would fight for the throne.

"I am sorry, Adelaide." Christopher bent close to me again. "I did not mean to hurt you—"

"*Your Majesty*," I prompted in a tight whisper. "I desire that you address me as *Your Majesty* henceforth."

"Very well," he said hesitantly. "Your Majesty."

Guilt swiftly panged in my conscience, but I silenced it with anger. If he planned to treat me like his queen and only his queen, I'd allow him to do so.

I glanced at the glowing horizon, then to Captain Theobald's camp, still quiet with slumber, although I suspected very few soldiers were sleeping but laid in wait for us just as we did for them.

"It is time," I said.

"Do not leave in anger," he said hoarsely. "Please."

"I shall give you what you have asked for, Christopher," I whispered. "A queen who will make Mercia great again."

With that, I crawled forward on my belly, using my elbows to propel me.

His hissed whisper urged me to stop. I moved quicker, fighting back my frustration and the sense of loss in knowing that Christopher would never be more than my counselor and loyal subject.

As I drew nearer to the camp, I glimpsed the log attached to the back of a cart. In the faint light, I could see it was suspended at a slight angle, likely to keep Mitchell from being crushed altogether but not enough to prevent scrapes and knocks as he was dragged along.

My stomach twisted at the thought of Mitchell's suffering during the past days of traveling. He'd done it for me, to set me free. If not for his actions, I'd already be in Delsworth married to Prince Ethelrex, abdicating my family's right to the throne, and leaving the people of Mercia to the subjugation of King Ethelwulf and his descendants forever.

At the base of the log, I skimmed along the rough bark until I brushed against Mitchell's feet. He'd been stripped of his boots and his ankles were tightly bound. The ooze of blood at the rope bindings as well as along his feet told me the ride had indeed been torturous.

"Mitchell," I whispered.

He didn't respond.

Above the bindings at his ankle, I was surprised to

discover his legs were bare except for his linen drawers. I drew back in horror at the realization that most of the tissue on his legs and thighs was raw and bleeding with deep cuts and wounds, raked open from being pulled over rough terrain.

I rapidly moved upward to gauge the status of the rest of his torso, only to find his chest was butchered too. The bloody flesh was coated with dirt and dust and pebbles. His arms were stretched high above his head abnormally tight, and his sockets were torn out of their joints.

"Mitchell," I said again, my voice quavering. Christopher hadn't been exaggerating after all. Mitchell was in terrible condition. Was he even alive?

I grazed his face. From what I could tell, his skin there wasn't in such desperate straits. The angle of the log had kept his head from scraping the road. I trailed his cheeks until I reached his mouth, praying I'd find the breath of life.

A soft whoosh of air greeted my fingers.

"Thank you, God," I whispered. He was alive.

Quickly, I slipped out my knife and sawed through the cord around his wrists. Once his arms were free, I lowered them onto his chest. In the process, he released a strangled cry. Without waiting to comfort him, I crawled to his ankles and sliced at the rope. By now, the guards surely had to be aware I was there. Were they allowing me to cut Mitchell loose before seizing me?

When the bindings fell away altogether, I caught him as he slid off the log, only to realize his back was just as torn and bloody. Gently, I laid him on the ground, and this time he whimpered like a wounded animal.

My stomach roiled with the need to be sick, but I took a deep breath and forced myself to proceed with what I'd come to do. We were seconds from a battle, and I needed to transfer him away from the enemy camp.

Before I could move him, he issued a guttural sound, as though attempting to speak to me. If Captain Theobald and his men hadn't heard us before, they surely would now.

"It is I, Adelaide," I reassured him softly. "We shall speak once we are safely away."

"No," he said more distinctly, his voice urgent. "Leave me."

"Shhh." I glanced at the shadows beginning to creep toward us. "Say no more."

I attempted to lift him to a sitting position and slip my arm around his waist to help him to his feet. But even as I did, his anguished cries rose into the air and were followed by the shouts of Ethelwulf's men surrounding me.

One of the guards thrust a torch at me, illuminating my face and at the same time casting light upon Mitchell. He was battered beyond recognition. In addition to the torn flesh, his body was riddled with bruises and burns. The skin around his eyes was puckered red and nearly swollen shut.

As he lifted his head toward me, only then did I realize his brown eyes were no longer there.

Captain Theobald had plucked them out.

My stomach roiled again, and this time I couldn't stop the bile from rising. I fell to my knees in the grass and vomited.

Chapter 21

CHRISTOPHER

From my hiding place, I counted two dozen soldiers congregating near Adelaide. That meant the others were lurking around, likely in hiding just as I was. My heart raced and my pulse pounded with the need to charge after her, carry her back into hiding, and force her to remain out of harm's way.

As she fell to her knees, I pushed up and almost stood. Had she already been wounded? I nocked my arrow and aimed at the elite guard closest to her. We'd agreed to wait until our men had joined in the battle, distracting Theobald's forces from noticing us as we rapidly picked them off. In spite of our plans, I'd shoot at anyone who attempted to hurt Adelaide, regardless of how it might affect my concealment.

Although the darkness shadowed Adelaide, the torchlight from one of the black-cloaked knights showed her heaving into the grass, sick to her stomach. I was surprised when the closest guard, a burly giant, offered her a scrap of linen and then gently aided her back to her feet.

Before I could make sense of what had happened to Adelaide or of the guard's kindness, our men charged forward, some on horseback, others on foot, all with weapons drawn. Their shouts of fury echoed in the air.

My muscles tensed in anticipation of the skirmish. I aimed for the weak spot in the armor of the guard closest to Adelaide. With my bowstring taut against my jaw, I slackened my hold. But when the guard lowered himself to one knee, thrust his sword tip into the ground, and bowed before Adelaide, I lost all concentration.

Several more knights around Adelaide did the same thing. They dropped to their knees, planted their swords into the ground, and lowered their heads.

At the sight of the elite guards bowing in subservience to her, Adelaide shouted and waved her hands at our men. "Cease the attack! Cease the attack!"

More of Theobald's knights surrounded Adelaide, kneeling before her in a clear act of goodwill and allegiance. I could only stare with slack bowstring and an open mouth. The other men in our group reined back, their war cries tapering to silence.

In that moment, I realized Adelaide had already won the hearts and loyalty of Theobald's knights. They had no intention of raising their swords to fight against her. Rather, they respected her and wanted to serve her. And they were defying Ethelwulf as well as their captain to do so.

As if my thought of the captain conjured him, he suddenly appeared out of the shadows on his horse, a small band of his soldiers on their mounts behind him.

"You are all traitors!" he called to the rest of his army as they continued to kneel before Adelaide. At Theobald's shout, the giant guard rose and stood beside Adelaide protectively, his weapons unsheathed.

"Mark my word." Theobald glared disdainfully over the bent heads. "When I capture you—and I will—you will die a traitor's death."

Adelaide straightened her shoulders. Though she wore her battle armor, she was more beautiful and regal than any woman I'd ever seen. "Mark my word," she replied, her voice ringing in the quiet of the morning. "When I have captured you—and I shall—what you have done unto my cousin shall be done to you."

Like everyone else, I glanced at Mitchell's mutilated body lying motionless in the grass. I could only pray that he'd blessedly passed out. Or died. At least then he wouldn't have to experience any more suffering.

"After your refusal to accompany me to Delsworth peacefully," Captain Theobald said in a cold voice, "I have no doubt the king will put a bounty on your head and ask for you dead or alive."

My spine went rigid at the implication of the captain's words. Before I could ready my arrow, the captain's knife sliced through the air aimed directly at Adelaide's throat. It flew with a precision and speed impossible to outshoot or outrun. Captain Theobald didn't wait to see if he succeeded but instead shouted an order to his loyal followers to ride out. While I knew I ought to stop him with one of my arrows, I could only watch with helpless terror as the knife glinted in the torchlight, its sharp blade destined to kill.

"No!" I shouted.

The enormous guard who'd been the first to kneel lunged in front of Adelaide and spread out his arms to shield her. The knife slammed into his broad chest with such force that he toppled against her, and the two crashed to the ground.

Shouts erupted around us, but my thundering heartbeat drowned out everything save the need to hold Adelaide. I scrambled forward, jostling through the knights, desperate to be by her side. Even if she hadn't been struck by the blade, the impact of the knight's body landing upon her could have harmed her.

When I reached her, the elite guard was already rolling away. She lay still and unmoving on the ground, her eyes closed. The knife had deflected off the guard's armor and landed a short distance away in the grass. I shuddered with the realization that it would have impaled Adelaide's throat if not for the quick reflexes of the guard. I would thank him and offer him a reward later.

As it was, I dropped to my knees next to her, felt for her breathing, and ran my hands over her head for any injuries. After a moment, her eyelashes fluttered up, and she expelled a breath. "I am unharmed," she whispered. "Just stunned."

My chest squeezed with gratefulness so overwhelming tears stung at the back of my eyes. Before I could rationalize my actions and stop myself, I lifted her into my arms, needing to feel her warmth, life, and strength and reassure myself she'd survived.

The giant guard hovered a moment longer before rising to his feet and once again resuming a protective stance next to Adelaide. Tall John also stood over us, but at the sight of Adelaide unharmed in my arms, he moved swiftly toward Mitchell.

I lowered my face against Adelaide's head, my mouth near her ear. "For the love of the saints, Adelaide. Do not ever take such risks again."

"Why?" she asked testily as she squirmed and

attempted to free herself from my hold. "Because Mercia cannot afford to lose her queen?"

"No, because I cannot bear to lose the woman I love." The words came out in spite of how reckless they were. However, the moment I spoke them, I knew them to be true—truer than anything else.

She ceased struggling and grew motionless.

I closed my eyes and fought the emotions drawing me to this woman. My duty to Mercia and the future stability of the country beckoned to me and demanded I let her go. I wanted Mercia to flourish, to succeed, to be at peace. And Adelaide was the key to that, wasn't she?

Mitchell's accusation about using Adelaide rose up to challenge me. Was I using her in my quest to rid Mercia of Ethelwulf? Pushing and driving her, regardless of all else?

I swallowed hard and in doing so let go of my need for Adelaide to be the savior. Being the savior was a burden too heavy for any one person to bear, and I could place it upon her no longer. I'd still encourage and advise and help her. But I couldn't expect her to be the perfect queen at the expense of all else.

She would face many challenges in the days to come, and she would have to make many sacrifices. But she shouldn't have to sacrifice everything that was important to her, including love. Although she hadn't spoken of her love for me yet, she'd hinted at her feelings—or at least her desire to explore what was happening between us. Until I'd cut her off.

"Adelaide," I whispered. For better or worse, I didn't want to cut her out of my life. If she truly wanted me the same way I did her, then we'd find a way together to make a relationship work. Couldn't we? "I love you more than I love Mercia. Your happiness and well-being are more important than anything else. And I am sorry for not understanding that sooner."

At my apology, she seemed to melt in my arms, molding against me. She started to raise her arms around my neck when an anguished cry drew her attention.

"Mitchell." She pushed up.

I reluctantly released her, knowing our conversation was far from over. But now was neither the time nor place to discuss what kind of future might lie between us.

Adelaide scrambled toward Mitchell and dropped to her knees beside him, opposite Tall John. Reaching for Mitchell's hand, she tenderly brushed her fingers across his forehead. Then I noticed what I hadn't been able to see from afar. Theobald had blinded him. While I had no doubt the loss of his eyes caused him pain, I guessed that what he suffered outwardly was only a fraction of the trauma his body was suffering internally. He likely had numerous broken bones and organ damage.

From the moment I'd seen him attached to the log, I'd known he wouldn't survive. Captain Theobald had made sure of that. The captain was an expert at taking people to the cliff of death, holding them there, and then finally dropping them over.

My fingers went to my dagger with the need to end Mitchell's agony. If I'd been in my brother's place, I'd want someone to put me out of my torment. But at the sight of Adelaide's compassionate ministrations, I withdrew my hand. She'd do everything within her power to save Mitchell. Even if her efforts were for naught and would only prolong his pain, she had to let him go in her own way and in her own time.

As angry as I'd been at Mitchell for locking me in the Wellmont dungeons and turning Adelaide over to Captain

Theobald, only sadness remained now. Sadness he would die, just as my father had, with a huge rift between us. I'd believed my father was a spineless fool. It shamed me to remember the words I'd spoken to him the day I'd left home. "You are a traitor to the true king," I'd spat at him. "I despise you for how weak you are and pray I shall never be like you."

He'd stood inside the stable door as I'd finished tying my packs to my horse. He hadn't responded except to lower his head. I'd assumed my words had brought him disgrace, that he couldn't rebut my accusations.

Now I realized he'd lowered his head in sadness—sadness for a son who was so arrogant, ignorant, and stubborn. In my immaturity, I'd never guessed the depths of my father's loyalty to Mercia and the extreme sacrifice he'd made for the kingdom by sheltering Adelaide. I hadn't trusted him even though he'd always been the fairest, kindest man I'd known.

In part, Adelaide had become a great woman because of who my father and mother were. They'd lived and died with honor, and they'd raised Adelaide—raised all their children—to do the same, to be valiant and noble and good.

Even Mitchell.

My sights shifted to him again, to Adelaide's loving caress against his battered face. If she could so easily forgive him for his betrayal, then how could I not follow her example and do the same?

The need to forgive and be forgiven pulsed through my chest. Maybe I hadn't been able to make things right with my father, but I had the opportunity with Mitchell.

Heedless of the soldiers swarming around us, I knelt next to Mitchell. Adelaide's touch must have soothed him, for he'd ceased thrashing.

"We must find a manor house nearby," Adelaide whispered to me urgently. "Someone loyal to the house of Mercia who would be willing to give us aid and shelter for Mitchell."

Words of caution immediately sprang to the tip of my tongue. We didn't have time to delay. We needed to make haste in chasing after Captain Theobald. If we could eliminate the captain before he reached Delsworth, we'd send a clear message to King Ethelwulf that he wouldn't so easily defeat us.

Before I could formulate a plan, Mitchell gasped and tried to sit up.

"Brother," I said.

My voice drew his attention, and he tilted his head in my direction.

"I want you to know," I started slowly, "I regret the way I parted with Father when I left Mercia. I was a fool to reject my family. I hurt all of you. And I am deeply sorry for that."

While I could have left my home under peaceful circumstances and should have made an effort to stay better connected, I could not apologize for going. In God's providence, I'd been meant to leave my home and country. Doing so had allowed me to amass a loyal following of dissenters while gaining an invaluable ally with the king of Norland. Both would be helpful to Adelaide in the days and weeks to come.

Instead of turning away from me, Mitchell nodded. I wasn't sure what the nod meant, but I took encouragement from it and continued. "I do not deserve your forgiveness for my callousness and abandonment. But I would ask for it anyway."

At my plea, Mitchell expelled a breath. For a moment, he was so still I was afraid he'd died. As if sensing the same, Adelaide brushed her fingers across Mitchell's forehead again. Though her expression remained composed, her hand trembled.

Mitchell's silence stretched, making the voices and barked commands of the other knights all that much louder.

A heaviness settled over me. Mitchell had decided not to forgive me. I held in a sigh and then placed my hand upon his mangled arm. "I love you, Mitchell. And I always shall." With that, I started to rise.

Before I could move away, his fingers captured mine in a surprisingly strong grip. "Love. You. Too." His whisper was stilted and hardly audible. Then he squeezed my hand, and I knew he'd forgiven me.

A lump formed in my throat.

"Vow. You will. Protect. Adelaide. With your life."

"I vow it."

He attempted to lift his hand but the movement only caused him to tremble with pain.

I knew what he wanted, and I bent my head and kissed his hand three times to seal my vow.

At my assurance, he turned his sightless eyes toward Adelaide, his expression taut as though he was attempting to see her beautiful face one last time.

"I kept. My promise. To Mother." His words were faint but distinct. "You are. Safe now."

A tear escaped and slid down Adelaide's cheek. "She would be so proud of you, just as I am."

He gave the barest of nods. His expression was earnest as though he wanted to say more, but his body began to shake. He convulsed for several seconds and

finally grew still. His chest ceased its rise and fall. His hand grew limp. And his head slipped sideways.
　　My brother was dead.

Chapter 22

CHRISTOPHER

THE FAMILIAR HIGH, ROCKY PRECIPICES OF NORLAND'S GREATEST seaport, Brechness, towered above the ship, the granite showing hues of rose threaded with lines of ebony. The bulk of the city sat on the cliffs, nearly impenetrable by the rock fortress that surrounded it.

Because of its secure position, King Draybane made Brechness his primary residence. He had several other castles throughout Norland where he dwelled from time to time. But I'd gained word from a passing vessel that the king was currently in Brechness, confirming my own knowledge of where I'd expected him to be.

I inhaled the salty air and savored the mist rising up from the waves splashing against the bow. Even in early July, Brechness was cooler than most places due to its far northern location as well as the cold winds blowing in from the ocean.

During our voyage, I'd expected to encounter any number of Ethelwulf's ships that still roamed the East Sea preying on merchant vessels. After countless battles on both land and sea against Ethelwulf's raiders, I'd been prepared to fight them as I had the past years of serving King Draybane.

However, we'd had no trouble as we'd sailed, seeing only one of his ships from a distance. Now I was anxious to dock and set my feet on solid ground. Though I'd seen little of Adelaide over the past week of traveling, I had no doubt she was ready to land as well.

Due to seasickness, she'd been confined to her berth most of the trip. Lady Sybil, the wife of one of the older noblemen accompanying us, had become one of her ladies-in-waiting and gave me frequent reports on Adelaide's condition.

I glanced starboard to the second ship. Many of the noblemen who'd joined us had brought their families to Norland fearing retribution from Ethelwulf once he learned they'd left with the queen. While some of the single young knights had opposed the additional passengers, Adelaide had insisted that any knight who fought for her would be allowed to protect his family in any manner he saw fit.

Her continued compassion won the hearts of not only the noblemen but their wives and children. Many of the women vied to serve her, to become trusted ladies-in-waiting. Rather than picking the most beautiful and poised of the noblewomen to be her attendants, as was Mercia's tradition, Adelaide chose the oldest, wisest, and most experienced at life.

"My lord," came Lady Sybil's voice behind me.

I spun to find the petite but graceful woman wearing court attire with her graying hair pulled up into an elegant knot. Her face was plain and marred by pockmarks from a childhood disease. But because Adelaide had proven she valued the woman's inner beauty more than her outward, Lady Sybil had become a devoted servant for life.

I bowed my head. "Lady Sybil, is the queen ready to disembark?"

"She requests proper attire, my lord."

I smiled. "Then she is finally agreeing to put aside her armor when she meets King Draybane?"

Lady Sybil returned my smile. She was my co-conspirator in my efforts to convince Adelaide to present herself like royalty rather than a knight for her visit to King Draybane's court. "It has taken some persuading, my lord. But she sees the wisdom in it."

"Then she has relinquished her notion to participate in King Draybane's tournament?" I'd made the mistake of mentioning I wanted to reach Brechness before the Summer Bounty Festival. The king of Norland always had a tournament to celebrate the occasion, and I knew the purse of gold he gave the winner would be helpful to our cause.

"She has made no more mention of it."

"Excellent." I exhaled another breath, this one of relief. Mitchell may have given in to her every whim to join in mock battles and jousting tournaments and other contests. But I was not my brother. And I would not allow Adelaide to partake in such activities, not even if I had to lock her away myself.

At the thought of Mitchell, sadness gripped my heart. We had buried him over a fortnight ago on the same day we'd recovered him from Captain Theobald. Though we'd pursued the captain, we'd been too late. He and his remaining guards had ridden swiftly and had found security behind Delsworth gates before we could overtake them.

Knowing our forces were yet too small for an offensive attack against Delsworth, Adelaide had agreed with her newly-formed council to withdraw from Mercia and join with the rebels already living in Norland.

Her main concern was that Ethelwulf would no longer search for her, but instead would pursue and capture her sisters. If he couldn't make her queen, then what was to stop him from forcing one of the other princesses into a marriage with his son? Or perhaps even use the other princesses to bait Adelaide back to Mercia to do his bidding?

So far, we'd heard no word of Ethelwulf discovering the princesses, which meant Mitchell had most likely not revealed their locations to Captain Theobald. At least we prayed he hadn't and that the twin princesses would remain safe until we could send men to secretively retrieve them—if we could find them in the places Sister Katherine had divulged to us.

Lady Sybil steadied herself against the mast of the swaying ship. "The queen has agreed to the suggestion to have several new gowns created once we arrive at King Draybane's castle. She says she will await her presentation to the king and court until she is properly attired."

"Thank you for exerting your womanly influence upon the queen, my lady."

Lady Sybil bowed and then retreated toward the cabin where Adelaide had confined herself. A deep longing cinched inside my gut. I wanted to follow Lady Sybil, enter Adelaide's room, and gather her into my arms. I'd already done so once around the knights, the day Firmin had fallen onto Adelaide after saving her from Captain Theobald's knife.

As a reward for saving her life, Adelaide had given

Firmin the position of captain of her elite guard. He and the other elite guards were aboard the second ship. After being in service to a cruel master, one who used fear to retain their loyalty, they'd eagerly pledged their lives and loyalty to Adelaide. They were slower to accept me and my commands. But at least they trusted and loved Adelaide.

No one had mentioned my passionate embrace with Adelaide. Mayhap the noblemen wouldn't be so bold as to ask me about the nature of my relationship with Adelaide. And mayhap they wouldn't outright condemn me for being her closest friend and advisor. But I could sense the disapproval from some of the older noblemen, the ones who expected their queen would marry nothing less than royalty.

I tried to cling to my resolve not to care what anyone else thought, but I also didn't want to hurt her reputation or position in any way. Besides, I'd confessed my love for her, and she hadn't responded. Granted, I'd picked a lousy time to tell her. Even so, she'd given me no more indication she reciprocated.

Perhaps once she watched me in the tournament, once she saw me fight, I would win her favor and heart. Perhaps then we'd be able to talk openly about our relationship again.

Even as I plotted how I might find more time with her, my sense of duty told me I had to let her go. If she didn't love me and considered me nothing more than a passing infatuation, then I'd be wise to keep from stirring emotions where there should be none.

Whatever the case, I had to inform King Draybane I couldn't accept his offer of marriage to his daughter. I couldn't marry one woman, no matter how favorable the match, when I was completely in love with someone else.

Adelaide

"This is the last measurement, Your Majesty," Lady Sybil assured me.

I stood on a stepstool at the center of the large chamber King Draybane had provided, wearing my simple linen undergarments. The dressmaker and her assistants seemed oblivious to my state of undress and had drawn up designs for new gowns, shifts, and nightgowns.

With half the morning spent, I'd allowed Lady Sybil and my other ladies-in-waiting to assume I was merely anxious to be finished with the poking and prodding and preening. In truth, the jousting tournament had started, and I had to sneak away soon, or I'd miss my chance to participate.

I understood why Christopher didn't want me to joust. But I wasn't in Norland to win a purse of gold. Rather, I was here to impress King Draybane and persuade him to loan us supplies for our war against King Ethelwulf. Since we had no treasure or coffers to draw from, at the very least, we needed his financial support. At best, we hoped he'd be willing to lend us his army.

Though I would put off my official appearance at court until I had an appropriate gown, I'd met the king last evening when we rowed ashore and climbed dozens of stairs. He'd been waiting for us in the gatehouse of his magnificent Brechness royal residence that graced the bluffs. A short, stout man with a round face made rounder by his full head of curly red hair, he greeted me with exclamations of how much I looked like my beautiful mother. Attired in the only garments I'd brought along—my men's tunic and breeches covered by chain mail—he surely exaggerated my beauty. Nonetheless, I'd accepted his praise graciously.

The king had enveloped Christopher in a fatherly hug and then proceeded to speak at length and with pride of Christopher's many feats and daring deeds. With such high adulation, I'd finally understood why the king had offered Christopher his youngest daughter's hand in marriage.

I'd never begrudged praise to those who deserved it. But the king's esteem of Christopher had kept me awake throughout the night. When dawn broke, I'd realized how weak and inconsequential I must seem in comparison to a skilled warrior and dynamic leader such as Christopher. If I'd been a man, would King Draybane offer Mercia his support more readily? If I'd been a man, would the rebels be willing to follow me for who I was and not merely because of Christopher's leadership?

I'd been praying for wisdom again and realized the joust would prove I was a strong woman, one equal to any man. The only problem was I had to make sure I didn't face Christopher in any of the early rounds. He'd recognize Roland, brought ashore last night along with some of our other horses. Even with the caparison that covered the bay roan's body and the chanfron protecting his head, I couldn't take any chances.

I'd given Firmin the task of secretly securing a

nobleman's name and place in the tournament. At dawn, my new captain of the guard had assured me he'd found a sick young nobleman, Lord Vaughn, who'd agreed to let a substitute ride in his stead using his name and coat of arms.

"I thank you for your assistance," I said to the dressmaker as she finally removed the last pinned sleeve from my arm. "You are most kind to willingly put aside all of your other projects to work on mine."

The woman curtsied and fumbled through a response before backing away. I didn't have the means to pay for the gowns yet. But apparently, Christopher had amassed a significant fortune from his raids on Ethelwulf's ships, and he'd commissioned the dressmaker on my behalf.

Was my poverty one more weakness in King Draybane's eyes? Perhaps I should have insisted on finding King Solomon's treasure before leaving Mercia.

I shook off the doubts. I was here in Norland, and now I would make the best of the situation. And I would do my utmost to show I was a worthy queen.

Lady Sybil and the other noblewomen made a move to follow me to my private chamber, but I halted in the doorway. "I do not wish to be disturbed for the next two hours."

They bowed their heads in deference to my order. When Lady Sybil lifted hers, her keen eyes held questions. What she lacked in size, she more than made up for with her intelligence. It was one of the reasons I'd liked her. She had proven knowledgeable about many things, including all I'd needed to learn about court life not only in Mercia but also Norland. Additionally, she had a tactful and kind way of conveying information so I didn't feel incompetent.

I closed the door of my private chamber behind me and walked across the room past the richly canopied bed to the other exit. As I opened the door and found Firmin standing in the servants' quarters, I let the tension ease from my muscles.

"Your Majesty." He held out a sack that contained my armor, hopefully freshly oiled and ready to don.

I nodded my gratitude. "How much time do I have?"

"Lord Vaughn is next."

"I shall need to get into my armor with all haste." A thrill shot through me. It had been too long since I'd jousted. The last one had been at Lord Mortimer's tournament before Aunt Susanna died.

Much had changed in the passing months. This would be my first tournament without Mitchell. As I pictured his thin, aristocratic face, his warm brown eyes, and quirky grin, tears rose swiftly. We'd made a good team. And I would miss conspiring with him.

I blinked back the moisture and straightened my shoulders. "This tournament is for you, Mitchell," I whispered. "In honor of your memory. May it live on forever."

Chapter 23

Adelaide

My breath was hot inside the great helm, and rivulets of sweat ran down my forehead into my eyes. I blinked away the perspiration and attempted to calm my anxious thoughts and settle my nerves.

Beneath me, Roland whinnied, sensing my unease.

After three days of jousting as Lord Vaughn, I'd reached the final competition. To escape from my chambers, I deceived Lady Sybil and the other ladies-in-waiting on several occasions. I'd been late to one of my jousts because of another dress fitting. And my return had been delayed so that I'd neglected to wipe the dust and sweat from my face before greeting the ladies.

I had the feeling Lady Sybil had figured out what I was doing and where I was going. To my surprise, she hadn't said anything to me. More importantly, she hadn't notified Christopher, though I was fairly certain she reported to him daily.

I was relieved Christopher had been eliminated

from the tournament in the last course. Otherwise, I would have been jousting against him in the finals, something I wasn't sure I could have done. Likewise, he'd never knowingly fight against me.

I cannot bear to lose the woman I love.

His declaration came rushing back as it oft did. Even though he'd made no mention of his love again, even though he'd likely only spoken the words because he'd been in a state of panic, and even though he hadn't acted upon the words and probably never would, I still savored them. Much more than I ought to.

Firmin had coated Roland with charcoal to turn him into a black horse. In spite of the disguise, I feared Christopher, who would be standing alongside the list with some of the other knights, would see through my charade and stop me. I could only pray I had the chance to show a little of my strength and prowess before he unmasked me.

"Are you ready, my lord?" the squire asked as he placed the oak lance in my gauntlet glove. While I'd wanted Firmin to be at my side, I'd realized such a move would cause suspicion. Instead, I'd used Lord Vaughn's squire.

I gripped the weapon and nodded, refraining from speaking so he wouldn't hear my voice. The squire knew I wasn't his master, but I'd disguised my true identity. I hadn't wanted my gender to interfere with his devotion to me, which had increased with every battle I'd won. He'd taken extra care to make sure my horse was well shod and outfitted, my weapons readied, and my armor in perfect condition.

Even now, I sensed his awe and respect for my skills.

With my spurs jangling and Roland's armor clanking, I rode to my end of the list just as my opponent did the same. At the sight of us, the crowds broke into exuberant cheering and whistling.

Out of my narrow eye slit, I caught a glimpse of the king and queen and their courtiers seated within the royal pavilion at the center of the corded off field. Several other smaller, yet no less elaborate, pavilions provided seating for the nobility. No one expected the queen of Mercia to be in attendance since tonight I was due to make my first grand appearance at the ball the king of Norland was holding in my honor. One of my new gowns was finally complete, and I needed to return to my chambers with all haste to allow Lady Sybil and the others to begin preparations for the big evening.

I could sense the gazes of the other knights upon me and my opponent, sizing us up, likely placing wagers on which of us would win. I guessed Christopher was doing the same, and although I was tempted to glance in his direction, I forced myself to stare straight ahead. I didn't want him recognizing me before the first round began and chance his interfering with the competition.

Instead, I focused on my rival and whispered a prayer: "God, You know what I have longed for—a discerning heart to govern the people and distinguish right from wrong. I have not asked for wealth or strength, only wisdom. May You grant that wisdom today."

As my opponent lifted his lance high into the air, I did likewise to signal my readiness. Then I couched my lance into my armpit and prepared for the ride.

A bugle call silenced the crowds and was our signal to begin the joust. Roland lowered his head and moved forward with a fluidness I loved. I bent into him, giving in to the oneness I felt with him during these moments. His pace quickened, and I focused on his rhythm, making it my own.

I trained my sights on my challenger's cuirass, the part of his armor above his heart. I secured my lance and urged Roland to move faster. From the steadiness of my rival's charge coupled with the bulk of his frame, I guessed I required more speed if I had any chance of winning.

My breath quickened, and I braced myself for impact. With his long arms, my opponent's lance hit my chest first. In the moment of his collision, I thrust hard against him, letting Roland's speed provide the momentum I needed.

Splinters flew into the air even as I jolted backward. My head snapped, my bones jarred, and my teeth rattled. I felt myself slipping to one side of my saddle. As if sensing my dilemma, Roland swayed in the opposite direction, which gave me the ability to right myself upon my saddle.

By the time I reached the end of the list, I was firmly in place, the reins gripped tightly in my hand. Only then did I turn and notice that my opponent and I had both split our lances and yet had remained upon our steeds, which meant we were tied.

Out of my eye slit, I caught sight of my squire racing toward me with a fresh lance. At the same time, I detected a commotion among the knights along the side of the list. "No!" one of them was shouting. "Do not give her the lance."

It was Christopher, and he was calling to my squire.

My heart dropped. He'd seen past my disguise. From the frantic nature of his calls and the worry creasing his face, he was obviously determined to stop me from riding again.

All around him, the other knights were watching in confusion. If I didn't act immediately, Christopher would soon be standing in the middle of the list and would have the attention of the entire gathering, including the king and queen.

I nudged my steed toward the squire, grabbed the lance from him, and raised it all in one motion. Thankfully, my competitor already had his new lance. At my readiness, he lifted his as well. Even as the bugle rang out, I kicked Roland with a force that contained all my desperation.

He thundered forward faster than our usual pace. But I was too eager to complete this round, and I refrained from slowing him down. It would be my last joust. Somehow I sensed it. And since it was my last, I'd unleash Roland and myself. We'd hold nothing back.

This time, my lance hit my challenger before he could get near me. The driving force shattered my lance and threw him from his horse in one move. He landed a dozen feet away on his back and laid motionless.

The crowd erupted into cheers, heedless of the injured knight on the ground. I, on the other hand, veered Roland around and cantered to my rival. I was off my horse and beside the man before his squire could reach him. At the sight of the heavy rise and fall of his chest, the crazy gallop of my heartbeat steadied.

He was alive.

He shifted enough that I could see into his eye slits while he blinked as though attempting to stay conscious. I offered him a hand. He took it and allowed me to help him to a sitting position. By then his squire was at his side.

The cheers of the crowd told me I needed to acknowledge my win. I stood, straightened, and then raised my hand.

The multitude roared their pleasure. Amidst the cheers, I crossed the list to the king's pavilion. Beneath my helm, my hair stuck to my cheeks and head, and sweat fell into my eyes. The padding underneath my armor was suffocating, and I ached from the blow I'd received. Nevertheless, I walked with confident steps, knowing this was one of the most pivotal moments in my life, one that would define me as queen not only to Mercia but quite possibly to the rest of the world.

When I reached the cord, I realized Christopher was waiting for me there. Through the opening in my great helm, his eyes met mine. Anger blazed in their honey brown amidst flames of fear. Later I would explain my actions. But for now, I silently pleaded with him to trust me.

After an instant, he nodded.

Without further hesitation, I positioned myself below the king and queen of Norland, straightened my shoulders, and saluted them with my lance. The onlookers shouted their approval again. At that moment, I knew it was time.

I lifted the great helm, let it drop to the ground, and then quickly untied the padded coif, letting it, too, fall to the grassy field. A shake of my head released the long strands of hair I'd carefully tucked into the coif. Waves of blond fell over my armor and down my back. With each passing second, the silence lengthened until the only sound was the king's standard at the top of his pavilion flapping in the sea breeze.

At the sight of my face and the realization of my identity, King Draybane stood, the shock in his expression mirroring that of the other royals and nobility surrounding him.

"I am Adelaide Constance Dierdal Aurora, the true queen and heir of the house of Mercia." I'd spoken loud enough that my voice carried over the entire gathering. At the gasps and ensuing commotion, I knew my words had their desired effect. The crowds had not expected a woman, much less a queen, to win the tournament.

The king's reaction moved from surprise to curiosity to interest. He studied my face with more care than he had the night we'd arrived. Then he glanced to Christopher before returning his attention to me. He raised his hand, and the crowd hushed again.

"As the winner of this tournament," I continued, "I ask for only one thing from the king of Norland."

The king's red brows rose high on his forehead, touching his fiery red hair.

"I do not ask the king of Norland and his people for gold or supplies or fighting men." I paused, enjoying the surprise that again rippled across the king's features. I had no doubt his advisors had already been diligently at work attempting to figure out how much Norland was willing to risk in my pursuit of Mercia's throne. To be sure, they were eager to see King Ethelwulf ousted after years of defending their borders against his attacks, costing them countless lives and resources.

Precisely for that reason, I understood what the king of Norland and his country longed for more than anything else.

"I ask for only one thing," I repeated, raising my voice so it could be heard far and wide. "In the spirit of King Alfred the Peacemaker, I ask Norland for peace."

Murmurs rippled around the field and through the royalty and nobility in their pavilions. The king sat back in his cushioned chair speechless, staring at me with a respect that hadn't been there previously.

"As the rightful queen of Mercia, I promise I shall never ask for anything I am not willing to give. And since I ask you for peace, I vow to offer it in return."

I could feel Christopher's presence next to me. What did he think of me now? Was he still upset that I'd jousted even though he hadn't wanted me to?

King Draybane raised his hand, calling for silence. When the chatter faded, he stood again and addressed me. "I have seen many rulers who excel at either war or peace. I have yet to meet one who can excel at both." He paused and swept his sights over the people listening to him with rapt attention. "Until today... Today the queen of Mercia has proven she is not only a skilled warrior full of valor and courage and strength, but she has also proven she is peace-loving."

The nods and murmurs of affirmation warmed my heart. Although I'd have much to prove in the days and years to come, I prayed my words would solidify King Draybane as my ally, not merely because of our mutual dislike for King Ethelwulf but because he respected and trusted me as a ruler.

"Long live King Draybane!" Christopher called out. Then, before I realized what was happening, he reached for my hand, lifted my arm high in the air, and shouted, "Long live Queen Adelaide Constance!"

He shouted the accolades again, and this time the onlookers joined in, chanting the words louder until the crowds were on their feet in a frenzy of cheering. I stood with my back straight and my chin high and silently offered a grateful prayer. God had granted me wisdom this day, and He was the one who deserved the praise.

Christopher squeezed my hand through my glove, and I peeked sideways at him. Still chorusing with the others, he gave me one of his endearing lopsided grins, his eyes shining with pride. Later, he'd chastise me sorely for putting myself at risk in the jousting tournament, but at least for now, I'd made him proud.

My chest swelled with gladness, and I smiled back. For a long moment, our eyes held. The joy of triumph mingled with something infinitely sweeter, something that made my heart flip.

As our connection broke, I caught King Draybane watching our interaction with narrowed eyes. I tried to pretend I didn't care if he saw my affection for Christopher. But Christopher's words of caution came back to me—the reminder my affections were not my own, that I would be expected to form alliances out of need and not love.

After all I'd gone through over the past month, I realized I was willing to sacrifice much for Mercia. But I wasn't sure I could relinquish the one thing that mattered most to me: Christopher.

Chapter 24

CHRISTOPHER

My fancy court clothes made my skin itch. The blue cotehardie was tight with a high collar and trimmed with a thick gold braid. My wool hose were form-fitting and uncomfortable beneath my knee-length breeches. And my chaperon hung from my head at an odd angle.

Without my chain mail and armor, the only part of my attire that felt familiar was my belt, low on my hips and holding a long gold dagger with a jeweled hilt.

"You keep looking at the door," King Draybane said through a mouthful of sweetmeats. The servant positioned next to his throne on the dais held a silver bowl of the sugared nuts and dried fruit.

"I beg your forgiveness, Your Majesty." I gave the king my full attention once again. The tantalizing aromas from the feast had drifted into the great hall—roasted wild boar, jellies, puddings, and dozens of other dishes that servants would bring out during the five courses. My stomach was rumbling with hunger. But my hunger wasn't the distraction this eve.

No, like everyone else in the crowded hall, I was waiting for the queen of Mercia to finally make her appearance at court. My nerves tightened with the need to see her and be with her. I wanted nothing more than to feast my sights upon her beautiful face.

"I take it you have made your decision," the king stated.

"My decision?"

King Draybane lifted his goblet. A squire standing near the buttery raced forward with a jug. Once the squire had poured the wine and moved to refill others, the king took a sip and then spoke again. "You have decided not to marry Princess Violet."

My attention shifted to the king's youngest daughter, sitting at the head table next to the queen. She was a lovely woman who was much more reserved than her father but still resembled him with her goodness and kind spirit.

The king was right. I wouldn't marry her. Even if I couldn't have Adelaide. "Your Majesty, I am indeed honored with your offer. It is a great privilege for a man like me. But I had planned to speak with you and let you know that regretfully, I must decline—"

"Then you admit you love the queen of Mercia." He spoke matter-of-factly without a trace of anger.

Even if he wasn't upset at my refusal of his daughter, I wasn't ready to confess my love for Adelaide to anyone else, at least until I had the chance to discover her true feelings. "I do care for the queen," I replied, carefully choosing my words. "She is a good friend—"

"Anyone with eyes in his head can see you look at her as more than a friend."

One of the qualities I appreciated about King Draybane

was his bluntness. He never refrained from sharing his thoughts. But in this case, his directness made me squirm. Was my attraction to Adelaide that obvious? Did others see and recognize it as well? "I am quite sure many men will desire the queen. I am not the first, nor shall I be the last."

King Draybane paused with a handful of sweetmeats halfway to his mouth. "Is there another nation vying for a union with her?"

"None yet except Ethelwulf, who would marry her to his son, the crown prince. But once she secures the throne and her fame spreads, I have no doubt every foreign king will send ambassadors with their princely proposals of marriage."

"Aye, she will soon be in demand among nations."

His words echoed the warning I'd uttered all along. The queen must marry royalty. Who was I to consider having any kind of relationship with her except that of a loyal servant?

The king stuffed the handful of honeyed treats into his mouth and chewed thoughtfully. "Now that the queen has vowed to be at peace with Norland, I have no wish to jeopardize those plans."

Adelaide's request of King Draybane at the tournament had been brilliant. After the years of turmoil and unrest Norland had experienced, she couldn't have offered anything more desirable to the king than peaceful relations. Where my talks with King Draybane and his council thus far had netted nothing secure, in that single act she'd won his admiration and devotion and perhaps even his support in our efforts to fight Ethelwulf.

"The queen will remain true to her vow," I assured King Draybane. "She is a woman of her word."

"Her intentions might be noble. But intentions cannot always withstand reality, especially with other nations involved and her husband exerting pressure upon her."

"The queen will not be easily influenced." While Adelaide was reasonable and teachable, she was also a strong woman and wouldn't be moved by the whims of her advisors or a husband.

King Draybane crossed his arms over his portly stomach and assessed me with the astuteness I liked about him. "She listens to you."

"Not always."

The king chuckled. "What woman *always* listens to the man she loves?"

Man she loves? My pulse tripped. Did the king know something I didn't? Before I could voice my question, the double doors at the front of the hall opened wide.

A bugle call silenced the room and was followed by the announcement, "Adelaide Constance Dierdal Aurora, the queen and heir of the house of Mercia."

I straightened to my full height and refrained from scratching my neck beneath the collar. Instead, I held myself stiffly, hoping I appeared worthy to introduce the queen on behalf of Mercia.

As she entered, she stopped for a moment within the doorway, which acted as a frame for the regal portrait she made. All functions within my body ceased and all thoughts within my mind fled save one: she was beautiful, exquisitely so.

Attired in a new gown of the richest ruby, her pale skin glowed with radiance. Fitting her to perfection, the dress revealed her to be every inch a woman in a way her armor had not. Her hair was piled on top of her head in glorious cascading curls of gold, surrounded by a simple diamond-studded crown.

When she started down the long center aisle that led to the king's throne, I couldn't tear my sights from her.

"Breathe, my good man," King Draybane said with a chuckle. "Breathe."

Only then did I realize I had indeed been holding my breath. I expelled the pent-up air but couldn't stop my pulse from pounding like a drumbeat.

"You must marry her with all haste," the king said. "Before anyone else can win her."

At the unexpected words, I shifted my stare from Adelaide to the king.

Taking in the surprise that was surely etched in my expression, the king grinned. "You love her. And it is clear she cares for you. What is to stop you from getting married?"

"You would approve of a wedded union?"

"It would allay my fears to know the queen of Mercia has my most trusted servant and friend by her side."

The sincerity of his tone and the warmth in his eyes arrested my heartbeat. He'd called me his friend, and I could ask for no higher compliment than that. "Your Majesty, I shall remain your servant and friend regardless of what the future may bring."

"I know that," he replied. "Even so, I would rest easier at night if I was assured you are the one who holds the heart of the queen of Mercia."

"No matter how we may feel for one another," I said, "I fear I may have irreparably pushed her away." Over the past few days, she'd held me at arm's length, had even gone out of her way to avoid me at times—or so it appeared. I'd accepted the distance, knowing I deserved nothing less for rejecting her after our kiss at Wellmont ruins.

"Then you must find a way to pull her back."

"How?"

The king thumped my arm good-naturedly. "God gifted you with a handsome face and a charming smile. Use them. Why else do you think you have them if not to win the woman you love?"

My grin broke loose.

"Besides, every woman appreciates when a man takes the time and effort to demonstrate his love, not for what he can get out of it but for what he can give."

She was halfway through the great hall, close enough now I could see the delicate lines in her elegant neck that rose to her softly rounded chin and beautifully proportioned lips. Her nose and cheekbones were sculpted so perfectly. And her eyes... I shifted my attention upward to the bright blue outlined with impossibly long lashes.

It took me a moment to realize she was looking directly at me, that our gazes had collided, that she was waiting expectantly for something. My approval? My praise? My pleasure?

Though I had the urge to stalk toward her, crush her in my arms, and show her how I truly felt, I held my emotions in check and gave her what I hoped was an encouraging smile.

"Of course, kissing her might help your case too," the king murmured.

I couldn't keep from choking at his bold statement. I pressed a closed fist against my lips to hold the cough back. But nothing could hold back the thought of doing exactly as he'd suggested.

Adelaide

The feast and the festivities were more lavish than anything I'd ever experienced. If King Draybane had set out to impress me, he'd succeeded. More than that, however, I sensed I'd impressed him, too, that he genuinely respected me. Because of his respect and consideration toward me, Norland noblemen and women followed his example, and I truly felt as though I was a guest of honor.

At the start of the ball, the king offered me the first dance, which I graciously received. Though he looked nothing like my uncle who had been like a father to me, I sensed in him a kindred fatherly spirit.

Several young unattached noblemen claimed the next few dances. I couldn't deny I was wishing Christopher would dance with me, but he'd disappeared after my dance with the king and hadn't returned.

I'd just completed a dance with yet another single wealthy nobleman when I heard Christopher's voice behind me. "Your Majesty, I would be honored to have the next dance."

I made myself count to five before pivoting and assessing him in what I hoped was a composed manner. His hair was slightly wind-tossed. But otherwise, he was just as handsome in his dashing courtier garments as he was in his armor.

"Lord Langley." I curtsied.

"Your Majesty." He bowed. Then he offered his

hand. When I accepted, his fingers circled around mine in an almost possessive way that sent a frisson of heat up my arm and into my chest.

As though he felt the same current, his gaze snapped to mine, revealing dark, almost bottomless depths that drew me in with their intensity. The music started again, and yet I couldn't make myself move. Apparently, neither could he.

"I had begun to conclude you had no wish to dance with me this eve," I finally said, trying to break the strange sizzle between us.

"Then you missed me?"

"You are one of the guests of honor. Of course you were missed."

His lips curled into the beginning of a smile. "You can admit you noticed I was gone."

A dancing couple passed by and peered at us with curiosity.

I quickly reached for Christopher's other hand, placed it on my waist where it should be, and moved my feet, forcing him to do the same. His fingers tightened, and the touch seared through my gown, making me much too aware of how close we were. If I dared to look up, his face would be only a handbreadth away.

He led me around the great hall in the steps of a simple dance we'd learned during our childhood.

"I know you want to ask me where I was and what I was doing." His voice was low and filled with a teasing that made my breath quicken.

"My lord," I managed evenly. "I am not so enamored with you that I must know where you are every minute of the day."

The pressure of his hand on my waist drew me toward him another inch. His breath brushed against my cheek, and I had to close my eyes to fight away the pleasure of his nearness.

"I would that you were so enamored," he whispered.

My eyes flew open, and I tilted back enough that I could see him. Was he teasing me again?

Earnestness lined his face, and sincerity swam in his bottomless eyes. Something else swirled there. Was it love? Was it possible his declaration the day we'd rescued Mitchell held steadfast, that he still felt the same?

A tiny thrill wound through my middle.

I dropped my sights to his chest. I didn't want to allow my hopes to escalate as I'd done before only to have him put me in my place again.

He stopped dancing. "Come with me." He retained his hold on my hand and tugged me off the dance floor. I didn't resist, though part of me warned that I should, that I couldn't withstand another rejection. Besides, what would people think when they saw me disappearing with Christopher? It would surely cause a great deal of gossip at court.

"Christopher," I hissed as we passed bystanders. "Where are we going?"

He glanced over his shoulder, a spark of amusement in his eyes. "I have a surprise for you."

"What kind of surprise?"

"It would no longer be a surprise if I told you."

I could feel the king's attention upon us. "What will King Draybane think of us disappearing together?"

"He will be glad of it."

"He will?"

"Aye. Most certainly."

The king stood near the head table, his arm around his slender, petite queen. He continued to watch us with a wide, almost pleased grin.

Christopher tugged me faster so that I had to bunch my skirt to keep from tripping over it. Once out of the great hall, he led me down a long passageway, turning several corners until at last, we arrived at the base of a stairway that rose into one of the castle towers. Two guards stood at attention on either side of the door. They bowed, and then one of them opened the door for us.

"No one is to disturb us," Christopher ordered as we passed through.

I shivered with anticipation as he led me up the spiraling staircase. "The guards were expecting you." I was winded, the climb much longer than I'd realized.

"Mm-hmm," he answered without stopping his ascent. The wall sconces were lit and guided us through the darkness of the stairwell.

"Can you not give me at least one tiny clue regarding the nature of our escapade?"

"No." He laughed softly. "You never were patient with surprises, were you?"

I laughed in response. "I have never been patient with anything."

He reached back for my hand again, and I gladly placed mine in his. When we finally came to the landing at the top, he circled behind me, and before I knew what he was doing, he slid his hands over my eyes. The tender hold made me want to recline into his embrace, especially because I could feel his presence behind me, the strength and warmth of his body, the rapid rise and fall of his breath.

"No peeking," he said.

"You ask too much," I teased.

Gently, he steered me out of the stairwell and into the turret of the tower. The coolness of the night air brushed against me, soothing my skin, which had become overheated from the climb—certainly not from Christopher's nearness.

He led me forward a few paces and then stopped. With his hands still covering my eyes, he bent in, his mouth close enough to my ear that his breath tickled me. "Are you ready?"

"Yes." The word was a breathless whisper.

"Are you sure?" he asked, closer and lower.

I swallowed my need to feel his kiss against my heated skin and managed a nod.

Slowly he moved his hands away from my eyes.

At the sight before me, I gasped in delight. A table for two sat in the center of the circular turret. A tall silver candelabrum with half a dozen long candles had been lit, revealing a three-tiered cake covered in white cream and adorned with vibrant pink roses that reminded me of home, of Langley and Mercia.

I approached the table, which was decorated with white linen, silver tableware, and a crystal vase bursting with more freshly cut roses. With the canopy of bright stars overhead and a full moon reflecting on the bay that spread out below the city, the scene took my breath away.

"It is beautiful!" I smiled at Christopher and noticed Tall John retreat into the stairwell and hide in the shadows there, apparently intending to give us the feeling of privacy even if we weren't completely alone.

Christopher moved to stand next to me, close enough that his fingers brushed against mine. At the faint touch, I wanted to tangle my fingers in his, but he shifted away before I could gather the courage.

"I know how much you love sweets." He reached for a long-handled silver knife next to the cake. "The cook assured me this was her sweetest cake."

"It is much too pretty to eat."

He quirked a brow. "Are you sure? I could take it back."

I nudged him playfully. "Of course I cannot resist tasting a cake as lovely as this, especially if you insist."

"I insist."

"Very well. Then since I always do as you bid, my lord . . ."

He snorted.

I laughed, my delight in this moment sweeter than any bite of a sugared confection.

Christopher sliced into the top circle, cut a thin triangular wedge, then picked it up with his fingers. He shifted to face me. "Ready?"

"Do you intend to feed it to me?"

"Of course." His sights zeroed in on my mouth. "You must have a taste to ascertain whether the cake is worthy of an entire piece."

My stomach fluttered like ribbons wavering in a warm breeze. As he raised the piece to my lips, our eyes locked. I opened my mouth and he very gently inserted the bite. As I closed my lips around the soft delicacy, I brushed his fingers, remembering when I'd fed him gingerbread on my birthday.

At the contact, something blazed in his eyes. The

same something sparked in the air between us and ignited a flame inside me.

Neither of us moved for a long second, not even to breathe. Finally, he sucked in a shaky breath and withdrew his hand. "How does it taste?"

Was he asking me about the cake or his touch? I let the morsels melt against my tongue before swallowing. "It is like none other."

"Do you desire more?" His eyes held mine, and somehow I sensed we weren't talking about the cake anymore.

I swallowed again and nodded.

"I do too," he whispered, lifting his thumb to the corner of my mouth and brushing away a crumb.

I trembled at his touch and the implications of his words. "You once told me I belonged only to other royals and that you must sacrifice your desires."

Instead of lowering his thumb, he skimmed it lightly across my jaw and yet in such a way that seemed to indicate I was already his.

"I was wrong." He made a trail to the pulse pounding in my neck. "I have realized I can make many sacrifices for Mercia, even giving my life if needed. But I cannot give up the woman I love, not for any cause or country."

At his confession, my heartbeat bounded forward. "Exactly what kind of love do you have for this woman? Is it friendly concern or something else altogether?"

"Allow me to show you, Your Majesty." His lips curved into a slow grin as his fingers circled to the back of my neck.

In those endless seconds as he bent and angled his

head, I nearly swooned with anticipation. He took his time brushing his nose against mine, letting his lips and breath tantalize the corner of my mouth. I was so eager for his kiss that I lifted up on my toes, grasped his cotehardie, and pressed in giving him no choice but to finish what he'd started.

For an endless moment, his lips tasted mine with such thoroughness and enjoyment it was as though he was truly savoring a bite of the sweetest cake.

"Oh, Adelaide," he said, finally breaking the kiss. "I must be careful lest I am tempted to feast before the banquet."

"You speak in riddles again, my lord." My mind was too clouded with thoughts of the kiss we'd just shared to make sense of anything else.

To my surprise, Christopher lowered himself to one knee before me, reached for my left hand, and then brought it to his lips. "I love you, Adelaide. And I long to spend the rest of my days showing you my love and serving you with my life. Will you grant me that desire?"

I wanted to jump up and down and shout yes, but I was no longer a little girl infatuated with Christopher. I was a full-grown woman, the queen of a nation, with responsibilities to handle and many people to please. I understood now why Christopher had been so cautious before. We were not at liberty to rush into any decisions about our future.

Even so, I loved this man kneeling before me, and I couldn't imagine a future without him beside me encouraging, advising, teasing, laughing, and even crying together. He was the man I needed. There would never be another like him, never be another I'd love a fraction as much.

Whatever the future held, whatever opposition we encountered, we would face it together and be stronger for it.

I began to lower myself to one knee, and he shook his head in protest. I knew he was thinking a queen should not kneel to one of her subjects. "No, Adelaide—"

I leaned in and silenced him with a kiss, a tender blending of our lips that I held as I finished kneeling. When I was firmly on the ground in front of him, I drew back and reached for his left hand.

"I have always loved you and I always will." I raised his hand to my lips and placed a kiss on his knuckles. "I would be satisfied with nothing less than showing you *my* love and serving you with *my* life."

Christopher lifted my hands, pressed our palms together, and intertwined our fingers. "Then you are answering my question with *yes*?"

I smiled. "Yes. Evermore."

Chapter 25

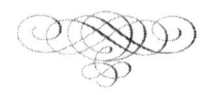

Adelaide

The bishop made the sign of the cross above where I knelt next to Christopher. "Forasmuch as the Earl of Langley and Her Royal Majesty, the queen of Mercia have consented together in holy wedlock, and have witnessed the same before God and this company, and thereto have given and pledged their troth each to the other, I pronounce that they be man and wife together, in the name of the Father, and of the Son, and of the Holy Ghost. Amen."

Christopher squeezed my hand, and I glanced at him sideways to find his head bent in prayer. I squeezed back, my assurance to him that we had done the right thing.

Since his proposal of marriage the night of the ball a week ago, the court had been in a frenzy of preparations for the royal wedding. Christopher had wanted the ceremony to take place as quickly as possible and would have married me the next day if I'd agreed.

"The sooner, the better," he'd said. "Once Ethelwulf learns of our plans, he may try to stop us."

Even with the short notice, the servants had decorated Brechness Cathedral with garlands of flowers, glowing candles, and a royal carpet up the center aisle. Those who'd traveled with me from Mercia as well as nobles from all over Norland crowded the benches and stood along the sides and back of the cathedral.

"Those whom God hath joined together let no man put asunder," the bishop said. Then he bid us rise.

In another of my long, elegant gowns, this one the color of brilliant opal, I could hardly maneuver through the layers of silk. Christopher's steady grip upon my arm as we stood was a reminder of the steady help he would be to me for the rest of my life.

Iron sharpens iron. We were both made of iron and would continue to challenge each other to grow. With Mercia's royal signet ring now upon my finger, I could already feel him bearing me up, lending me his strength, and making me a better queen because of it.

The bishop closed his eyes in a final prayer. "The Lord mercifully with his favor look upon you; and so fill you with all spiritual benediction and grace, that ye may so live together in this life, that in the world to come ye may have life everlasting. Amen."

"Amen." King Draybane's echo came from his position beside Christopher.

I'd been relieved the king had so readily accepted the news of our betrothal. I'd expected a measure of resistance, particularly regarding Princess Violet. But Christopher had assured me King Draybane supported our union and had even encouraged him to marry me with all haste. With Christopher like a son to him, in some ways our marriage served to form an advantageous alliance for both of our countries.

As we turned to greet our crowd of witnesses as man and wife, King Draybane clamped Christopher on his shoulder and grinned. "Go ahead, my good man. Seal your vows with a kiss. We can all tell that you want to."

The king's words elicited laughter among the nobles and cheers of encouragement.

Christopher bowed to the king. "I am your humble servant, Your Majesty. Who am I to deny your command?"

The king released a boisterous laugh.

Christopher then bowed his head toward me. "Will you graciously grant me the pleasure of sealing our vows with a kiss?"

Since our night eating cake on the turret, I'd longed for another kiss, but he'd held himself back out of respect and integrity. Even now, our eyes connected as they had many times throughout the week, and a familiar spark flamed between us.

"Let it be known," I said loudly enough for the gathering to hear, but I had eyes only for my husband. "The Earl of Langley may kiss the queen of Mercia without permission. I grant him free license to kiss her whenever he so chooses or so desires."

My proclamation brought more cheers, the loudest from King Draybane.

Without waiting for a second invitation, Christopher stooped and pressed his lips to mine, effectively wiping out the rest of the world save the two of us for a brief moment. Much too brief.

When he lifted away, the king had already claimed Christopher's attention, slapping him on the back as if he'd just become the victor in a tournament.

"Before we depart for the wedding feast," King Draybane shouted out as the wedding guests began to rise. "I would like to announce my gift to the newlyweds."

Christopher shook his head. "Your friendship is gift enough—"

"No, no," King Draybane said, the mirth in his features giving way to a seriousness I hadn't seen there often. "Lord Langley, you are like a son to me, and Queen Adelaide Constance has proven herself to be like a daughter."

As he spoke the kindly words, his gaze shifted from Christopher to me. The sincerity in his eyes brought a lump to my throat, and I understood once more why Christopher had served this king so loyally the past five years.

"My gift to you is resources and men to aid in your fight against the black-hearted King Ethelwulf."

I had not brought up his involvement in our war against King Ethelwulf even though this past week some on my advisory council had urged me to do so. I'd been adamantly opposed to asking King Draybane for his help. I'd already made my request of him after the jousting tournament, and I would not diminish or add to it.

Had Christopher worked out a plan with the king without my knowledge?

I glanced at him, our eyes meeting again. His expression told me he was as taken aback as I was by the king's generous offer.

"I may not be able to provide much for your cause," the king continued. "But Norland will do whatever it can to restore Mercia's rightful queen to her throne."

I bowed my head in deepest gratitude to the king. I didn't know how or when we'd return to Mercia to fight King Ethelwulf. But when we did, we would need every bit of assistance we could get from the people of Mercia, the king of Norland, but most of all, from God.

The all-wise God had given me the wisdom to accomplish everything I had so far. And perhaps His wisdom was the only part of the ancient treasure I truly needed. For the Holy Scriptures said: "Happy is the man that finds wisdom, and the man that gets understanding."

If I gained nothing else, I knew I'd already been blessed.

Chapter 26

KING ETHELWULF

I CARESSED THE KEY, STARING AT THE DETAILED PATTERN OF THE pomegranate as I had a hundred times. I was no closer to understanding its meaning than I was the day Captain Theobald had brought it to me. I'd had my best scholars study the golden relic. Other than informing me the pomegranate was an ancient symbol for wisdom, they could tell me nothing else, especially about the location of the treasure.

So far, every possible lead had been futile. And I was growing more frustrated by the day.

Across from me in my antechamber, the captain stood, awaiting my permission to deliver the latest news on Princess Constance. I finally leaned back in my stiff chair. "Do you have good news for me, Captain? You must know I am weary of the failures. If you had not worked so faithfully for so many years, I would have hanged and replaced you by now."

"I have both good and bad news, Your Majesty." Theobald's severe expression remained unchanged. If my words bothered him, he was adept at hiding his feelings.

I rolled the key over and over in my hands, praying somehow the key itself would speak to me and reveal whatever I was meant to know. I might be obsessed, but Sister Katherine's words from many years ago still haunted me, the words she'd spoken to me the day I'd captured and imprisoned her in the tower. *The princesses will have Solomon's treasure to aid them, and there will be nothing you can do to stop them.*

Princess Constance wouldn't have access to the treasure now that I had her key. But neither would I be able to get the treasure until I had the other two keys.

Curse the person who had divided the keys among the princesses. They were supposed to stay together and had remained together for centuries. In fact, when King Alfred the Peacemaker had divided the kingdom between his twin daughters, he'd kept the keys together. Of course, he should have given them to his oldest daughter, Queen Margery, my grandmother. Instead, he'd allowed the younger twin, Queen Leandra, to become the keeper of the keys.

As the younger twin, Leandra shouldn't have been given anything, neither land nor keys. I'd spent my years on the throne accomplishing what others in my family hadn't been able to do. I'd restored the order of birthright, regained Mercia, and united the kingdom. Now my last task was to bring the keys back together. They belonged to my lineage.

I placed the key into the leather pouch at my side and closed it tight. I would find the other keys. And once I did, I would finally begin the quest to unearth Solomon's treasure. It was something I'd dreamed about my entire life, something I'd longed to do ever since I'd first learned about the ancient wealth.

It didn't matter that throughout the ages many other kings had searched for the treasure and hadn't located it. At least none had ever recorded finding anything. And it didn't matter that an old prophecy foretold a young wise ruler who would use the treasure to rid the land of evil. At forty-seven, I was still young and determined enough. Eventually, I would become the most powerful king in the world since King Solomon.

I gestured impatiently at Theobald. "Well, get on with it. What is your news?"

The jagged scar on the captain's cheek twitched, the only sign of his discomfort. "The Princess Constance is married."

I slammed my hand on my writing table, irritation flaring to life and causing my head to pound with the beginning of an all-too-familiar ache. "You were not able to prevent this?"

"I sent my secret guards just as soon as we received news of her betrothal, but she married the Earl of Langley within a week, and the men were too late to stop the ceremony." The captain stared straight ahead.

I mulled over the news of the princess's marriage, steepling my fingers against my beard. If she was married, then she would be of no use to me anymore. A union with the Earl of Langley posed no threat. He may have made a name for himself as a skilled warrior in Norland and had King Draybane's ear, but he was insignificant in the greater scheme of things.

In fact, the princess had aligned herself with a nobody when she could have formed a marriage alliance with the Franks—her mother's relatives. Instead, she was in Norland with King Draybane, who was a weak man with no ambition. If not for the Highlands along the northern border, I would have conquered Norland long ago.

I'd resorted to raiding Norland ships and coastal cities, until King Draybane had hired mercenaries to protect his towns. Only recently I'd learned Christopher Langley was one of those mercenaries. If I'd discovered that earlier, I might have questioned the Earl of Langley and his wife more carefully. As it was, I'd presumed the earl was a loyal and trusted advisor when really he'd been hiding the oldest princess all these years.

I seethed every time I thought about the earl's betrayal. With anger stirring in my gut, I stood and stalked to the antechamber's only window, the one that overlooked the training ground for the elite guards. Ethelrex was in the middle of a sword drill. His tall, strong, and fierce stature stood out from the rest.

I watched him easily deflect the blows of the men fighting around him, and my chest swelled with pride. In the few months he'd been in Delsworth, he had proven himself to be dedicated to the kingdom and loyal to me. During his infrequent visits over the years, I'd feared that perhaps he'd be too soft, like his mother, and that Magnus would be a better heir.

But now I'd put my concerns to rest, especially with his willingness to obey me in everything I asked of him, even in marrying the enemy.

He was the solution to the growing unrest among the people. His marriage to one of the lost princesses would surely placate the people. How could they complain if one of their own was back on the throne and in line to become the next queen?

"We need to find another lost princess for the crown prince to marry."

"We shall, Your Majesty," Theobald responded. "The good news is that our tracking dogs have finally picked up Sister Katherine's scent again."

"Do you think she will lead you to one of the other princesses?"

"It's what we're hoping for."

We'd hoped Princess Constance would lead us to her sisters. At the very least, I'd expected Lord Mitchell would release information on their whereabouts of his own volition. As it turned out, he hadn't divulged anything helpful, even when Theobald had used his most persuasive methods for extracting secrets. Either Lord Mitchell hadn't known any more details about the princesses, or he'd been stronger than I'd assumed. Not many could withstand the captain's torture.

Sister Katherine had been one of the few to do so.

"Do not lose the nun's trail," I cautioned the captain.

"We won't."

"Shall I remind you of all that is at stake if you fail?"

The captain opened his mouth to respond but then closed it tightly. He knew as well as I did that we could not fail to track down the other lost princesses. We must find them. No matter the cost.

Jody Hedlund is the best-selling author of over twenty historicals for both adults and teens and is the winner of numerous awards including the Christy, Carol, and Christian Book Award. She lives in central Michigan with her husband, five busy teens, and five spoiled cats. Learn more at JodyHedlund.com

Young Adult Fiction from Jody Hedlund

The Lost Princesses

Always: Prequel Novella

On the verge of dying after giving birth to twins, the queen of Mercia pleads with Lady Felicia to save her infant daughters. With the castle overrun by King Ethelwulf's invading army, Lady Felicia vows to do whatever she can to take the newborn princesses and their three-year old sister to safety, even though it means sacrificing everything she holds dear, possibly her own life.

Evermore

Raised by a noble family, Lady Adelaide has always known she's an orphan. Little does she realize she's one of the lost princesses and the true heir to Mercia's throne . . . until a visitor arrives at her family estate, reveals her birthright as queen, and thrusts her into a quest for the throne whether she's ready or not.

Foremost and Hereafter coming soon . . .

The Noble Knights

The Vow

Young Rosemarie finds herself drawn to Thomas, the son of the nearby baron. But just as her feelings begin to grow, a man carrying the Plague interrupts their hunting party. While in forced isolation, Rosemarie begins to contemplate her future—could it include Thomas? Could he be the perfect man to one day rule beside her and oversee her parents' lands?

An Uncertain Choice

Due to her parents' promise at her birth, Lady Rosemarie has been prepared to become a nun on the day she turns eighteen. Then, shortly before her birthday, a friend of her father's enters the kingdom and proclaims her parents' will left a second choice—if Rosemarie can marry before the eve of her eighteenth year, she will be exempt from the ancient vow.

A Daring Sacrifice

In a reverse twist on the Robin Hood story, a young medieval maiden stands up for the rights of the mistreated, stealing from the rich to give to the poor. All the while, she fights against her cruel uncle who has taken over the land that is rightfully hers.

For Love & Honor

Lady Sabine is harboring a skin blemish, one, that if revealed, could cause her to be branded as a witch, put her life in danger, and damage her chances of making a good marriage. After all, what nobleman would want to marry a woman so flawed?

A Loyal Heart

When Lady Olivia's castle is besieged, she and her sister are taken captive and held for ransom by her father's enemy, Lord Pitt. Loyalty to family means everything to Olivia. She'll save her sister at any cost and do whatever her father asks—even if that means obeying his order to steal a sacred relic from her captor.

A Worthy Rebel

While fleeing an arranged betrothal to a heartless lord, Lady Isabelle becomes injured and lost. Rescued by a young peasant man, she hides her identity as a noblewoman for fear of reprisal from the peasants who are bitter and angry toward the nobility.

A complete list of my novels can be found at jodyhedlund.com.

Would you like to know when my next book is available? You can sign up for my newsletter, become my friend on Goodreads, like me on Facebook, or follow me on Twitter.

Newsletter: jodyhedlund.com
Goodreads:
goodreads.com/author/show/3358829.Jody_Hedlund
Facebook: facebook.com/AuthorJodyHedlund
Twitter: @JodyHedlund

The more reviews a book has, the more likely other readers are to find it. If you have a minute, please leave a rating or review. I appreciate all reviews, whether positive or negative.

Printed in Poland
by Amazon Fulfillment
Poland Sp. z o.o., Wrocław